"Why do you c̲_____ ____ ____ ____ y the wounded card so w̲_____ ____ ____ ____ ̲oing it. I can't just walk ̲_____ ____ ____ feeling like an ass."

"If you want to walk away, do it. I'm fine no matter what you do, and I'm not playing anything at all."

"You're not fine," he countered. "You think I don't see it? You think I can't tell that you're hiding secrets you don't want people to know?"

"So what secrets are you hiding?" she retorted.

"I'm not here to share secrets, form friendships, or anything else."

Rolling her eyes, Macy threw her hands in the air and bent down to scoop up the receipts. "Yeah, I get it. Family, work. Simple life."

"Nothing about my life is simple," he snapped, his voice growing louder. "If things were simple I wouldn't want to close this gap between us and kiss the hell out of you like I nearly did months ago. . . ."

Books by Jules Bennett

WRAPPED IN YOU

CAUGHT UP IN YOU

LOST IN YOU

Published by Kensington Publishing Corporation

LOST IN YOU

JULES BENNETT

ZEBRA BOOKS
KENSINGTON PUBLISHING CORP.
http://www.kensingtonbooks.com

ZEBRA BOOKS are published by

Kensington Publishing Corp.
119 West 40th Street
New York, NY 10018

All Kensington titles, imprints, and distributed lines are available at special quantity discounts for bulk purchases for sales promotion, premiums, fund-raising, educational, or institutional use.

Special book excerpts or customized printings can also be created to fit specific needs. For details, write or phone the office of the Kensington Sales Manager: Attn.: Sales Department. Kensington Publishing Corp., 119 West 40th Street, New York, NY 10018. Phone: 1-800-221-2647.

Zebra and the Z logo Reg. U.S. Pat. & TM Off.

First Printing: April 2017
ISBN-13: 978-1-4201-3912-9
ISBN-10: 1-4201-3912-6

eISBN-13: 978-1-4201-3913-6
eISBN-10: 1-4201-3913-4

10 9 8 7 6 5 4 3 2 1

Printed in the United States of America

To Roxanne St. Claire,
for her pep talks, friendship, Snapchats, and
all the right words just when I need them.

Chapter One

Macy tried to ignore the footsteps overhead as she went through her evening routine. As the owner of Knobs and Knockers, the only hardware store in Haven, Georgia, Macy ran a bustling business and often stayed after hours to accommodate customers.

Which was why she now found herself listening as her new tenant moved around upstairs. Her new tenant who drove her out of her ever-loving mind, who kept her awake at night, who monopolized her every thought . . . well, most of them anyway. On occasion she also thought about tacos, so there was that.

And if Liam Monroe ever knew just how much mind time he inspired, he'd never let her live it down. Or he'd use it against her, which would be mortifying, because if he rejected her . . .

Ugh. She ignored the path her thoughts had traveled and focused on something she could actually control. Control . . . something she prided herself on, something that had gotten her through the past several years.

Macy shoved the cash and receipts into her bank bag and tucked the bulk beneath her arm. She needed to get out of the store before she had a run-in with Mr. Sexy Tenant.

Liam had moved in a few months ago and she'd tried to avoid any face-to-face time when no one else was around to buffer. . . . So far so good.

Even though she'd known him since she was a teen, she'd never been more aware of her feelings where he was concerned. That teen crush had vanished, replaced by something intense and much more grown up. She couldn't describe how she felt now that he was back home. Knowing he was so close made her want to reach out to him, but then that fear from her past, the fear of his reaction, had her hesitating.

Damn fear. Why did she let that control her? She'd wanted one man for years, and now that he was here, she went on about her life like everything was perfectly normal.

Nothing could be further from the truth.

Slinking in and out the door of her own business was absolutely *not* normal. Her heart accelerating each time she heard heavy footsteps upstairs was *not* normal.

Yet here she stood with bank bag in hand, just like every night the past two months he'd been here. The internal battle between her angel and devil never more prominent. He wasn't in town to pick up where he'd left off years ago. Not that they had shared anything to pick up. Her attraction had clearly been one-sided because she was pretty sure he didn't even flick a glance her way other than on friendly terms.

No, what brought Liam back to Haven—reluctantly—had been his family. He and his brothers, Zach and Braxton, were now owners of Bella Vous, a women-only resort and spa. The fact that three rough-around-the-edges men now owned something so dainty and feminine would be laughable if the circumstances surrounding their decision weren't so tear-jerkingly sweet.

Their late sister, Chelsea, had created this vision, going so far as to keep notebooks and journals about a place for women to go and relax, take a break from reality, or just have a fun girls' trip. When Chelsea unexpectedly passed away, the guys banded together to make her dream a reality.

Granted, it took Liam a bit longer to come around, but the bad blood between him and Zach had been somewhat settled . . . as much as possible, considering their past and the ordeal they had been thrust into.

Just before the grand opening, Bella Vous lost its chef when the lady who'd been hired opted to take off with her boyfriend on a cross-country trip. Needless to say, the Monroe brothers were in a bind, and since Liam had been let go from his hoity-toity position at an upscale place in Savannah, he decided to fill in.

Macy knew Liam didn't want to be here. He never came out and said the words; he didn't have to. His actions, his apparent unhappiness, spoke volumes. But as much as Liam wasn't keen on being back in the town that reminded him of the tragic night that had altered his life, he wasn't about to let his family down when they needed him most.

And the last minute change of plans had left him with nowhere to live . . . until Zach's intended, Sophie, mentioned the apartment over Knobs and Knockers.

So, now Macy had to hightail it out of her own territory because the man she'd been infatuated with since high school was invading her space.

As soon as she grabbed her keys from the shelf beneath the counter, Macy froze. Those footsteps overhead were now on the steps . . . as in coming down the steps. Toward her. She'd hung around too long. It wasn't like she could make a mad dash for the door now.

Gripping the keys in one hand, she grabbed the bag from beneath her arm and whirled around to the back of her store. Clad in well-worn jeans and a black T-shirt that molded to his muscular form, Liam met her gaze as he crossed the wide aisle toward the counter.

The scar running along the left side of his face might have been intimidating to some, making him appear harsh, but to Macy he was the sexiest man she'd ever met. And that scar was a reminder of how close they'd all come to losing him. His broad frame, those dark eyes fanned with dark lashes, and an intense gaze only added to the appeal. The ink peeking from beneath the short sleeve didn't hurt, either. Would it be too forward to ask him to take the shirt off? Just to see the rest of the tattoo, that's all. Maybe she could trace it with her finger . . . or tongue.

Yeah, this was no teenage crush anymore. This was full-on adult hormones with very adultish images scrolling through her mind each time she saw him.

"I need some putty for the faucet in the bathroom upstairs," he told her in that low, gravely tone that covered her entire body with chills in a very delicious way.

Focus, Macy. The man needs putty, not drool.

Macy loved this old building, which was full of charm; however, charm and old often went hand in hand with renovations and repairs. She'd lived above the hardware store her entire life. Her grandparents had started the business and saved money by living upstairs.

Then the store was passed to her parents when they married. Macy had never known another home until a few months ago. She and her father had moved when Macy decided to build a house, with an apartment built on the back of her garage for her father. Needless to say, she was adjusting to a new life from every possible angle.

"I'll come up and fix it." She sat her bag and keys on the counter. "Let me grab the putty."

Macy moved around the old, scarred wrap counter that sat in the middle of the store. Liam didn't budge as she approached him. She'd always been tall, but next to him she felt tiny, feminine. For a woman being five feet ten inches and owning a hardware store, Macy relished the simplest things that made her feel like a woman . . . like her slight addiction to pretty lingerie. She'd always been athletic, not the type to paint her face with makeup or wear the latest styles. Sports and tools had been her staples growing up. Oh, and her cowgirl boots. She never left home without them.

"I'll fix it." He tipped his head slightly to the left, a habit she noticed and knew he didn't even realize he was doing. The vain attempt at hiding his scar came second nature to him. "Just give me the tub."

Macy crossed her arms, her elbows brushing slightly against his chest. Well, hello there, glorious muscle tone.

"You're my tenant," she reminded him, though she was mentally reminding herself as well. "I'll take care of any problems."

"I can fix the damn sink, Macy."

Why did she have to watch his lips as he said her name? Did she enjoy the torture? Apparently masochism was another trait she possessed. He didn't say her name often, but when he did she took a moment to savor the way his low, throaty tone delivered the simple word.

Macy placed a hand on his chest, to move him *and* to get a feel for those pecs again, and pushed him aside. She made her way to the front of the store where she'd just finished the plumbing display with all the essentials for a DIY project. Had she not stayed after to finish this project, she wouldn't be dealing with her sexy tenant.

The second she wrapped her fingers around the tub of putty, Liam reached over her shoulder and covered her hand. The warmth from his body radiated against her back and Macy closed her eyes, gritted her teeth, and willed herself not to whirl around and plaster herself against him. Would that be coming on too strong?

Still, she could take just a moment and memorize the way he perfectly curled his fingers against her own.

Flirting was second nature to her. Liam wasn't the only one with scars; Macy's just happened to be on the inside. Physical relationships were all she did. One time she'd allowed herself to foolishly fall into young lust, and she'd never been the same since.

Men were too easy. They tended to want one thing, so she gave it . . . on her terms. She always remained in complete control over what she would give. Never again would a man hold any power over her—power laced with undeniable strength.

But Macy knew Liam wouldn't be easy. She knew he wasn't going to just go away or get out of her mind. Liam was a complication she couldn't afford. She'd barely recovered from the last time she opened herself and that had been years ago. She'd come back to heal from the assault, and she was still here.

"Go on home," he told her, prying the tub from her hand. "I've got this."

When she could pull in a good, solid breath, Macy turned. "Do we have to argue about this?"

One broad shoulder lifted in a shrug. "I'm not arguing. I'm going upstairs to fix my sink, hit the punching bag, then try a new recipe."

That combo pretty much summed up Liam Monroe. He was as complex and simple as that.

Her eyes raked over that form-fitting T. "You don't dress like a chef."

"My whites are in the wash."

He never missed a beat to come back with some sarcastic reply. That dry humor of his had always been another pull for her. Damn him for being appealing even when his snarky side kicked in.

"Dad has a poker game tonight, so no rush for me to hurry home with dinner," she said.

Macy tried to make sure her father had a nice meal each

night, though she bought takeout and brought it back to her house. Cooking definitely wasn't one of her skills. Buying for two was actually cheaper than going to the store and cooking, especially considering she'd most likely burn the dish and they'd have to buy anyway. She was frugal that way.

Actually, Macy liked having her dad close. Though they each had their own space, he was in and out of the store often, most likely checking up on her. This was the first time ever they hadn't lived under the same roof except that brief period she was away at college.

"It's Friday," Liam commented. "Go get ready for your date and just deduct the putty from my rent."

It took her a moment, but the words sank in. "I don't have a date tonight," Macy stated, propping her hands on her hips. Of course he'd assume she had a date. She dated often. She knew what people thought, though they were usually discreet about saying anything. Nobody knew she used her social life as a mask for the pain. Nobody would ever know.

Liam stared at her for another minute before shaking his head and turning away. Without a word, he started for the back of the store and went right on up the steps. Seriously? Did he think because he said so that she would just go on home? Apparently he didn't know her at all.

They'd been a few years apart in school and Macy had been swamped with keeping her good grades up and being the star player of her softball team. But she still made time to daydream and appreciate the sultry, sexy Liam Monroe. The oldest of the Monroe boys and the quietest. Why were those silent types the most intriguing?

Since she had been friends with his late sister, Chelsea, Macy had been able to get a little closer to Liam than just random passes through the hall at school. But when Liam was in an accident that left him scarred, he pulled away from people, his family most of all. That all happened around the same time Macy went off to college on a softball scholarship.

Little did she know her entire life would change in the most drastic of ways.

Shoving aside her mother's untimely death and the incident she refused to give her thoughts to, Macy made sure the store alarm was set, the outside lights turned off. Then she marched right up those steps and pounded on the door to Liam's apartment.

The entire second floor was an open living space, save for the two bedrooms and bath. Her grandparents had bought the old building with a dream and a vision. They'd established the hardware store and when her mother took over, she'd put a small shop on one side of the store that had home accents. Her grandparents had been too poor to do so. So they had lived in the upstairs, but they let nothing stand in the way of their dream.

Macy's parents had eventually renovated the space during their married life and never moved. Her father always joked that the commute was too convenient.

Macy had grown up here and the place still felt so much like home. A home when her entire world had been right, had been all sunshine and rainbows. These walls could tell so many stories of laughter, Christmas mornings, slumber parties, and late night movies. Reality and fate hit her hard when she'd been eighteen, though.

And now Liam lived here. She'd never had an intention of renting the space out, but he needed a place to live and she'd lost her mind for a split second and extended the invitation when Sophie suggested he stay.

Macy waited, but the door remained closed. Blowing out a frustrated sigh, she turned the knob and let herself in. She'd see his stubborn and raise him one.

As soon as she stepped inside, memories rushed back to

her. Her father had left nearly all the furniture when he'd moved out. The familiar old brown couch sat against the wall to the right. Her mother had always wanted it in the middle of the floor with a sofa table behind it. She'd wanted people who came to visit to mingle and feel comfortable. The television wasn't in the same spot as she'd remembered, either. So many things were the same, yet completely different.

Liam's stamp now imprinted the only home she'd ever known. Tennis shoes to the left of the entrance, wallet and keys on the small table by the door. A single coffee mug rested on the corner of the sink; a large stand mixer that looked quite expensive was on the counter. There were massive-looking free weights by the coffee table. The visual image of Liam pumping iron and sweating wasn't something she needed. She was trying to mentally detach herself.

Apparently Liam wasn't too keen on unpacking. The entire wall separating the living room from the main bedroom was lined with stacked boxes. Each one labeled with thick, black marker indicating the contents.

Macy had lived up here with her father until just a few months ago, when she'd gotten her own home. But this simple space would always be hers, no matter who else lived here.

Her eyes drifted to the wood trim around the door. The pencil lines and dates had her reaching out, trailing her fingertips over the visible memory. Such innocent times, such sweet nostalgia.

"I didn't invite you in."

Macy glanced over her shoulder, blinked back the moisture, and shrugged. "You didn't lock the door, either."

Liam stood in the doorway of the room she used to call her own. If he noticed her getting all teary, he didn't say anything. Macy pushed her hair away from her face, cursing herself for leaving it down today. Ponytails were her best friend.

"I'm not being difficult," she started. "I would be here no matter the tenant. I don't expect you to do any repairs and I actually meant to replace the entire sink and faucet before you moved in, but I didn't have time. That was the only thing I didn't get to when we renovated."

"I don't need anything new, so don't replace it on my account. I hope I'm not here very long."

Macy froze. He'd leave Haven? His family? "What?"

Liam muttered a curse and turned toward the kitchen, which was only separated from the living area by a large center island. "Nothing. Just go on, Macy. I have things to do."

He turned his back to her and started pulling things from the cabinet and the refrigerator. Macy wasn't going to beg him to explain himself, nor was she going to beg him to let her fix the damn sink.

There was so much more going on between them than landlord/tenant. Whether he wanted to admit anything or not, Liam had feelings for her. Granted, most of the time it was disdain, but Macy could read men pretty well and she honestly thought he was masking his true feelings.

At least, that's what she told herself, because the possibility that Liam truly thought of her as annoying and forgettable was too hurtful. But she had her pride and she damn well wasn't giving any man power over her. She'd done that once in her life . . . and it cost her everything.

Liam waited until the door closed behind Macy. Damn it, he felt like an absolute jerk, but he couldn't have her in his space.

Okay, fine, technically the apartment was hers. He was already reminded over and over of the fact she had grown up here. But he couldn't have her physically in the apartment and maintain any form of sanity. Macy was everything he wasn't and he didn't need the reminder that she had her entire life all sorted out in perfect detail.

She knew what she wanted and went after her goals with a smile on her face. She'd been raised to be a third-generation business owner and she was doing just that. With her brand new house Zach had built, she was thriving.

What shocked Liam, though, was when he'd caught her touching the trim where her growth chart had been recorded. The shimmer in her eyes had rendered him speechless for a second because he'd never seen Macy as anything other than upbeat—or smart-mouthed, when she was talking to him. But never sad, and Liam knew for certain he never wanted to see her that way again.

Before that moment, he hadn't thought of how difficult stepping into this apartment would be for her. He'd been thinking of this space as a personal failure, a hit to his pride, in coming home and having to stay here. This wasn't what he wanted, what he planned. He'd had a great life in Savannah, one he desperately wanted to get back to.

But for Macy, this apartment, the store, and Haven were her entire life. She knew the path she wanted and hadn't let anything steer her off course.

Bracing his palms on the edge of the island, Liam tried to focus on the recipe he'd thought of earlier today. Giving Macy too much of his mind time or inner emotions would only lead down a path he sure as hell wasn't willing to go. Work was what he needed to hone in on so he could figure out how to keep his brothers happy, honor his late sister's memory, and get out of Haven without damaging already rocky family relationships.

Monday a group of ladies were coming in, apparently for a week-long bachelorette party. An entire week of pampering, wedding chatter, and who knew what the hell else.

Lord help them all. He'd never heard of such a thing, but whatever. Women were odd creatures and he wasn't about to begin to try understanding them—he had enough of his own issues.

The thought of catering to a group of women celebrating marriage made him cringe, made that bitterness burn deeper in the pit of his stomach. But just because his relationship hadn't worked out didn't mean others wouldn't, right? Besides, Chelsea had dreamed of this exact thing. Had hinged her entire life savings on women coming to Bella Vous to celebrate themselves, relationships with their friends, their families.

Chelsea had taken every bit of money she'd saved and bought the old Civil War–era home on the edge of town. Liam and his brothers had had no clue what she'd wanted to do with the place when she'd made the investment and she'd passed away before she could tell them. It was only after she was gone when they discovered her detailed notes on the dream she had for the old plantation. Their free-spirited sister was gone, but he'd do whatever he could to make sure her vision lived on.

He'd tried to avoid this town at all costs after the accident. He'd actually done a pretty stellar job, but now his family needed him. Liam thought he could just be a financial partner and stay in Savannah, but when he'd asked for time off to help with the renovations and start-up, he'd been given an ultimatum. As much as he wanted to stay in Savannah, even he wasn't that much of a jerk to turn his back on his family . . . on Chelsea's dream.

She might be gone, but she was still the glue that held the family together. When Zach, Sophie, and Liam had been in the accident, Chelsea was the one who kept trying to offer support, to offer advice. When Zach had been sent to prison for a year because of the drinking and driving and all the injuries Liam and Sophie endured, Chelsea had been the one to beg Liam to go visit Zach. Liam hadn't been able to bring himself to go, hadn't been so willing to forgive. Still, Chelsea had wanted her family back together; she'd not been able to handle all the tension, the brokenness.

Liam couldn't keep dwelling on the past. He'd worked hard to get beyond all of that and getting swept back to that time threatened what he was living for right now. As much as he wanted to help his brothers with Bella Vous, Liam also wanted out. He didn't like being in this tiny town. He'd gotten so used to being away, had created a life that worked for him. He was too vulnerable, too exposed here, where everyone looked at him—at his face—and instantly remembered the accident.

There were just too many emotions associated with this place. Losing his mother at a young age had ruined ever going back to his hometown, over an hour away, and the accident when he'd been in his early twenties had put a dark stain on Haven. Being here pushed him way too close to a past he'd outrun—and way too damn close to Macy.

How had he let his soon-to-be sister-in-law talk him into living above Macy's store? Sophie was a real estate agent, for crying out loud. Surely she knew a slew of places that were perfect for him. But for a few months he'd been living in Macy's old apartment, right above where she worked. Thankfully she was usually gone by the time he got home and he had a separate entrance up the back of the building.

But tonight he'd needed some stupid putty and had to face her. Stubborn woman thought he'd just let her come in and fix the sink? He could fix a damn sink.

When he'd first come back to Haven, he'd listened to her talk about her dates. He hated the jealousy that speared him each time he overheard her talking to Sophie or Cora. The other two ladies were his future sisters-in-law and Macy's closest friends. Damn it. There was no way to avoid her entirely. She was literally in every aspect of this new life of his. Another reason he needed to get out of Haven and back into his comfort zone—because he sure as hell wasn't comfortable here.

One night he'd been returning from the resort and she'd been coming in the back door. It was late, the sun had set, and they'd started a simple conversation, which turned into an argument. He honestly couldn't recall the contents of the argument now because the fact he'd lost his mind and nearly kissed her overrode everything prior. He'd gripped her face, in an attempt to shut her up, but the second he leaned in, his lips barely brushing against hers, he pulled back. She was too much temptation and he had a whole host of issues that kept him detached. Besides, he didn't want to stay in Haven forever.

Getting involved with Macy on any type of physical level would only lead to one or both of them getting hurt.

Being a financial backer for Bella Vous was all the commitment he wanted, but he couldn't just leave his family in a bind, so he'd stay until they found another chef. Of course, he'd have to actually tell his brothers to start looking for a replacement, and he wasn't quite mentally prepared to have that conversation with them.

But he'd been unable to save his mother from the brain aneurism, unable to save Chelsea from her skiing accident, so here he was paying some sort of penance in an emotionally warped way because he needed to do *something* to justify all of this guilt.

The only time he ever had complete power over anything was in the kitchen. What started out as a hobby with his mother had quickly turned into a passion. Some might have seen this as an immediate man-card removal, but they didn't know the science that went into cooking, the skill, precision, patience, and control.

The control. Every facet of his life came back to that.

A shrink would get lost inside all the various tunnels and sharp turns in Liam's mind. Even Liam knew that he was a mental mess. He was well aware of the fact he clung to his profession in an attempt to keep that bond with his mother, but it went so much deeper than that. His mother's dream had always been to open her own restaurant, but they'd been too poor for her to even consider such a notion.

Somewhere along the way, Liam had inherited that need to have his own place. And while he didn't own anything of his own in Savannah, he had been the head chef in the city's most sought after restaurant. Everything that he'd made for himself was back in Savannah, waiting on him to return and pick up where he'd left off.

On a sigh, Liam cursed himself. Between the Macy mind games and thinking of why he chose to be a professional chef in the first place, he was having a Dr. Phil moment with himself. And if that wasn't the most pathetic thing ever, he didn't know what was.

Liam grabbed the spices he needed and started mixing together his own concoction. He'd had the greatest idea for an herb bread and dipping sauce, but he needed to try them out privately first. He had two very important ladies in his life who were all too eager to sample his made-up recipes.

A year ago his youngest brother, Zach, had reconnected with sweet Sophie. Their reunion had been bittersweet as they were all still reeling from the death of Chelsea, who'd been Sophie's best friend. Sophie had played a huge part in getting Bella Vous up and running, and out of the clutches of the mayor, who wanted to turn the house into some stuffy museum.

Then Zach had discovered a runaway teen hiding out in the old house during the renovation stage. Brock had been abused, emotionally and physically, and Zach, who didn't do commitment, suddenly found himself taking the boy in.

Add in a stray dog who had puppies in his laundry room, and Zach had an instant picture-perfect family.

Liam couldn't help but laugh at his brother, who had always avoided any type of relationship at all costs. Their childhood home was now filled with a moody teen, dogs all around, and a woman who doted over Zach's every move.

Liam ignored the tug of jealousy. What did he have to be jealous of? He didn't want that life. Not at all. But his younger brother Braxton had found himself falling head first into love as well, and Liam was beginning to wonder what the hell was in the water in this town.

Just before Christmas, his college professor brother got tangled up with the town's new masseuse, who just so happened to be the heiress to a chocolate company known around the globe. The most shocking part about Cora was the fact she was blind. Not that her lack of sight defined her by any means; the woman was so talented and she could rely on her other senses to hone in on those around her. There was constant praise from clients at the resort. Cora was helping to get their name out there, and Liam couldn't be happier for Zach and Braxton.

Happy endings weren't for everyone, though. Liam adored the women his brothers were bringing into the family, but he wanted his old life back. He wanted to be out of this little town. He hated walking down the street and having people stare. The old people who knew the story behind his scar looked at him with pity, while the newbies who had no clue what had happened often looked at him with repulsion. Yeah, the scar wasn't a pretty sight, but what could be done at this point? Plastic surgery would only fix so much, and no way in hell was he subjecting himself to more pain, physical or emotional. He didn't need to be pretty to pursue his goal of owning his own restaurant.

No, he'd live with the ugly reminder of a night that still

haunted him. If he'd only insisted on taking the keys. If he'd only been more forceful and adamant about being the driver, perhaps there wouldn't have been an accident. He wouldn't have a scar, Sophie wouldn't have a limp, and Zach wouldn't be a felon.

But nothing could be done now. The past was over and Liam needed to move on. And he had. He'd gone to Atlanta, had attended culinary school, and made a name for himself in Savannah. He'd been just fine working behind closed doors where he could hide from the world and do what he loved.

Unlike Zach and Braxton, Liam actually had had an amazing upbringing with his single mother. She was the first woman he'd ever loved, the one who always put her needs last and often went without new things in order to pay for Liam's spot on the Little League team or for those karate lessons. He didn't realize at the time just how much she had sacrificed.

Liam pulled the dough from the refrigerator. He'd mixed it the other evening and sat it inside, knowing it needed to chill for a while so he could mess with it later. He needed this outlet, needed to escape. And though he worked all day at the resort preparing meals and snacks for guests, when he was home he still found the task relaxing. Not many people could say they loved their job this much.

When a passion coincided with a career, there was so much joy. At least, there should be.

So why was Liam in such a pissy mood lately? Part of him hated that he'd been technically forced to move back to the town he loathed. Okay, "loathed" might have been too strong a word, but he'd rather live anywhere than in the place where people knew his backstory and thought they could relate.

Unless you had your mother die when you were twelve, you had been abused at your foster homes, and you had a tragic accident leaving you scarred in every single way, there was no way you could relate.

And the pity party he was mentally throwing himself had to cease. Just being back in Haven put his mind in an uneasy state. He'd overcome that time in his life, or at least tried to move past it. He'd literally run from everything and started fresh.

Of course he'd lost his job when he'd asked for time off to help his brothers get the resort started. But his skills were unlike any others' and he knew he could find a job in another prestigious restaurant.

He vowed one day to have his own. The ultimate objective of any chef, he figured, but he had his sights set high and he didn't plan on stopping until he reached his goal.

After Liam got the bread ready, with just the right amount of spices coating what would be the crusty top, he popped the pans into the oven and sent off a quick text to Sophie and Cora. No doubt the ladies would be eager to see him in the morning once he arrived with fresh bread and dipping sauce, which he still needed to make.

His phone buzzed, but instead of a reply text he saw the message was from one of his old coworkers. Liam didn't make many friends, but John was the closest thing to one in Savannah.

As he read through the lengthy text, Liam became increasingly intrigued and a bit hopeful. The place where he used to work was rumored to be going up for sale. Liam and the owner hadn't parted on the best of terms, even though Liam had been a loyal worker for ten years. When push came to shove, Liam had had to walk away from his dream job in order to come home and Mark Pritchard hadn't even tried to keep him.

Liam didn't reply to the text. What could he say? There were too many questions. Why was it for sale? What did John want Liam to do? It's not like Liam had funds to purchase another business. At the moment, all of his savings were tied up in Bella Vous.

But having his own restaurant was the top contender on his bucket list. Buying Magnolias would be a smart move for anyone. The business was already established, the location was perfect, and no doubt all the employees would want to stay on. Getting a loan shouldn't be a problem.

If Magnolias was actually going up for sale, Liam wanted it. He had to at least try; the opportunity was everything he'd been hoping for. The timing sucked, but everything in life worth having usually came with some type of risk. The dream his mother had was now a potential reality for him.

He needed to put his pride aside, and the sting of being let go, and talk to Mark to see if they could settle on a price. Then the hard part would come and Liam would actually have to talk to Zach and Braxton.

Blowing out a breath, Liam checked on his bread. Within minutes the apartment filled with familiar, comforting smells. His phone vibrated several more times with excited messages from Sophie and Cora. Women were so easy to please, especially with food. Wait until they tried the macaroons he'd have on hand for the next Wind Down with Wine event.

Liam wondered what pleased Macy, but quickly shoved that thought aside. He didn't need to know what pleased her. He didn't need to know any more about her than necessary.

Macy wasn't like most women he knew. She was simple, her clothes, her style. She was breathtaking without an ounce of makeup, her hair pulled back, and her flannels and jeans. The T-shirt and jeans were equally as sexy. A tall woman with curves in all the right places was enough to attract any man, and Liam figured that was why she dated so much. She could have any man she wanted and he was a fool for spending so much time thinking about her.

He should have been a little more grateful for her help, for her giving him a place to stay so he didn't have to intrude on his brothers and their new love lives. Still, something about Macy made him edgy, irritable. He knew what that "something" was, but he didn't want to admit anything, even to himself.

From now on, he needed to keep his distance from Macy whenever possible. He wasn't looking for anything, much less an unwanted attraction. The last thing he needed was to make more ties here. He was working on a way to get out of this town, keep supporting his sister's dream, and live his own life . . . away from Haven. Away from Macy.

Chapter Two

"Marry me."

Liam laughed at Sophie as he piped frosting through the center of the cream horns for breakfast the next morning. He absolutely loved working in this kitchen. Because of his profession, his brothers had given him all the authority to pick and choose how this room should be set up. At the time, Liam had no idea he'd be the one benefitting from the double wall ovens, the six burner gas stove, and the dual commercial size refrigerators.

The large quartz top island was any chef's dream. The storage beneath held so many of his baking needs well within reach, the far side he'd requested would have six bar stools so they could eat in here comfortably while the guests used the formal dining room.

The bright window over the sink looked out onto the pond. There was no way he could be in this room and not be in a good mood. As much as he wanted his own restaurant, for now this wasn't a bad gig.

"If I was looking for a wife, you'd be a perfect contender," he told Sophie.

"If you flirt with my fiancée again, I'll kick your ass."

Liam glanced up as Zach strode into the renovated

kitchen, a brown sack beneath his arm. Sophie tore off another hunk of bread and dipped it into the creamy sauce he'd made the night before. If her moans, sighs, and marriage proposal were any indication, he'd say the new recipe was a hit.

"She proposed to me," Liam defended. "Maybe she has a thing for a man who can cook and owns something besides denim and flannel."

"Like those tight-ass T-shirts you wear?" Zach grunted as he kissed Sophie on the cheek and took a bite from the bread she held. "Damn, Liam. I'll marry you for that. What did you do to that bread?"

The unexpected compliment took Liam by surprise. It was no secret the two of them didn't always mesh. At one time there was pure hatred, but over the past year they'd grown closer. Chelsea would've loved to have seen this, and perhaps because of her untimely death and the dream she'd envisioned, Liam and Zach were actually repairing their damaged past.

Even before the accident, the two would butt heads. Their type A personalities seemed to clash on a daily basis. They had been in the midst of an epic argument when the accident happened. They'd been circling each other for months, griping at each other about anything and everything. Their egos were constantly clashing. They'd both attempted to date the same girl, and that had turned out about as well as it sounded.

Then that tragic night struck and they'd never been the same.

They'd both grown since, but the old hurt had never disappeared. Neither of them made any attempts to take that first step and merge their differences onto some common ground. Liam and Zach had just had to learn to deal with their pain and attempt to move on into some normalcy—in their own directions.

"Just mixed some spices in a blend I'd never tried before," Liam stated with a shrug, hating he wasn't sure how to even reply.

Compliments weren't something he was comfortable with. Working in an upscale restaurant like Magnolias, Liam was used to getting feedback from customers and he enjoyed it, but it always made him feel awkward. He wasn't cooking for others for the praise. He'd taken the passion his mother had instilled in him, turned it into a science, a meticulous hobby that just happened to pay the bills. In the kitchen, he was in complete control of his life, of the outcome of what he was doing. It was the other mess in his world that he kept losing his grip on.

"What's in the sack?" Sophie asked, leaning against the large center island.

Zach took the brown bag and sat it on the counter. Liam instantly recognized the logo on the front. He continued his work, cursing the way his heartbeat kicked up at just the sight of a bag from Macy's store. Ridiculous. He seriously needed to concentrate on moving on, making a plan and not letting his mind get so wrapped around a woman who had no place in his life.

A near miss kiss, a few months of living in her old apartment, and randomly seeing her and hearing about dates was enough to have him grinding his teeth and clenching his fists nearly every day.

He'd let one woman into his heart years ago. He'd let her so far in, he thought they'd spend their lives together. Foolish, really. She'd been a player, looking for nothing more than using Liam as a stepping stone until someone better, with more money, better looks, less facial scarring, came along. Liam had a great job, lived alone, and had very little debt. His savings and investments were a nice cushion, but he'd never dreamed she was looking for a sugar daddy. Liam still felt betrayed, used, and deceived.

His ex never came right out and said his looks bothered her, but he wasn't naive. He'd seen the man she'd left him for and Liam was convinced the attraction was about more than a hefty bank account.

After that relationship ended, he became even more detached than before and vowed never again to let a woman work her way under his skin. He'd been doing just fine at staying closed off . . . until moving back to Haven.

The fact that he allowed Macy to have power over him only made him angry. The scar wasn't his only excuse, though he let people believe that. The jagged line that ran down the left side of his face was not a big selling point with the ladies. And Macy was definitely all lady. She ran a hardware store and knew more about PVC pipe and cement mix than the average woman, and likely some men, but the way she filled out those jeans and her plain T-shirts was damn near a sin. On cool mornings she'd throw a plaid flannel over her T, but by the end of the day, he'd see her with the shirt tied around her waist, flaring out over her hips.

"I had to stop in and order some materials for that house I'm building over on Peach Tree Lane," Zach stated. "I went ahead and picked up some extra lightbulbs for here as well."

Zach had followed in their adoptive father's footsteps, taking over the family business of construction. Zach had definitely hit some major hurdles in life, but he'd jumped over them and kept going strong. At one time he'd tried to give up, but then Sophie entered his life, and Liam knew for a fact that the woman literally saved Zach from himself.

"Haven't seen Phil for a while, now that he's pretty much passed the store on to Macy," Zach went on, tearing off a piece of bread for himself.

"I'm sure it's hard for him to just let go," Sophie added. "Even though he still hangs out there and helps, passing that down has to be bittersweet."

"He was the only one working today," Zach replied around a large bite. "Said Macy texted him and said she couldn't make it in. He didn't say why, but that's definitely not like her."

Liam placed the final cream horn on the glass platter and refused to let his mind wander. Most likely she had been on a date. She'd probably left his place last night and headed straight home to get all fixed up. She'd told him she didn't have a date, but a woman like Macy didn't just stay home on a Friday night.

He'd heard the rumors of her social life, had actually heard her talking enough firsthand to know she wasn't a recluse like him. Probably stayed out too late or maybe slept over somewhere. The thought knotted his stomach.

Still. None of his business.

"I hope she's okay," Sophie added, oblivious to the internal argument Liam was waging with himself. "I'll call later and check on her."

"Brock will be here after school." Zach took another hunk of bread, this time dipping it in the sauce. "I told him to come by and help with cleaning since we have those two groups coming in. So we can put him to work."

Sophie sighed. "I think we're working him too hard."

"He's wanting to save for a new car," Zach countered. "He can put in the time and save some money."

This was not an area Liam wanted to be involved in and sure as hell not something he had experience with. Parenting was just as terrifying as a relationship. No thanks to both.

While the two argued about what was too much for Brock to handle, Liam continued getting the snacks prepared for tomorrow. They always offered wine and some type of little finger food or pastry around eight in the evening. According to Sophie, there were four ladies coming in tomorrow morning who would stay two days, in addition to the bachelorette group arriving.

Whatever the reason for the getaways, this was exactly what Chelsea had wanted. She'd had a vision, and so far, her dream was becoming a beautiful reality and really taking off.

"I need to get back to the site," Zach said, brushing the crumbs off his hands and onto his holey jeans. "Call me if you need me."

He kissed Sophie good-bye and nodded to Liam on his way out the back door.

"Not that I agree with my brother often, but Brock is a hard worker." Liam wiped a damp towel over the work space on the oversized island. "He's like me as a teen. He wants to stay busy, to feel needed. Trust us on this one."

Sophie chewed on her bottom lip and nodded. "I know. I just don't want him to feel like we brought him into our family just so he could be an extra pair of hands."

Liam loved her soft heart. They'd shared a special bond since the night of the accident, when they'd both been critically injured. Sophie had needed several surgeries on her hip and leg, and still walked with a slight limp. Liam had taken it in the face, had suffered a broken jaw and collarbone, and irreparable laceration to his face. Hard not to feel a connection after all of that, so Liam definitely had more patience and more concern for Sophie than most people.

Moving around the edge of the counter, Liam took Sophie's shoulders and turned her toward him. "He doesn't think that. He loves you guys. You saved him. He'll do anything he can to make you proud, even if you tell him to go scrub the toilets. He'll grumble and complain, but he's a teen so that's his job right now. If he's not rolling his eyes, that's when you need to worry."

"You're right." Sophie's mouth tipped up into a smile,

just as he'd hoped. "I have some of my sketches getting delivered today. I sent them off to get custom framed. I'm adding more to the library."

Sophie was a master at pencil sketches. They'd tried to get her to sell the things, but she refused. She claimed she only did them as a way to relax and unwind. But Zach had talked her into using each piece to decorate the rooms of the resort house.

"Do you need me to hang around and sign for them?"

"Actually I have to put all the sheets on the beds, so I'll be here for a bit longer. I can sign when they arrive. Do you need me for anything down here?"

Liam shook his head and stepped back. "I'm done for the day. I'll be back around six in the morning to make sure everything is set up. I know the first group of ladies wanted a breakfast when they arrived, so I fixed the majority of the food today."

Most resorts or bed and breakfasts didn't allow an early morning check-in, but Bella Vous catered to every client. No matter their request, Sophie went out of her way to try to accommodate every single one. Actually, they all did. Sophie was still swamped with her real estate business, but she did all the bookings for the resort—which were mostly done online anyway.

Without a doubt, the resort wouldn't be what it was without her. Oh, the guys would've eventually managed, but Sophie had kept them on track with a limited amount of fists flying.

"You're not held to certain hours," Sophie told him. "You're part owner, so you definitely don't answer to me."

"I know, but I wanted you to know what I was doing."

Sophie went up on her tiptoes and wrapped her arms around him. "I'm so glad you're here. Chelsea would be, too."

Damn it. Guilt slid through him. He didn't want to be

here. Going back to Savannah was all he was looking for. His heart wasn't in Haven, had actually only been here when his adoptive parents were alive. Now, he felt like an outsider—story of his life. But in Savannah, he could blend. He didn't have many friends, and even those were kept at a distance. He was looking for a way to sneak out of this awkward life he'd been thrust into and hoped his exit would go smoothly.

Most likely it wouldn't, but until Liam had a solid plan for his future, he'd stay right here and not express his need to get out of town. Before he made any major decisions, though, he needed to check into the rumor of Magnolias being for sale. The idea that the restaurant he'd loved for years, had considered his home, could be his was overwhelming and thrilling.

Liam patted her back and stepped away. "Call me if you need me. I'll just be home."

Sophie's brows drew in. "Why don't you date? You've never mentioned anyone to me and I can't believe you literally spend all your time working."

He gritted his teeth, but attempted to control his response because Sophie wasn't being nosy, she was legitimately concerned. "Don't worry about my social life. I'm happy just the way things are."

"Really?" She tipped her head to the side, a clear sign she didn't believe him. "I actually just sold a house to a new teacher—"

"No." Hell no. He didn't want to be fixed up on some blind date. "I need to go."

As he grabbed his phone and keys from the counter by the back door, Sophie called out, "Stop running."

He froze, keeping his back to her, his eyes locked on the pond in the distance. The sun was just setting, spreading a vibrant orange glow across the horizon and reflecting onto the water. Such a peaceful evening, quite a contrast to the turmoil inside him, the instant tension in this room.

"Don't run from your fear," she added in a softer tone. "You can't overcome it if you don't face it."

Liam glanced over his shoulder, pasted on a smile, and lied to her face. "I'm not afraid of anything."

Macy let herself in the store and quickly disarmed the security alarm. Usually the best times to tackle the dreaded paperwork and invoices was when she couldn't sleep and she was confident there would be no interruptions.

She knew the store better than her own house, so she maneuvered through the aisles. Security lights helped illuminate the layout as she headed toward the back where she had a tiny office—her dad's old office, which had belonged to Macy's grandfather. That whole generational bond made staying in Haven so much easier. Here is where she felt safe, where nothing could touch her, hurt her.

Macy remembered being little and playing with a block of wood, an old hammer, and nails on the floor while her dad worked on invoices. While she didn't have a family on the horizon, that didn't mean she didn't envision having a child at her feet someday. Though it sounded clichéd, she had that small-town dream of having a family, a devoted husband and children. She wanted to be able to pass the business down one day, too.

The option of adopting had interested her months ago and she'd already started the process of becoming a foster parent. That next step for her in her quest to be a mother was to adopt. Even though she would be a single parent with a full-time job, she wasn't going to let that steer her away from her dream of being a mother. There were many single parents out there and there were so many children who needed a good home.

So what if she wasn't married? She didn't need a man in her life.

Macy might date, quite a bit, but that was all for show, for herself really. To prove she had control, to prove to her eighteen-year-old self that she didn't have to be bullied around by a guy and his friends who wouldn't take no for an answer.

She hadn't found a man yet who fit the bill for someone she wanted to commit to, but that didn't mean she was giving up. She'd seen the love between Zach and Sophie, Braxton and Cora. She'd seen the love between her own parents before her mother passed away. Macy wanted that. Even with all she'd been through, she still held out hope that there was a nice guy somewhere, that she could get her own happy ending with a man who loved her.

As she rounded the corner to her office and reached to flick on the light, a strong hold circled around her shoulders, way too close to her neck. A scream tore from her as she jerked in an attempt to get away. She'd been held against her will once; instant flashes of that night consumed her. Never again would she be a victim of anything.

She screamed louder, fought harder. She kicked, clawed, and arched back in an attempt to break free. Fear gripped her tighter than the strong arms.

"Macy, it's me."

Liam's low, firm tone in her ear calmed her instantly. Her heart beat in a frantic rhythm as she closed her eyes and willed her breathing to regain some sort of normalcy. She was safe. This was nothing like what she'd endured. Nobody would hurt her here. Nobody would ever hurt her again.

"Liam," she whispered, cursing herself for shaking. She needed to get control over the trembling before he noticed. "What are you doing?"

He remained behind her, his arms wrapped around her

midsection, her back against his rock hard chest. "I heard something and came down to catch the intruder."

With unsteady hands, Macy shoved her hair away from her face. Random strands clung to her mouth, making her realize how much she'd struggled. Her weak knees barely held her in an upright position.

"I'm not an intruder and I was quiet. How did you hear anything?"

"I wasn't asleep."

He also hadn't let go, which would explain why her heart continued to thump an unsteady rhythm in her chest. She'd known he was big; she just hadn't been this close to him to realize how powerful he was. Power had once instilled a crushing panic in her. . . . She refused to ever be that woman again.

"You can let go," she muttered, not because she feared him, but because she might want to lean into him. If she was ever going to fully move past that night, she needed to do it on her own.

His arms remained around her. "Are you okay? You're trembling."

"I—I'm fine." She wasn't about to explain the nightmare that continued to haunt her. "I just wasn't expecting you to be guarding the store."

Slowly, he pulled away from her body and Macy instantly felt the chill. Strong arms used to terrify her, still did actually, but the strength Liam possessed was controlled, caring. Until now she didn't know such a power could be combined with gentleness. Tears pricked her eyes. She didn't want to feel vulnerable, but damn it, she had no choice here. Liam pulled emotions from her that she'd just as soon leave buried.

When Macy turned, the glow from the security beams behind him cast a light around his broad shoulders. His very bare shoulders, which led to his very bare chest and ink she couldn't quite make out over his left pec and up over his shoulder, spreading down over his bicep. Mercy, the man was sculpted better than she'd ever envisioned—and she'd done plenty of envisioning.

That tanned skin wrapped over taut muscle didn't come from kneading dough or frosting a cake. His broad frame tapered into lean hips and had Macy pulling herself together to form a coherent thought. Whatever he had going on with that punching bag he mentioned was doing some glorious things to his physique.

She couldn't see his facial expression very well, but he was close. Too close. Or maybe not close enough.

Macy had been known around town for her dating, and some people presumed she was promiscuous. That was their business. She couldn't change what people said or thought of her and she wasn't going to spend her time trying. Yes, she'd purposely dated quite a bit, mostly to prove to herself that she was in charge.

But she wouldn't lie. She felt a pull toward Liam that unnerved her. In his presence there was always a rush of emotions she didn't know how to handle. Sometimes she wanted to throw caution to the wind and make a move with Liam, but then that worry of rejection nipped at her mind. She'd never cared or worried about rejection before, so why was she letting this man matter so much? He'd been back only a few months and each day that passed had her more revved up than the day before.

"What are you doing here?" he asked, propping his hands on his hips.

He needed more clothes. Something to cover up all that scenery, because she was having a difficult time recalling exactly why she was in the store in the first place. And her damn head was starting to pound.

Invoices. Right. The things she needed to get to customers so she could get paid and keep her business up and running. Moments ago she'd been dead set to get some work done, but suddenly invoices were the last thing on her mind.

What would he do if she actually reached for him, ran her hand along those hard muscles? Maybe if she leaned forward to just briefly touch her lips to his. Would the controlled, quiet Liam snap or push her away like he had a few months ago? They'd yet to talk about that moment. How long would he pretend he didn't want to kiss her? How long would she let him pretend?

"I had some work to do," she replied.

"Out too late last night to come in today?"

Confusion had her jerking back. "Excuse me."

Liam shook his head. "Nothing. None of my business."

He started to move, but Macy stepped in his path. "Tell me what you meant by 'out too late.' I wasn't out last night at all."

"Phil looked exhausted when I saw him. I thought he turned this place over to you."

Her dad looked tired? She hadn't seen him and he'd never tell her if he needed help. Stubborn man. She'd talk to him about that, but for now she had other matters to deal with. Namely the half-naked man who clearly had a bad impression of her.

And the migraine she'd nursed all day was threatening to rear its ugly head once more. The twinge behind her eyes was always the first sign this was no regular headache.

"He did turn this over to me," she defended, suddenly angry. "And you're right, this isn't your concern. If you'll excuse me, I'm going to my office to finish the invoices I wanted in the mail earlier this afternoon."

Macy knew her blood pressure was rising. She jerked around Liam and headed to her office. Stupid to get this worked up over a man who'd only been back for such a short time. She'd never cared what people thought before, but Liam was different. There was a pull toward him that she couldn't deny, and the fact he fought it, too, was only more frustrating.

She clicked on the small antique lamp and braced her palms flat on her desk. From the corner of her eye she spotted Liam as he filled the doorway. Sexy and intriguing as he was, she just wasn't in the mood for an argument. She'd barely recovered from her earlier migraine and all she wanted to do was get back home and crawl in bed. She'd thought once the last one passed that she was relatively safe to get some work done. Clearly she'd been wrong.

"Do you need help?"

Macy glanced over her shoulder, intent on meeting his eyes and not all of those displayed muscles. "Is that your way of apologizing?"

"I was out of line."

He lifted his arms and held on to the door frame above his head. Oh, no. Now he was playing dirty with taut muscles that flexed and rendered her stupid and mute.

Macy looked back down to the stack of papers on her desk and sighed. It would be best if he went back upstairs and left her alone. The way he kept tilting his head out of habit, as if to shield his scar, the way he almost seemed to want to know more about her, yet pushed her away at the same time . . . it was all getting to her. She didn't know what to do with all these mixed up emotions, and in the middle of the night, when they were completely alone together, was the last place and time to try to figure things out.

Liam wasn't trying to purposely play games. The man just held so much sex appeal, she couldn't fault him for the power he held over her. He had no clue and this was her problem. A problem she was having a hard time dealing with, considering her migraine was starting to turn her stomach. Stupid nausea.

"I've got it," she replied, rubbing her temple. "Don't let me keep you."

Bare feet shuffled across the old checkered linoleum floor. He'd truly run down the stairs half naked, sans shoes, to take on an intruder. Said quite a bit about a man's integrity.

"You look ready to fall over." He stood right next to her, the warmth from his body enveloping her. "Go on home, Macy. These invoices can go out tomorrow after you've had a good night's sleep."

Macy turned, but the defensive words died the moment she looked at him. The lamp from the desk shined directly onto his scarred cheek. The angry red pucker did nothing to deter from his appeal and she wanted to get closer, wanted to know the man who kept himself so closed off.

Without fully thinking, she reached up. In a flash, Liam's hand gripped her wrist, stopping her approach. Why did he have to put up a wall every single time she attempted to get close? Did everything have to be a battle?

The intensity of his glare should've had her backing down, but she wasn't one to shy away from conflict. Liam was too strong, too stubborn, to let insecurities run his life.

"Don't let this have all the power."

He kept his tight hold on her. "You know nothing about me. Leave it."

Macy stepped in closer, narrowing the gap between them and ignoring his hurtful words spoken out of pain and anger. "I know you won't let people in and you keep to yourself."

"You know the man I used to be. I've changed."

Liam dropped her hand, but shifted forward to loom over her. It took a mighty large man to make her feel small, but Liam did just that. It wasn't just his height—it was the dark gaze, the clenched jaw, firm shoulders. He was indeed the entire package of brooding man . . . and yet his vulnerability rolled off him in waves. Did others notice? Did they even try to see how damaged he still was?

Macy swallowed. He wasn't saying a word, wasn't touching her, but they were no more than an inch apart. His warm breath tickled her face, his eyes held hers, and the headache that threatened to return wasn't even a priority now.

"Are you going to tell me how I can't possibly know you since you've only been back a few months?" she finally asked when the silence became too much.

"No. I'm going to ask how you recognize someone who's hurting." His eyes traveled over her face, to her mouth, then back up to her eyes. "Who hurt you, Macy?"

For a split second, she wanted to tell him. How freeing it would be to finally get the demon out of her, but she couldn't. The harsh reality was he would look at her differently, and that was a risk she refused to take.

"Don't turn this around on me."

She jerked away and turned back to the desk. Pulling in a deep breath, she tried to regain some of her courage and focus on what she came to do. The ache now turned into a throb she might not be able to ignore for much longer.

"Don't dig into my life if you don't want anyone digging into yours."

With shaky hands, she gathered the invoices and tapped the edges on the desk to make them all neat and orderly. She needed control of something right now, even if it was these stupid papers.

"Want to share stories?" he asked.

She nearly called him on the rhetorical question. What would he say if she came out and told him what she'd been through? What would he say if he knew she'd never told another soul what happened to her that night? She might not wear her scars on the outside, but she had plenty on the inside.

"I want you to stop being a jerk," she told him as she turned back around. "Obviously you're not used to people caring about you, so I'll try not to make that mistake again."

Something flashed through his eyes. Regret, guilt, fear? Maybe all three, but the emotion was gone as fast as it had come.

"That's for the best." He delivered his reply as he turned and walked out.

That was it? He wasn't going to say anything else? What on earth was going on in his head? What had just happened? Seriously. Because her entire system had gone into overload in the past twenty minutes. Between being wrapped in his arms, held by his strong grip, and stared at with such intensity, Macy didn't even know how she should react. She prided herself on keeping the upper hand when it came to men—she had to—but Liam rocked her world in ways no one had before, and she didn't like it. Okay . . . she did. But she didn't like being so emotionally confused when her body was so revved up.

In all honesty, the crazy ambiance and invisible pull was most likely why Liam had made his exit. Maybe he wasn't sure how to respond either, so leaving was the best option.

Macy sank into the old wooden chair. Propping her elbows on the desk, she rubbed her temples and concentrated on deep breaths. That stupid migraine was coming back full force. Trying to come into work tonight was obviously a complete waste. She'd felt fine when she'd left home, was able to tolerate the dull ache when she'd first arrived, but she was at a point where she needed to get back, take her medicine, and get into bed.

Liam Monroe was throwing her for a complete loop. She didn't know if she wanted to scream at him or grab him and kiss him.

Both. She wanted to do both.

The sharp pain shooting from behind her eyes had her reaching blindly to click the lamp off. Stress tended to exacerbate these migraines and she really didn't know what she was so stressed about lately. Day-to-day responsibilities hadn't really increased once she took over. She'd always worked at the store, but now that she was the sole owner, maybe she was doing more so she could give her dad the time off he so deserved. And she didn't want to let him down.

As the third generation owner, she wanted the next few decades to be just as successful as in the past. She wanted her father to be proud. Regardless of the fact that this wasn't necessarily her dream job, she was here and she'd do the job she was supposed to do.

Macy continued to massage her head in a vain attempt to ease the pressure. Her purse with her medicine was out at the counter where she'd dropped everything when she first came in. Now she just needed to get to it.

Maybe if she just rested for a moment. Macy folded her arms and lay her head down, keeping her eyes closed.

The soft brush of footsteps in the room was her only warning before familiar arms banded around, this time lifting her from the seat. She must've fallen asleep, because she was a bit confused as to where she was for the briefest of moments.

Macy whimpered as the movement jarred her head. She hadn't realized how fast and how far gone she was. Apparently the rest hadn't done a thing to help her state.

Leaning against Liam's bare, broad chest was a comfort she hadn't even known she was seeking. With her eyes closed, she leaned against his warmth and let him carry her away. That dizzying state of sleepiness continued to envelop her.

"You shouldn't have come in if you're that tired."

"Migraine," she whispered.

"Do you have medicine?" he asked, his voice low, caring.

"My purse. By the front counter."

She couldn't say more, couldn't move. Nausea started to build as it did when she got these sudden attacks. She only prayed she wouldn't toss her cookies all over Liam.

He barely slowed as they passed by the front counter. Then he kept going and was heading up to the second story.

"I'm sorry," she whispered, humiliation sweeping through her.

Liam didn't say a word, just carried her up the steps as if she weighed nothing. When she felt better she'd appreciate his masculine skills and the fact he wasn't even breathing hard. A strong man didn't have to be scary; strength could be extremely sexy. Again, something she'd have to analyze later, when thinking didn't feel like a jackhammer in her head.

Moments later he eased her down. A bed, she realized as she brought an arm up to cover her face. She could tell from the direction he'd walked when she heard him from downstairs that he was sleeping in her old room, and the cool sheets smelled like him, all manly and rugged.

Sounds registered around her: Liam shuffling from the room, coming back, rummaging through her purse, shaking the pill bottle.

Easing up, Macy held out her hand. He dropped the pill onto her palm and then held a glass to her lips. If she didn't feel so bad, she would be embarrassed at how she was acting like an invalid, but there was no other option.

Once she swallowed the pill, she eased back down. The bed dipped beside her as Liam sat next to her hip.

"Does this take long to kick in?"

"Long enough," she murmured.

How humbling was it to be infatuated with a man only to have him witness you at your absolute worst possible time? She only prayed the nausea didn't become worse.

Macy started to sit back up, risking opening one eye and

grateful to find the room was dark. "I'll just wait out in my truck for this to pass."

Instantly, hands covered her shoulders and settled her back against the pillows. "You'll sleep here. I'll go to the couch. What else can I get you?"

No way was she staying the night. As soon as she felt like moving without throwing up, she was out of here. Despite the dark room, Macy kept her eyes closed and sank further into the soft sheets. Why did this have to feel so good? Why was letting him take care of her so annoyingly wonderful? The only person she'd ever let help her was her father. This went against everything in her "I am woman, hear me roar" attitude.

"You're not arguing, so I know you feel awful." He brushed the hair away from her face and she wanted him to keep touching her in that soft manner. Had anyone ever done that?

"I'll leave the door open in case you need something," he went on, pulling away and easing off the bed. "Don't worry about waking me. If you get worse, I want to know."

"I'll be fine. As soon as it eases, I'm leaving."

Liam grunted and his heavy footsteps carried him from the room. Macy didn't want to think about lying here in his bed, didn't want to think about how one minute he was infuriating and the next he was nurturing. Why did he have to be so . . . ? She couldn't even pinpoint one word to describe him. When she was better, she vowed, she'd think of a whole host of adjectives to describe her tenant.

Macy shifted to her side and brought her hand up over her eyes. She prayed the prescription would kick in soon. It was already around midnight and she really didn't want to have to call her dad in to open the store in the morning. Two days in a row wouldn't look too good. Even though he completely understood her condition, she didn't want him to think she couldn't handle the responsibility of taking over. She hadn't been able to finish her degree, had let fear grip her and take over momentarily, and she refused to fail at this, too.

All she needed was to wait, let the meds kick in, and she'd be good to go. She'd just lie here, inhaling the woodsy scent on Liam's sheets, and try to recall a time when any man treated her with such care.

Chapter Three

"Do you think I should ask her or not?"

Liam rolled out the dough that would become a cherry cheese Danish. Brock sat across the center island, ready for some advice. He'd come straight to the resort after school and apparently Liam was the chosen one to spill those teenage insecurities to.

"I'm the last person you should seek relationship advice from." Liam tried not to take his frustrations and anger out on the dough, but past memories threatened to destroy the pastry he was forming. "You're better off asking Zach or Braxton."

Brock shook his head. "Nah. They're getting married. I don't want to get married. I just want to know whether or not I should ask Alli on a date."

Liam glanced across the counter to the teen. That look in his eye seemed so familiar. The confusion, the sliver of hope in what could happen if he pushed the panic aside and went after what he wanted. Liam had been so much like Brock at that age. Brock was a mix of all the Monroe brothers and the boy wasn't even remotely related to any of them. Yet fate had brought them all together, sending them each on a path that led to this moment.

Last year when Brock was discovered homeless and living in the resort, which was in the midst of renovations, Zach had instantly taken him in. Through the proper legal means, Brock was no longer a runaway from an abusive father and was now surrounded by a family who loved him as their own. They'd all come from various places, so they understood the need for security, for some sense of stability.

And though Liam was honestly the dead last person to offer his opinion in regard to women, he couldn't ignore Brock's questioning gaze.

"If you want to go on a date, ask her." Liam resumed rolling out the dough, making sure to get the edges nice and even with the middle.

"It's more than a date," Brock muttered. "It's the prom."

Hell. Prom. Liam recalled his prom night. He'd only been worried about how to maneuver his date out of her dress. Damn it. Teenage hormones were definitely not an area he wanted to venture into. That would be a hell of a lot worse than relationships.

"Then ask her to the prom. It's just a dance."

"To chicks, the prom is everything. I don't care about a dance—I just want a date and I heard she and her boyfriend broke up, so she doesn't have a date."

High school days. Liam wouldn't go back if someone paid him. Between still trying to cope with the loss of his mother, living with the Monroes, and just being a teenage boy with all the pressures of that age, Liam had absolutely hated that time in his life.

"Then if she's free, sounds like the perfect time to ask."

Brock's finger traced the marble pattern on the quartz counter. "What if she says no?"

Liam withheld the sigh. Were teenage boys always this fearful? Liam may have hated those days, but he'd also had a chip on his shoulder when he'd been a teen. But in Brock's defense, the boy's father was an ass. He'd belittled

Brock for so long, the poor kid was just learning what it was like to have a support team.

"What if she says yes?" Liam countered without looking up. "What if you guys go out and you have the best time and she wants to see you again?"

"I have no clue," Brock snorted. "I'm still working on the first date and you've already got me on the second."

Liam laughed and reached for the bowl of flour. Spreading a light coating onto his rolling pin, he eyed Brock. "Have you always been this nervous about asking a girl out?"

Brock's bright eyes drifted to the floor. He gave a slight shrug. "I've never asked a girl out before."

Well, great. Nothing like making him feel even more insecure. Brock had been living with Zach and Sophie for a year and Liam had been in Savannah for the majority of that time. He'd just assumed Brock would've gone out and had more of a social life. Perhaps they were more alike than Liam first thought.

"I mean, I've been with groups and we've done stuff, but I've never flat-out asked a girl to go on a date."

This was a total game changer. Setting his rolling pin on the counter, Liam rested his hands on the surface and leaned forward. "Listen, when you ask her make sure you are confident. Even if you have to fake it."

Brock blew out a sigh and came to his feet. "Why do guys always have to do the asking?" he muttered as he searched the cabinet for food. He ended up grabbing a bag of BBQ chips and settled back down on his stool.

"I know of women who ask guys out." Liam was leaving it at that because his ex had found it rather easy to ask quite a few guys out while they were still together. "But if you ask, that shows you're taking charge and confident."

Brock shoved a handful of chips in his mouth. Liam watched as the crumbs fell onto the counter. "Um . . . I'm working here."

With a mouthful, Brock stopped chewing, muttered an apology, and swiped the crumbs onto the floor.

"Great. I needed you to sweep and mop today anyway," Zach stated as he entered the kitchen, the screen door slamming at his back.

Brock groaned and took his bag of chips to the other side of the kitchen, thankfully away from the dough. The last thing Liam needed was a BBQ-flavored Danish. He turned to the industrial-sized stainless steel refrigerator and pulled out the container of filling he'd mixed up earlier.

"So what's this about Macy spending the night at your place?"

Liam nearly dropped the bowl, but managed to get it onto the counter before turning to glare at Zach. Damn it. With a crooked grin and a quirked brow, his brother leaned against the island. Whatever the hell Zach was trying to start, Liam needed to put a stop to it. The last thing he needed was damn gossip spreading about what he and Macy definitely were *not* doing.

"You told me you shouldn't give advice on women and you had one sleep over last night?" Brock accused, suddenly not concerned about shoveling in the chips.

Zach glanced between the two. "You went to *him* for advice?"

And this was just one of the many reasons Liam missed his job in Savannah. The large, posh restaurant had so many employees and they were so swamped, nobody had time to stand around and chitchat like teenage girls. Besides that, nobody cared. He'd always done his job and gone home. End of story.

Now that he was back, suddenly everyone wanted to know about his business . . . and his overnight guest, which sounded so much more interesting than what truly happened.

Liam jerked the sealed lid off the filling. "She came by

the store late last night to do some work, she got a migraine, and couldn't drive. That's all."

Brock snorted in disbelief.

"Don't you have floors to clean?" Liam growled.

"They're not going anywhere."

Yeah, Brock fit in perfect in the family with his quick wit and snarky comebacks. Damn if Liam wasn't proud that the kid felt so at home here he could just be himself.

But Zach wasn't easing up. He continued to stare, waiting on more of an explanation. Damn nosy family. And Liam loved them. He couldn't help but love this crazy bunch—he just wished he had some privacy.

"You can stand there all day," Liam told his brother. "But that's the entire story. How did you know, anyway?"

"Ran by Knobs and Knockers earlier. I asked Macy if she was feeling all right. She just didn't seem like herself."

Liam scooped the filling onto the dough. Stubborn woman was going to make herself worse if she didn't slow down. How did she expect to keep going when she was clearly burning both ends of the day trying to prove she could handle the store? She could more than handle it or her father wouldn't have entrusted it to her. But she was determined to kill herself to prove a point.

Liam had been up all night because he was afraid she'd need something and wouldn't tell him. He randomly went to the bedroom door to check on her, but each time he checked, she was sleeping peacefully, her dark hair fanned all around her, all over his sheets.

He hadn't had a woman in his bed in way too long. Macy shouldn't keep pulling him in, but she did without even trying.

Liam had left at six a.m. and tried to be as quiet as possible. He didn't figure she wanted an early morning encounter any more than he did. He couldn't imagine if they'd actually had sex because this morning after had been awkward enough.

And why was he thinking sex anyway? He told himself not to put sex and Macy in the same sentence . . . not even in his own mind.

But he was a guy, so . . .

"I'm not her keeper," Liam growled. He couldn't make her do anything, except last night when she'd been too sick to drive. And she would've tried to drive herself home had he not stopped her. He scooped more filling, leaving drops between the bowl and the dough. "She's a big girl."

"Maybe she needs someone to check on her," Zach suggested, reaching across to swipe the filling off the counter and lick it off his finger.

On a sigh, Liam faced his brother. "Spit it out. Whatever you're hinting at, just say it."

"He wants you to go see Macy," Brock stated.

Zach shrugged. "I'm just saying that she's always looking after her dad, looking after the store, and never dates the same guy twice from what I've seen. That tells me maybe nobody has taken time to get to know her and actually care for her."

"Are you kidding me?" Liam really, really didn't want to have this conversation, but he also needed to clear the air and get this out so they could move on. "I'm not looking for a date, a girlfriend, or whatever the hell else you're thinking. I'm here for you guys and to work. That's all. Don't try to dig deeper into my life."

Zach started to reach across, this time for the bowl. Liam moved it away just in time.

"Get out of my kitchen."

"You'll make a shitty housewife. You won't share and you don't communicate," Zach said.

Liam gritted his teeth and counted backward from one hundred. He made it to ninety-eight.

"Just because you fell in love, don't go around playing matchmaker." Turning his attention back to the job he was here to do, he added, "Both of you out. Brock, I'll be done in an hour and you can come back and clean the floor. Why don't you two go discuss Brock's female problems, because I don't have any and am not in the mood to talk."

"Mom is cranky today," Brock whispered.

Zach's laugh filled the spacious room. "She didn't get any sleep last night because of her roommate."

"Out," Liam yelled, pointing his spatula toward the door.

"Kind of hard to sound and look like you have authority when there's icing dripping on the floor," Zach said around his laugh.

Brock groaned. "Aw, man. I have to clean that."

Liam jerked the spoon again, sending another glob onto the ceramic tile. "I can keep going."

Brock grabbed the bag of chips and headed out the back door.

Zach started to follow, but froze in the doorway. "Seriously, man. Check on her."

Liam turned his back on his brother and ignored that niggling of guilt that pushed through him. He didn't want to form any extra feelings, didn't want to care about anyone else. His plate was full. He'd cared for one woman before—had gotten close, too close. Then he'd been taken for a fool. That experience had sucked out the little bit of his soul he'd rebuilt after all he'd been through. Attempting to feel again could very well destroy him.

But he did care for Macy no matter what he kept telling himself, and he didn't have to be a jerk. He could call her and see how she was doing, see if she needed . . . what? What exactly could he do for her? They weren't precisely friends, let alone anything more.

And he was leaving. So no commitments. None. No matter how much he was drawn to his sexy landlord.

Liam finished putting the Danish together and popped them into one of the two wall ovens. All he could do was call and check on her. Anything beyond that wasn't an option. Liam didn't have time for more, didn't want to make the time, because he refused to ever have his emotions or his heart used against him again.

By the end of the day Macy felt nearly human again. The headache was gone, but she was utterly exhausted. She flipped off the flashing OPEN sign—a sign she'd had to talk her father into getting because he was still turning over the old plastic one that clanged against the door every time someone would enter or exit. Just as she headed toward the door to lock up, a familiar face popped in.

"Do you have a minute?"

Macy smiled at her old high school softball coach, Diane Davis. "Of course. Flick that lock, though."

Diane closed and locked the door, then moved closer to the counter. As always when Macy saw her, Diane was dressed for practice. Today was no different; she wore a pair of track pants and a T-shirt with the school logo on the front.

"I was hoping to catch you when you closed so we wouldn't be disturbed. Is this okay?"

Intrigued, Macy nodded. "Absolutely. Is something wrong?"

Diane would pop in now and then and Macy would see her at the grocery. Haven was a small town after all, but she'd never stopped after hours to talk. During Macy's high school days, she tended to see Diane more than her own family. Practice and traveling for games made them close, more friends than just a coach and a player. Diane had even made it a point to go to a couple of Macy's college games . . . before her year was cut short.

"Not at all," Diane assured, then gestured toward the register. "Don't let me keep you. If you need to do other things, I can talk while you close out."

Waving a hand, Macy replied, "Come on back to my tiny office. I'm in no hurry to add up credit slips."

Macy led the way through the narrow aisle with screws and bolts and headed toward her office. Her eyes glanced to the stairs and an instant image of Liam carrying her flooded her mind. Not that he'd been far from her thoughts today, especially when Zach had stopped in and mentioned that she looked tired.

Without thinking, Macy had mentioned that she'd slept upstairs last night, but another customer had come up to the counter and she'd gotten busy before she could fully explain. Then Zach left and she had no doubt that he went to Liam for the scoop.

Only there was no scoop, only humiliation and embarrassment and leftover questions as to what was happening between them. She could guess by the passion she'd seen in his eyes and the shield he quickly put up whenever she tried to delve deeper that someone had hurt him; she would bet anything on that. And she didn't think it was the accident that had left the deepest wound, either. The emotions running within him were just as jagged as the marring on his face.

Later Macy would call and thank him, even though she would have liked to ignore everything that had happened and just move on. Clearly moving on and ignoring what Liam stirred within her wasn't an option. Besides, he didn't have to be so compassionate last night. He could've helped her to her truck like she'd requested and let her wait the pain out on her own.

Macy pulled out the step stool she kept in the corner and took a seat on it, gesturing toward her rickety desk chair for Diane. "Have a seat and tell me what's up."

The chair squeaked and groaned as Diane settled in. Macy leaned against the wall and waited to hear why this conversation was so important that her old coach needed privacy.

"I'm retiring after this season," she began.

Macy smiled. "That's wonderful. You've devoted so many years, you deserve some time to yourself. Wait . . . you're not sick or something, are you?"

Diane shook her head and rested her elbow on the desk. "No, no. Just tired, and I think a younger, more energetic coach is needed."

When Diane only continued to stare, then raised her brows, Macy finally realized what this talk was about. "Me?"

"I don't know of anyone more qualified."

Macy could name about five people off the top of her head. She hadn't touched a bat, glove, or ball since she left college midseason after winning a big game against their main rival. She'd actually burned her uniform when she returned home after her mother passed. Her father had been in his own state of grief and she never wanted him, or anyone for that matter, to know her secret. She'd handled everything herself, but she just didn't know if she could ever revisit the sport she'd once loved more than anything else.

"Oh, Diane, I'm flattered, but—"

"Don't say no." She held up a hand and leaned forward in the creaky old chair. "I'm not looking for an answer today. You have some time and I haven't told anyone I'm retiring. I wanted to discuss this with you because I know you'll be great. I didn't want to let the board know yet, because I didn't want them to post the position."

Macy's mind was spinning, something she couldn't physically afford at the moment. "Surely there's a teacher who wants to coach."

Diane had stopped teaching high school math two years ago, but stayed on as the softball coach. She was loved by students and parents. She demanded respect, but the adoration she had for every child she worked with showed. She always had a winning team because the determination and hard work she instilled in her players invariably paid off. Regardless of who replaced her, the school would feel that void.

Diane definitely had some big shoes to fill. Macy wasn't even sure if she could fill small shoes at this point.

"I doubt there's a willing teacher," Diane replied. "I've hinted for several months that I may start to slow down and nobody seems eager to step into my place."

"Because nobody can run that program like you do."

Diane beamed. "That's sweet of you to say, but it's time. My husband wants to travel, and to be honest, I do, too. We want to get an RV and just drive. I want to see the country while I'm still young enough to go on adventures."

Macy wanted that for her, but to actually agree to apply for the position of softball coach was quite a leap. A leap Macy never intended on taking. She couldn't explain to Diane why her love of the sport had been tarnished.

"Are you retiring no matter what my decision is?" Macy asked.

"I am. But I'm hoping you'll really think about this."

Macy swiped her hair back away from her face. She hadn't gone home this morning to change. She'd merely taken off her flannel and kept on her T-shirt. Thankfully she kept a few toiletries in her small bathroom here, but she'd been out of rubber bands. She'd twisted her hair up once using a pencil, but with the weight of all she had, the pencil had only held for so long.

"I'm really swamped with the store," Macy muttered, voicing her thoughts. She might have been looking for excuses, reasons to say no, but the store was a legitimate concern.

Not to mention, she had her own personal dream she was so close to fulfilling. The social worker had verified all of Macy's paperwork and fostering had been approved. The home visit and background check had been completed. Macy hoped it wouldn't be long before she could bring a child in and care for him or her. Her main goal was to adopt. Her father knew of her plans, but that was all. And the only reason he knew was because the social worker did a home visit with him as well, since he lived on her property.

Diane's smile didn't fade. "I understand, but before you say no, at least come to a game or two. Maybe you'll feel differently."

Macy wasn't sure how she'd feel stepping back into that world again. Would she pick up where she left off? Would she freeze and let that one night consume her? Would the cheers from the stands, the crack of the ball hitting the bat, thrust her back into a time that threatened to cripple her emotionally if she stayed there too long?

"You were the best player to ever come out of Haven."

Nothing like turning that guilt key just a bit more. "So you've told me before."

"Nobody has ever beaten your school records," Diane added.

"I've only been out ten years."

Diane shrugged and came to her feet. "Like I said, you were the best. I wouldn't want to pass my girls off to just anybody."

Macy stood and followed Diane to the front of the store. Footsteps overhead instantly grabbed Macy's attention. She wasn't getting out of here anytime soon because she planned to have an awkward conversation with Liam, which she felt she shouldn't avoid.

Diane glanced up. "I heard Liam Monroe was living

here. That new resort of theirs is really taking off. Talk around town is they have a killer masseuse and Liam's food is worth the visit all in itself."

Macy nodded and reached for the lock on the glass door. "They're really thriving. But he's only living here temporarily, until he finds a place."

She hoped. Surely he was looking . . . wasn't he? Perhaps after last night he was ready to move. Maybe the next time Macy saw Sophie she could casually ask if there were any houses or condos to rent in the area.

"I've heard only positive feedback," Diane added. "They are really drawing the tourists from Savannah. Looks like those Monroe boys have made something of themselves after all. I worried about them, but their parents and Chelsea would be proud."

Macy nodded. "They would. The boys came together for Chelsea, which says so much about the person she was. They wouldn't have let her dream just die."

Diane rested her hand on Macy's shoulder. "I don't want you to say no to the job because you're afraid, but I don't want you to agree out of guilt, either."

Did she think the boys launched the resort out of guilt?

"Our next game is Saturday at eleven." Diane flicked the lock on the door and stepped out, but threw a smile over her shoulder. "We have a new stadium you should check out."

Once Diane was gone, Macy locked up again. Coaching was a far cry from playing. All the stress was on the coach, as was all the worry for each player. Was she really ready to tackle a bunch of teenage girls with hormones all over the place, boy issues, drama? Just the thought threatened to bring on another headache.

But Diane had created such a remarkable program that the only girls who tried out for the team were those who truly wanted to be there. Girls just like Macy used to be, hoping for scholarship money to further their education and keep playing the sport they loved.

Still, the store was a full-time job, and fostering would be as well.

She leaned back against the door and closed her eyes. The words "no way in hell" kept ringing through her head, but Diane wanted her to think about it, so Macy would. How could she possibly juggle everything? The store was demanding, and provided her with job security, which was a blessing. To add another demanding job to the mix might just be more than she could handle—regardless of her personal issues.

"Is your head still hurting?"

Macy jumped, holding a hand over her heart, which nearly thumped right out of her chest. She hadn't even heard Liam approach. "You scared the hell out of me."

He stood there, wearing a perfectly fitted gray T, hands in the pockets of his well-worn jeans. There was something to be said about a man who could make cotton and denim look so sexy. And now Macy knew exactly what he looked like without that shirt on, and that visual reminder did nothing to squelch her desire. She reminisced about the rest of the tattoo that peeked beneath his shirt sleeve.

"Is your head hurting?" he repeated, taking a step forward.

"No. I'm fine."

"You don't look fine." Those dark eyes studied her. "Zach thought you felt bad earlier, too."

Without bothering to hide her groan, Macy started past him. "Zach might be stirring something up."

Liam's hand whipped out and gripped her elbow as she walked by. She turned, her face mere inches from his.

"Is there something to stir?" he asked.

Unable to help herself, Macy grinned, lifted a brow, and leaned into him. "You tell me. You want to stir something up?"

Instantly he dropped his hold, but continued to stare into her eyes. "Don't do that. I'm not one of the guys you date."

"You could be."

Had she just said that? She seriously needed to stop and think before opening her mouth sometimes. But the man got under her skin and she didn't like it. She needed control, and she couldn't let him have the upper hand. Even though Liam was nothing like the guys who'd hurt her, Macy couldn't relinquish power over her emotions.

"Apparently you're feeling better."

Liam turned and started walking away. The empty, sickening feeling settled deep in the pit of her stomach. Why did she do that? Why did she treat him like any other guy she'd flirt with—get all sassy and then never talk to him again? Liam wasn't like those guys; he was absolutely right. And she was a jerk for even thinking for a split second that she could pull this with him.

But, damn it, he threw her off and she didn't know how to act. This was completely new territory for her. When had a guy captured her interest in such a way? Even before her attack, there had been no one who stirred up so much in her.

"I'm sorry," she called across the store.

He stopped in the middle of an aisle. The evening sun beamed through a nearby window and Macy concentrated on the flecks of dust floating through the air and not the way Liam seemed to take up so much space in her life now.

Slowly, she was losing her tight grip where he was concerned and she knew there was no way to stop. All she could do was attempt to hang on.

"I don't know what to say to you," she said to his back. At least he'd stopped walking away, so he was listening. "You act like you don't want to talk to me one second, and the next you're caring for me."

Still, silence. Her heart beat so hard inside her chest. Macy sighed, tugging on the tied flannel around her waist.

"Thank you, by the way."

Slowly, Liam turned. Macy remained silent, waiting for him to say something, leaving the ball in his court. She didn't like feeling inferior or awkward, but with Liam things were much more complex—one label couldn't cover it all. She'd been interested in him for so long, but he'd never shown any interest whatsoever. Not even a little. Then they went their separate ways. Soon after, life intervened, changing them both. But now that they were living in the same town again, could she ignore her old feelings? Possibly, but why would she want to battle herself? Her feelings were stronger, deeper, and heart-pounding.

Were they dancing around something more? Should she just say exactly what she was thinking so they'd get everything out in the open? They'd had a moment last night, and she'd seen a side of Liam she hadn't expected.

Carrying her up the staircase—à la Rhett Butler—was sexy as hell, but she hadn't been able to fully enjoy the moment considering they'd been in a hardware store and she'd been praying she didn't throw up.

"If you don't pretend, then you don't have to apologize." He remained a good distance away, but he still tipped his head slightly to keep his scar concealed from her. "I'm not asking for anything from you, Macy. I'm only in Haven for a job and my family, that's all."

The veiled statement came through loud and clear. She wouldn't be making a fool of herself ever again where he was concerned.

"Duly noted," she replied with a nod. "I need to finish up closing and get out of here. Thanks again for last night."

She rounded the counter and started pulling out the credit card receipts from the small binder she kept them in below the register. Liam stood behind her; she hadn't heard him move away, but she refused to turn and see what he was doing. He didn't want anything to do with her other than a place to live. Fine. She was a big girl, she could handle this. He didn't need to come right out and tell her he wasn't interested. She was smart enough to read between the lines.

She just wished he didn't make her feel. What was it that made Liam get beneath her skin? Was it the fact she'd always wondered what, if anything, could've happened between them had she not gone away to school and had he not been in an accident? Was it the fact he was broken in ways she could only guess and she recognized another vulnerable soul?

"It's not you," he murmured.

Macy's fingers stilled in the midst of sorting the tiny strips of paper. His words hit her hard and she closed her eyes, refusing to show any emotion. But she also wasn't going to tell him everything was okay when it wasn't.

"No, it's not me," she agreed.

"I never want to date or get close to anyone," he went on. "My family is all I need."

Family loyalty. She totally got that aspect, but . . . forever? He *never* wanted to be close to another person? Clearly he was more broken than she'd thought. Not that she'd call him on it, because he'd surely deny it.

"You don't have to explain anything to me." She concentrated on making neat little piles of receipts, ignoring the way her hands shook. "I need to finish this."

"Damn it, Macy."

His booming voice seemed to echo in the open space. She jerked, spun around, and spilled those perfect piles right at her booted feet. The man continued to disrupt her life in every way imaginable.

"Why do you do this?" he demanded, settling his hands on his narrow hips. "You play the wounded card so well without even realizing you're doing it. I can't just walk away now without feeling like an ass."

"If you want to walk away, do it. I'm fine no matter what you do, and I'm not playing anything at all."

Maybe she didn't sound as convincing as she meant to. Liam dropped his head between his shoulders, then looked back up at her with that tilt of his head. Those dark eyes pinned her in place.

"You're not fine," he countered. The muscle in his jaw clenched as his lips thinned. "You think I don't see it? You think I can't tell that you're hiding secrets you don't want people to know?"

Macy crossed her arms over her chest. A little hope burst in her when his eyes darted down to the V in her T-shirt. Not that she thought she was sexy by any means in what she wore.

"So what secrets are you hiding?" she retorted.

"I'm not here to share secrets, form friendships, or anything else."

Rolling her eyes, Macy threw her hands in the air and bent down to scoop up the receipts. "Yeah, I get it. Family, work. Simple life."

"Nothing about my life is simple," he snapped, his voice growing louder. "If things were simple I wouldn't want to close this gap between us and kiss the hell out of you like I nearly did months ago. If things were simple I wouldn't have spent my day at work worried after Zach told me you didn't look well. If things were simple I'd be in Savannah where I belong and I wouldn't have to deal with a past I never wanted to revisit again."

Slowly, Macy came to her feet, work forgotten. Though silence settled between them, his words still seemed to echo.

"My life is complicated," he added, his tone calmer now. "And I can't deal with any more."

Now he did turn and walk away. His heavy footsteps seemed to pound on the stairs. The door to the second floor opened and closed. The resounding *snick* of the lock was all the exclamation point she needed to know that their conversation on this topic was over.

But for a moment, she just wanted to stand here and revisit some of the most beautiful words she'd heard in a long, long time.

Finally he'd admitted to wanting to kiss her.

If that moment was still in his thoughts, then she had taken up some real estate space in his mind. Maybe he wasn't immune to her after all. Maybe she didn't need to flirt with him. Perhaps someone like Liam found a basic woman attractive, one who didn't wear makeup, didn't play dress up, and didn't drive some cute little car.

Whatever he was dealing with had nothing to do with her. But it was nice to know she was a distraction. She wasn't sure if she'd ever been a distraction for someone before.

And now she had to figure out exactly how to handle this situation. Because Liam wasn't one to buy into her act. She was going to have to let go of her well-crafted self-image and be herself. She hadn't been that girl in so long, Macy wasn't sure she could. But baring her true self might be the only way to get him to open up, and for some reason, she wanted him to let go. Perhaps helping him would free her somehow . . . so long as she didn't have to reveal the darkest part.

Would her risk pay off or would he throw her attempts back in her face and become even more closed off?

There was only one way to find out.

Chapter Four

"You're cheating."

Phil Hayward laughed as he laid down his cards and raked in the chips, not caring that he took his daughter's meager winnings. "You say that every time."

Macy took a drink of her beer. "That's because you cheat every time."

She loved poker night with her dad. Since they technically lived separately now, she had him come to her house once a week after work. When they were done, he'd walk out, down the driveway and into the back of the garage where Zach had built an apartment. It was weird because Macy had never lived alone. She'd always been with her dad, both in the store and in the apartment above. Other than going away to college, she'd been right here in Haven.

But now that she had her own place, she rather liked the freedom. She was pretty sure she sucked at decorating, because she'd lived here for about five months and had yet to hang a picture on the walls. She couldn't stand the thought of putting holes in perfectly good sheetrock she'd be paying for over the next thirty years.

She might not have been the best decorator, but she had a hand in helping Zach and she knew for sure her house was rock solid with the finest of materials. A little more important to her than the right balance of candles and picture frames scattered around just to be dusted later.

Her dad came to his feet and groaned. "It's getting late."

"It's nine," she countered, sliding the cards together and tapping them on the edge of the table.

"And I'm an old man. I'll be sixty in a couple weeks. I should be in bed at this time."

She never thought of her father as old. Most kids always viewed their parents as ancient, but Macy never did. Old always meant death to her, so she never wanted to view him that way . . . especially after her mother passed. She wanted to hang on to him for as long as possible.

"Sixty isn't old," she argued. "And you're healthy as a horse."

"The doctor says so, but I think I'm supposed to moan and groan at my age."

Macy laughed as she stacked the cards.

"How are your migraines?" he asked, gripping the high back on her kitchen chair.

Coming to her feet, she started placing the chips back into the appropriate slots in their carrier. "Fine now. This last one came out of nowhere and lingered longer than usual."

Her father's silver brows drew inward. "Do you need to go back to the doctor?"

"I'm fine."

"You'd never tell me if you weren't," he muttered. "I worry about you."

Moving around the table, Macy threw her arms around her dad's neck. He was just a few inches taller than she was. She definitely took her height from her dad and her curves from her mom.

"I worry about you, too, but I promise if I need to see someone, I will." She gave him a reassuring squeeze and eased back. "Trust me, I hate having migraines. If I get another one like that I may make an appointment to see if we need to change the medicine. I definitely don't want to have them when I'm trying to take care of a little one."

Her father smiled, the creases around his eyes deepening. "Any child you take in will be so lucky to have you."

"I requested a little girl," she informed him. "I just thought that would be easier all around."

"Probably so," he said, nodding in agreement. "Are you sure you can handle everything? I don't want you to get overwhelmed."

She'd put in hours thinking on this exact subject. But she was more than confident she could do both jobs. "I can do it. Besides, you're my backup for the store and a built-in babysitter."

Apparently he was happy with her answer since he gave a brief nod. "Speaking of the store, everything okay? When I worked the other day I saw you had rearranged the plumbing section."

Yeah, she didn't figure he'd be good with any changes she made, but she'd had cause. "I got in a new line of products that had a huge rebate and catered toward the DIY crowd. I wanted to showcase that and the plumbing needed to be shifted."

"Customers don't like change," he grumbled.

Macy patted his smooth cheek and smiled. "But customers like rebates, so I think I'm still okay. Besides, I'll be changing it out again when the new spring items start arriving. All the pots, the seeds. I'm trying a new distributor this year."

He grunted before heading toward her back patio doors, which looked out onto the spacious yard. "I know it's your store now, at least in all the legal ways, but I'm still here. I can do more than just fill in when you have a headache."

Macy knew that's why he'd randomly stop by the store

when she was open. He would make the excuse of already being out running errands and say he just popped in to see the customers. But she'd caught him shifting the boxes of nails around, changing out a few sale signs, and one morning she'd discovered he'd already opened for her, claiming he'd gotten up early.

In all reality, her father wasn't ready to retire. She'd tried to talk him out of it, but he said it was time for the next generation to take over. She figured he wanted to still live his life and have a good time while he was young enough to enjoy it. He had a few buddies that had already retired and were living it up on the golf course. She couldn't fault him one bit for wanting to join them.

Macy always knew the store would go to her—that's what she was raised understanding—but part of her wished she would've finished her business degree. No one in her family had gone to college and she wanted to be able to prove she could, to make her parents proud. She didn't need the degree to run the store, but she wanted it. There would have been some sense of pride in knowing she'd been the first.

But she couldn't regret not getting her degree. Had she managed to finish, she would've missed out on several years of being with her father when he needed her most. Actually, they'd needed each other. All things happened for a reason, right?

Even bad things that altered your every decision in life.

"I know you're there for me, Dad." Her cell vibrated on the counter where it lay charging. She'd check it later. "I'm really fine, but it isn't my store. It's our store no matter what. Come in and do whatever you want. Now that we don't live together, I miss seeing you all hours of the day."

Her father laughed and shook his head. "I'm sure you're happy to have your own space. Now your dates can pick you up and not have to run into your dad."

"My last few dates I've actually met at a restaurant," she countered with a grin. "And I haven't been on a date in almost a month."

She refused to admit, even to herself, that she'd been preoccupied with a certain Monroe brother and she'd wasted time waiting on him to make a move. Granted, he did admit he wanted to kiss her, so . . . was that a move? If so, could he scoot his fine rear end a little quicker and make said kiss happen?

"I don't want to meddle in your love life, so I'll just stay in my apartment. You tell me if you need me at the store, to shoot a guy, or to walk you down the aisle. I'm always here."

Macy laughed. Her father had the driest sense of humor, but she adored him. He'd been her only stability after she returned from college a shattered teen who'd seen the cruelty of life and lost her mother all in the span of twenty-four hours. Even though her father didn't know everything, he'd held her while she cried, he'd wiped her tears, and he'd never questioned her need to be home. He'd never acted like her turning away from the scholarship was a disappointment. No matter the decisions she made, he always stood right behind her. And he'd done every bit of it through his own grief.

"I don't plan on walking down the aisle anytime soon," she told him. "And I don't really want you shooting anyone for me either. Feel free to come in to the store anytime, though. It's our home, Dad. It always will be."

"Speaking of home, how's Liam working out?"

Macy resisted the urge to sigh. Crossing her arms over her chest and shifting her feet, she tried to think of the proper words. "I haven't seen much of him." Okay, that might be a lie. "He tends to be getting in as I'm closing up and uses the back steps."

Well, that much was completely true. Best not to mention

the whole late night escapade. In reality, she wasn't even sure what had happened then. She'd wanted him to kiss her, to quit dancing around the friction that always stood between them. But he hadn't. Liam Monroe was the only man she just couldn't make herself take that first step with. She wanted him to make the leap. She wanted him to cross that line in the fiercest way . . . and the fact she was so hung up on him terrified her.

She'd promised herself she wouldn't let another man control her. Being physically controlling was one thing, but Liam had complete emotional power over her in a way that both thrilled and terrified her.

"That poor boy never was the same after that accident," her father muttered, shaking his head as if talking to himself. "Maybe now that he's back home he can put those demons to rest and move on. Family is the best medicine for healing."

She wouldn't bank on Liam recovering. From what she'd witnessed, he had enclosed himself behind a self-erected steel wall. What would it take for him to remove that outer shell and let someone in? He was loyal to his family, that much was obvious, but he even kept them at somewhat of a distance.

"I'm his landlord, not his therapist." There. That sounded convincing. "Besides, I've heard what an amazing chef he is. Bella Vous is one busy little resort, and between Cora's magical hands and Liam's dishes, Chelsea's vision is really exploding."

Raking a hand over his still thick, now silver hair, her father laughed. "A women-only resort. I'll be the first to admit the concept sounded crazy when I first heard it, but I know the determination of those Monroe boys. They were raised right, once they came to Haven. They may have had their share of hard times—they're human. But they've moved on and made something of themselves. Ed and Carol would be proud of their boys."

Each of the brothers, and Chelsea, had come from foster care when they'd been sent to Haven. Macy didn't know much about their lives before they came to town, before she met them at school, but those early years couldn't have been good considering none of the boys ever talked about their pasts.

She wondered what all Liam had endured before the accident, before he ever came to Haven. Were his only good years the brief window from when he came to live with the Monroes? Did he ever have an actual happy memory? Macy physically ached for him. She couldn't even imagine how much pain he carried around. What had happened with his biological parents? She had so many questions she wanted to ask, yet she had absolutely no right.

"The resort has definitely brought quite a bit of new tourists to the area," she added. "Especially those day trippers from Savannah who are just nosing around and want to know what all the buzz is about. They've been open since the beginning of the year and have more bookings than they expected right off the bat."

"A smart business plan is what it takes," he said with a firm nod. "Perseverance and motivation, too. Those boys had everything on their side from the beginning."

Macy's phone vibrated on the counter behind her once again. Someone clearly wanted to talk to her.

"I better get back home," her father sighed once again. "If you don't have plans for Saturday night, I'd like to take my favorite girl out to dinner."

Macy smiled. His favorite girl used to be the position of her mother, and now Macy held that title. She was honored.

"I have no plans and I'd cancel them for my favorite guy," she said, then remembered the game on Saturday she was invited to. An early game. "Would you mind watching the store for a bit on Saturday? Maybe from ten-thirty to noon?"

He cocked his head. "Something going on?"

She didn't want to discuss the position she was offered, but she didn't want to lie to him, either. "I need to check something out. Can I wait and tell you about it later? It's still new to me and I'm not sure how I feel, yet."

He eyed her another minute, then finally nodded. "Sure. I've got nothing else going on."

In all likelihood he would've been at the store anyway. "I know that's a busy time, so I'll try not to be gone too long."

Maybe if she just went and watched an inning or two she'd get a good sense of where her head was. Macy would no doubt know the second she walked up to the stadium if she could handle being there or not.

"You forget I used to work at that store alone when your mother had to run errands and you were too little to help," he reminded her. "I think I can handle an hour and a half. I'm more interested in what's pulling you away, though, but I'll be patient."

She closed the space between them and kissed his cheek. "Thanks."

He hugged her good night and left out the patio door, the motion lights instantly kicking on and lighting his path down the drive toward the back of the garage where his apartment was. The thousand-square-foot add-on wasn't too large or too small. The space was perfect for him and Macy figured he was finally glad to have his own space. At least, that's what she kept telling herself. For the first time in forever, he was living on his own. He'd married her mother right out of high school, then when she'd passed, Macy had moved back into the hardware store apartment, so he'd never truly been alone.

This whole new chapter in their lives would take some

getting used to, but this was for the best. She needed space and he did, too. Granted she'd never brought a man back to her house because this was her space and nobody had impressed her enough to deserve to come here.

She'd actually only been on a handful of dates since Liam came back. Suddenly, the appeal just wasn't there. But she needed to figure something out. Either she needed to be bold and make a move, forcing his hand, or she needed to move on before he completely turned her world inside out.

A sliver of giddiness spread through her as she realized that she was quite possibly turning him inside out, too. He wouldn't be so cranky, yet caring, and confess his need to kiss her if she wasn't getting under his skin. More than once she'd seen him barely hanging on to his control. What she wouldn't give to have him snap and just tell her what he truly wanted.

Macy crossed back to where her phone lay on her limestone countertop. She loved every aspect of her new home, loved even more that a friend had helped design and build it. Zach was definitely the only person she would've considered for the job.

Leaving her phone to charge, she thumbed through her texts. One was from a guy asking her out, and the other was from Sophie, wondering if Macy wanted to get together for girls' night one day next week.

Only one of those messages received a yes . . . which just proved how wrapped up with Liam she was. Really, it was absurd to allow her mind to focus on one man for this amount of time. This wasn't like her, but she couldn't help but wonder. There was so much energy surrounding them whenever they were together.

She'd always found him to be intriguing in high school, in that quiet, mysterious way. Now more than ever she wanted to dig deeper, to find out what made him tick. Macy wasn't one to throw herself at a man, and being flirty didn't count. All of that was superficial. She refused to be that clinging, I-need-attention girl, too. What she wanted from Liam was so much more. She wanted into his world for reasons she wasn't ready to explain even to herself.

With a sigh, Macy pushed away from the counter and turned. Her gaze landed on the calendar hanging on the side of her refrigerator. In bold, red letters she'd penned in her father's birthday. She should do something for him. Going out to dinner wasn't new for them, considering she couldn't boil water without setting off her smoke alarm. Besides, just taking him out to dinner wasn't special enough for a sixtieth birthday.

The idea hit her so hard, so fast, she wanted to squeal and jump up and down. A surprise party. That was so the answer. Phil Hayward was such a loved man in the community of Haven. He and their store were staples in the center of town. People would no doubt love to come and celebrate. But she was limited on planning time. She had no idea where to have the party, but worse yet, she had no idea what to serve. Store-bought cake and chips with dip were not options.

That initial idea snowballed into another because she knew someone who did cook. He was phenomenal, actually. But she didn't want to use this party as a way to get closer to him. That would be seriously pathetic, and the surprise wasn't about her trying to get Liam to face whatever feelings he may or may not have. She legitimately wanted to throw her dad an amazing celebration. . . . She just needed a little help.

One glance to the clock and she figured now would be as good a time as any to get this ball rolling. Excitement bubbled within her. She couldn't wait to plan this party and see her dad's face when he realized how many people wanted to share his special day.

Macy would definitely have to enlist the help of Sophie, who was a whiz at planning things. In addition to being a real estate agent, the woman was a meticulous organizer. Plus, she'd been diligent in getting the word out about Bella Vous, so spreading the word around town about a party shouldn't be a problem. Macy just needed everyone to keep it under wraps because she wanted nothing more than to catch her father off guard and surprise him.

But her entire plan all started with catching another man off guard.

Was Liam ignoring her? His black SUV was parked behind the store, but she'd knocked for a while now. Maybe she shouldn't assume she was welcome. He'd tried to keep his distance and maybe he didn't want to associate with her any more than necessary.

Well, too damn bad. Macy had a party to plan and a father to surprise. Her fist pounded once again, until the door flew open and—

Oh. My. Word. Whatever she'd come here for had completely slipped her mind because right now Liam Monroe stood in his doorway wearing black running shorts. *Only* black running shorts. Earbuds dangling around his neck, hands wrapped in tape, and a sexy amount of sweat all over that bare, broad chest completed that mouthwatering view. That ink across his pec and up to his shoulder glistened, rendering her speechless. Seriously, when someone was built like this, shouldn't spectators take the time to appreciate the entire package?

Her eyes traveled with the bead of sweat that trickled from the side of his neck, down his collarbone, and directly over perfectly toned muscles.

His heavy breathing only led to thoughts she shouldn't be having, not that scolding herself changed anything.

The images were still there. Sweat never looked so good on a man.

"Macy?"

She shifted her gaze up to his. He swiped his forehead with his forearm and tipped his head slightly to offer the smooth side of his face.

"I didn't mean to interrupt," she told him, but she wasn't about to apologize. Mercy sakes, she wasn't one bit sorry she'd persisted in getting him to open the door. This sight alone would fuel her dreams for weeks, months.

"I'm done now."

Which would explain why he hadn't answered the door before. Clearly he'd been working out with his punching bag, if the tape on his knuckles was any indicator, and the earbuds had been in place. Oh, yeah. This was definitely worth the wait of knocking for several minutes.

"I just needed to borrow some recipe cards or cookbooks. Whatever you have that you can loan me for a few days."

Liam's brows drew together, his fingers wrapped around the edge of the door as he shifted his stance. "Recipe cards?"

Why was he looking at her like that was an absurd request? He was a chef, wasn't he? Although right now he looked like he could do more heating up in the bedroom than the kitchen.

Okay, that was a cheesy thought, but her brain was malfunctioning at the moment due to the half-naked hottie before her.

"I want to throw a surprise birthday party for my dad," she explained, shoving her hands in the pockets of her jeans. The sharp stab to her palm from the teeth on her keys kept her in check. "I can't cook to save my life, but I can read, so I figure I can attempt to follow a recipe. I'll need to borrow some of your easier ones, though."

For a split second she couldn't read his expression and feared he was about to close the door in her face. But then he threw his head back and laughed. A full-blown laugh from the gut. She couldn't remember a time she'd actually heard him laugh. Surely she had when they'd been younger, but she couldn't place it. And she wasn't so sure she wanted to hear it now, considering she was the butt of whatever private joke he was sharing with himself.

Pulling her hands out, Macy crossed her arms and tilted her chin. "What is so funny?" she had to practically yell so she could make sure he heard her.

Once he composed himself, there was still a shimmer of pleasure in his dark eyes. Okay, so maybe she didn't mind taking the hit to the ego if he was going to have a moment of happiness. Now that she thought about it, she not only hadn't heard him laugh, she rarely ever saw him smile.

"I don't have recipe cards or a cookbook." His face sobered instantly. "Well, I have one cookbook, but I won't loan it out."

"How do you cook if you don't have anything?" Between the laughter and his obvious lack of wanting to help, Macy was more than done here. "If you don't want to help, that's fine, but I thought you would have something simple I could try to do. Forget I stopped by."

Macy turned and started for the steps, but a hand on her shoulder stopped her.

"Don't go. I didn't mean to laugh."

She threw a glare over her shoulder. "I'm pretty sure you did."

Liam dropped his hand and shrugged. "Maybe, but you showing up at my door to ask for recipes was about the last thing I ever would've expected."

Macy backed away from the top step and turned to face him. "Then how do you cook if you don't have anything to look at? Do you have recipes online you could print out or e-mail me?"

He shook his head. Why was he being so damn stubborn and hardheaded?

"I tend to make things up as I go along or I'll experiment at home, then try it out at the resort."

Macy watched him, but realized he wasn't joking. "I can't make a frozen waffle turn out right and you can pull random recipes out of your head on a whim?"

"We all have our talents."

And his talents were adding up. He was a master chef, he could console without a single word, and he answered the door looking like every woman's secret fantasy.

Macy started to wonder what her talent was, then realized the only thing she'd ever been good at was softball. But she didn't want to start thinking about that right now. She couldn't handle too much at once. Besides, all of that was in the past and now she was moving forward, inching toward that family goal she'd always wanted.

"I just thought this would be a simple fix," she muttered, mostly to herself. Starting to feel defeated, she shrugged. "With all that's going on, I was hoping for one easy thing. Sorry I interrupted your workout."

"I was just relieving some frustration with my punching bag." His eyes narrowed as he studied her. "What's your stress reliever?"

Macy laughed. "I don't have time for a stress reliever."

"All the more reason you need one," he replied. "Come on in."

Macy gave him the side-eye. "Why?"

A lopsided grin had her stomach doing flips. "You're about to get sweaty."

Chapter Five

What the hell had he been thinking inviting her in like that?

First, he hadn't expected her to show up at his door, but she'd been fidgeting, biting that bottom lip, and looking like she'd rather be anywhere else than asking him for help. Then she'd gotten frustrated and quite possibly embarrassed.

Macy had pride, a trait he admired in anyone, but she was strong, determined, and went out of her way to help others. Her father was the same way, but Liam knew there was something in her past that made her who she was today. He recognized that stubborn streak, recognized the brokenness she tried to hide, and damn if that didn't make him more attracted.

Which was utterly ridiculous. He'd made a huge mistake with her already and he couldn't afford to lose sight of his ultimate goal. And other than this obvious attraction, what did they have in common? Why should he push forward and allow himself to feel when he knew full well that this wasn't his forever home?

"Follow me."

He led her toward his bedroom, where his free stand

punching bag sat in the corner. His eyes traveled toward the messy bed, instantly remembering her wrapped in his sheets.

"Wow, you go from wanting to kiss me to saying let's get sweaty and leading me to your bedroom. You don't waste time."

Liam threw a glance over his shoulder. "Funny."

With a slight shrug and wide smile, Macy replied, "I thought so."

Damn it. Why did she have to make him feel? He didn't want to feel. Didn't want to find reasons to smile, to be drawn closer to her. She was everything he wasn't and he refused to succumb to her sultry charms. At least if he was alone, he couldn't get hurt.

"So why did you bring me in here?" she asked, crossing her arms over her chest. "Because I actually have things to do."

The boxing gloves he'd discarded moments ago were on his bed. Liam picked them up and extended them. "Yeah, you're going to let off some steam."

She clutched the gloves to her chest, her eyes holding his. "By fighting?"

"By hitting the bag." He motioned to the corner. "Trust me on this. You may want to lose the flannel."

The red and black plaid flannel might have looked frumpy and boxy on some women, but Macy wore it like she'd had it custom made to fit those curves. A white tank peeked out, so he knew she had something on underneath.

After a moment of hesitating, she sat the gloves on the end of the bed and began unbuttoning her shirt. This was such a bad idea. Because Macy with her flannels, or even her T-shirts, was a mouthwatering sight. But Macy with her toned arms exposed, her fitted white tank with lacy pale pink bra straps peeking out and lying against smooth, bare shoulders, was something that would make any man weak in his knees. Liam sure as hell didn't need any more help with being weak where she was concerned.

Macy focused on tying her flannel around her waist, then looked back up at him. "Now what?" she asked, her arms out to the side. "I've never done this before."

Liam forced himself to get the gloves and concentrate on showing her how to put them on. Once they were secure, he gestured to the bag.

"Step on up." He kept his unmarred side to her as he came in beside her. "Stay relaxed, don't lock up your arms. Don't try to move the bag, just literally punch it."

She hesitated, staring at the bag as if it were going to retaliate.

"It won't hit you back," he said with a laugh.

Had he enjoyed himself this much when he lived in Savannah? Had he even wanted to have fun or be with someone else? The more Macy was near him, even if they were battling tension, the more he wanted to be near her. Friends would be fine, right? It wasn't as if he could dodge her until he left town.

He'd left a message with the owner of Magnolias to find out if indeed the place was for sale. Although with Liam leaving on bad terms with his boss, perhaps his call would go ignored. But he'd been a top chef, bringing in more business than any chef before him, so Liam felt pretty confident. He also knew his boss's anger had stemmed from fear of losing Liam, but at the time Liam had an obligation to fulfill.

Now, though, he might be able to transition back into his old lifestyle and find a replacement for the resort. There had to be a way. To honor his mother's memory, to fulfill a dream they'd both had, he would find the loophole and jump through it.

Liam was just about to say something to Macy when her

right arm shot out as she made contact. The hit didn't budge the bag at all.

"Now what?" she asked, glancing over. "Nothing happened and I feel the same."

Wow. She was trying at times. "What are you frustrated with? What are you stressed about? Pretend you're hitting everything that takes up space in your mind and steals your happiness."

Hello, Pot, I'm Kettle.

Who the hell was he to give emotional advice? He certainly was no motivational speaker. He was as messed up as they came. Liam had no clue how to help someone else.

And that was the crux of his problem. He wanted to fix things, wanted those he cared about to always be happy, to have everything they ever wanted. If they needed saving, even from themselves, he would find a way to help. Unfortunately, saving people didn't always work for him. But damn it if he'd give up. Something was eating away at Macy, but he didn't have a right to pry, though that was precisely what he wanted to do.

At this point, he could only show her what he did to relieve frustrations and pent-up emotions. And perhaps this little exercise would help get that tension from her body and help with the migraines. She just needed an outlet.

"I don't have that much stress," she mumbled.

Liam tipped his head, eyeing her in that silent way to let her know he didn't believe her. "Fine. What about those secrets you're keeping? That past you don't want people to know about."

In an instant she transformed from soft to hard. Her eyes narrowed, the muscle in her jaw clenched, shoulders stiffened.

"We all have that part we keep inside," she defended.

Liam nodded in agreement. "All the more reason to let the

tension go without actually telling anyone your problems. Take control so it can't take control of you."

Again, who the hell was he to be saying these things? He'd been trying to exorcise these demons for years. Yet again, he may not know what he was doing, if he was even helping, but he refused to give up. He'd lost his mother, lost his adoptive parents, and was cheated on by a fiancée. Saving any of those relationships was impossible, but backing down from helping those around him wasn't an option . . . even if it did test his patience and his emotions at times.

"I haven't let anything control me for a while," she replied, turning to face the bag. "But I won't be a victim again."

Before he could even comprehend the chilling meaning behind the term "victim," Macy let loose and hit the bag. Once, twice, three times. She grunted on the last one and continued to glare as if she were truly facing her nightmare.

"Victims are weak." Punch. "I'm not weak." Punch. "I have no reason to be afraid of anything."

Liam propped his still-taped hands onto his hips and watched as she let out the pent-up anger and rage. This was the best form of therapy he'd ever found. He'd gone to a shrink one time, and that was enough to know hashing out his feelings to a total stranger who knew nothing about hurt and true pain didn't work . . . at least not for him.

He'd had an amazing childhood with his single mother. They were inseparable . . . and then they were ripped apart by her untimely death. The foster home he was sent to looked picture perfect from the outside, as most do, but he was in a choke hold on day two. By day five, Liam had discovered if he didn't hit back, he'd never make it.

Liam's foster parents were in denial about the behavior of the son they were raising. The teen boy, who was four years older than Liam, had about fifty pounds on him. Liam learned to sleep with a chair beneath his bedroom doorknob, and learned to stay in the same room as the foster parents as much as possible. But there were always times when they'd be at work, leaving their oldest son in charge.

Liam continued to watch as Macy fought her own past. Just how ugly were those images rolling through her head? Liam had a feeling once he learned—and he vowed to dig deeper to find out—he'd want to hurt someone. Macy deserved all the happiness in the world and the fact that she was a victim of anything made his blood boil. He never would've imagined her battling her own living nightmare. He'd been so sure she had the perfect life, which she deserved, but he'd been wrong. And more than ever, he wished he'd been right.

The pounding continued and before long, Macy had a sheen of sweat covering her shoulders, her arms. Her ponytail swung against her back, and her concentration was so intense, Liam didn't dare say a word to disrupt her. She needed this, and maybe he needed her here. Maybe he needed to see that just because they had this crackling chemistry they kept ignoring didn't mean they couldn't be in the same room together.

Chest heaving, Macy turned to face him. With pink cheeks, damp forehead, and strands of hair clinging to her neck, she made quite the picture. The scoop in her tank showed off damp skin and he had to fist his hands in an attempt to remind himself he had zero right to touch. The lace strap slid slightly down one toned shoulder. Liam clenched his hands at his sides. His wants and needs had no place here.

The fitted jeans and well-worn cowgirl boots only aided in the entire sexy package. She screamed down-home girl.

"I need to get one of these." Her eyes literally sparkled. Her face, void of makeup, lit up as she smiled. "No wonder you're so"—she waved a gloved hand up and down his body—"that way."

He shouldn't be enjoying this as much as he was. "What way am I?" he asked, tugging her gloves off and tossing them back onto the unmade bed.

With smile still firmly in place, Macy lifted a brow. "Seriously, Liam? Fishing for compliments?"

He didn't say a word. Compliments weren't something that came to him. Stares, whispers, questioning looks, all of that was the norm. He wasn't vain, but he knew he wasn't ugly before the accident. He'd dated quite a bit, had several girlfriends, in fact. There was a time he'd lost his mind and thought about looking for a long-term relationship, maybe one day even getting married.

He knew Macy had had a slight crush on him back in the day. Chelsea had hinted enough, but Liam didn't think getting involved with his sister's friend was the wisest move at the time.

Then Macy had gone off to college only weeks before his accident and Liam had regretted never asking her out. He'd planned to rectify that when she came home on break. Unfortunately, the next time she came home, he wasn't in Haven any longer. The accident had changed everything inside him. He'd been so angry at the world, at Zach, at his mother for dying and leaving him. He'd wanted out, had wanted to cut all ties, so he'd gone to Savannah, where he could blend into a larger city.

That's when he'd met Angela. She'd been amazing at first, everything he thought he needed at the time to heal. Then she showed her true self by cheating on him when someone better came along. Clichéd, yes, but there was no sugarcoating the truth.

After their relationship ended, Liam found out just how much she'd gotten around and he knew he'd been played for a fool. From then on he'd done a stellar job of keeping people at a good distance, staying alone and having a private life. He'd not let anyone even remotely close to him.

And his plan of being alone had all worked beautifully, until now.

Macy continued to stare at him. Silence surrounded them in that crackling way that made him twitchy. When she took one step forward, then another, every part of him tensed. Her eyes never wavered and he wished like hell he knew what was going through her mind—or perhaps he was better off not knowing.

The second her hand lifted, instinct had him turning away. Delicate fingers landed on his shoulder blade. "Why do you always do that? Turning won't make anything change."

The scar and the tension. Damn it.

"I turn away because this isn't why you're here." But he couldn't step back from her touch, not when it felt this good. He wanted her hands on him, so he was selfishly taking only a little of what she was offering.

"Look at me," she demanded, though her tone remained soft. "You know I don't care about a scar."

He whirled around. "Because this didn't happen to you. You have no clue what scars I carry." His heart beat fast in his chest. Never had a woman been so direct about his face. Then again, he'd never given any woman the opportunity. And Macy only knew the scar she could see.

Macy swiped her damp face with the back of her forearm. "Are you ready to spill your secret yet? Let me in so I can understand."

"Why don't you tell me all your secrets?" he countered. No way in hell was he going to get all emotional and allow someone so sweet into his ugly past.

For several moments he stared, waiting on her to say something, to call him on the fact he countered her question with one of his own. When she said nothing, Liam spun around and made it all the way to the door when her words stopped him cold.

"I was sexually assaulted when I was eighteen."

Reaching up, he gripped the door frame and willed himself to breathe. The image that instantly popped into his head had rage boiling within him. Just the thought of Macy alone and vulnerable made Liam want to kill this faceless bastard. He kept his hold on the frame so he didn't punch the wall. Damn it, no wonder she'd gone at that bag like it was her enemy.

"My mother died the next day," she went on, her voice wavering slightly. "We all have our own monsters to face. But running from them won't change anything."

There was something he remembered hearing, something that didn't jive with her statement. Running was something she'd know quite a bit about. Little by little Macy's past was falling into place and he didn't like the picture he was seeing.

Slowly, Liam turned to face her. "What's your degree in?"

Macy jerked slightly. "What?"

"Your degree. What's it in?"

Her lips thinned. "I didn't finish."

Bingo. That's what he'd remembered. She'd come back home when her mother died and stayed to help her father with the store. Everyone had assumed it had been because of her mother's death, but now Liam knew there was much more to the story. Why had she chosen now to tell him? Did she just need to finally get it out in the open?

"You stayed because you were afraid to go back."

Those expressive eyes that were so vibrant moments ago now filled with unshed tears, angry tears. Her jaw clenched as she tipped her chin up in defiance.

"Don't act like you know how I felt," she accused. "Don't pretend you know why I stayed simply because I gave you the abbreviated version."

"Then tell me the rest."

Liam purposely kept his tone down. She was upset

enough for both of them and he was trying really hard not to smash something because so many disturbing thoughts kept filtering through his head.

At this point he needed the details so he wouldn't explode. But on the other hand, he didn't want her to relive the experience. Didn't want her nightmare to come out into the open and settle between them.

"Your father doesn't know, does he?"

Macy blinked back tears and shook her head.

"Does anybody?"

"Billy Martin and two of his friends."

Friends. More than one guy had shaken her very foundation, had removed any light that she held within her, and had altered the rest of her future. They'd given her a reason to run away from her dreams and right back into this comfort zone. Now, years later, she still ran from the monsters who'd hurt her. But that was not an area he would tackle. Everyone ran from something at some point in life.

"Why are you telling me now?"

Macy swiped at a stray tear that slid down her cheek. "I only let you in a bit, Liam. This goes both ways."

The meaning of her words hit him hard. She wanted in to his dark past. Not going to happen. While he was more than ready to extend an olive branch and listen to her, there was no way in hell he was opening up about his life.

"I don't share bedtime stories."

For a moment he had no clue what she was going to say, how she was going to react. But then she stepped forward and placed her palms on his bare chest. When she tipped her head up, parted her lips, and stared at him with such intensity, Liam had to seriously concentrate on remaining perfectly still. From the corner of his eye that lace against her shoulder continued to mock him.

"Then what would you be willing to share?" she asked.

Anger continued to course through him. He reached up

and gripped her wrists. "I've told you before to stop this. I'm not other men."

"No, you're not. And I'm not other women. Maybe I won't let you hide behind your past or your scars or any other part of your life that prevents you from living."

"Macy," he warned with a growl.

"What? Maybe I'm done wondering what it would be like for you to kiss me, for you to actually admit that you have an ounce of feeling for me. Maybe I deserve—"

Liam's mouth slammed onto hers and the second their lips collided, she melted against him.

Not enough. Not nearly enough.

He needed her closer. He released her wrists and framed her face as he stepped into her, lining their bodies up perfectly. Macy's slender arms came around his waist, her fingers dug into his bare back.

She was everything he'd fantasized about and so much more. Since coming back he'd done his share of thinking of exactly this moment and absolutely nothing in his thoughts touched the amazing reality of Macy's kiss.

The tip of her boots hit his feet, but he didn't care. She was here, in his arms, and he was finally tasting her.

Just one more second. He only needed a bit more, though warning bells were sounding in his head. A second more wouldn't hurt.

But then she sighed, ran her hands up his back, and threaded her fingers in his hair. Her touch was something he could get used to, and just one kiss, potent as it was, could get out of control so fast, and he would be utterly powerless to stop. He lifted his head, but one look at her closed eyes, her parted, wet lips, and Liam went back in. He wasn't a saint, never claimed to be. He was selfish and human.

All of the reasons this was a bad idea vanished from his

mind. Macy was in his arms, kissing him, clinging to him, and any other thought ceased to exist.

When her fingertips traveled over his shoulders, he trembled. When her hands framed his face, he jerked away.

The second he stepped back, a chill took over. Macy stood only inches away, hands at her sides, her body taking in deep breaths.

"This was a mistake." One he couldn't regret, but wouldn't make again.

"Kissing me was a mistake?"

"One of them," he confirmed, hating that he needed to be noble and brutally honest. "Moving in here was probably my first mistake. Bringing you into my room was another."

Slowly, Macy ran a hand across her mouth. "I see." She jerked the knot from her flannel, loosening it from her waist. Shoving her arms back in, Macy adjusted the material around her shoulders and left it unbuttoned. "I'll make sure not to come around again. You can just give your rent checks to Zach to pass along. He's in the store often enough. And you may want to get Sophie started on finding you another place. She knows of several rentals, since you clearly don't want to set roots here."

There was no warmth in her tone. She'd have more emotion leading a board meeting to discuss a toilet paper campaign. He'd done that to her, but he couldn't let her leave without something of an explanation.

He backed up, blocking the doorway. "You have to know why this is a bad idea."

"Do I? Because moments ago you had your hands all over me and everything felt like a great idea."

He'd remember the feel of her beneath his palms for the rest of his life and that would be his penance for losing control.

"We want different things, Macy. We're night and day."

Bright eyes narrowed, then she threw her arms out. "You know what, forget it. Forget I came by, forget everything that happened in here. I thought we were making headway. I trusted you and opened up to you more than anyone else. I've wanted to kiss you since I was sixteen. But I didn't know how bad I would feel after. I didn't know you'd regret it."

At the risk of more torture to himself, Liam reached out and grabbed her shoulders. "I don't regret a thing that happened. I regret the fact that I can't be what you need in your life. I regret that you had to face a monster all alone and then felt there was no one to turn to. I regret never asking you out to begin with because maybe our lives would've turned out differently."

Macy placed a hand on his chest and gave a slight push. "Everything happens for a reason. I can't look back. I can't let my past define me."

"And you think you've moved forward?" he countered. "Because the other night when I found you downstairs, you freaked out when I grabbed you."

Her eyes wavered slightly as she glanced away. "I'll always have memories, Liam. I can't change that, but I can't let them run my life."

Risking so much, walking a fine line, Liam gripped her chin and forced her gaze back to his. "So when are you going to finish that degree and stop letting those bastards steal from you?"

When her chin quivered, he knew he'd pushed too far. He'd crossed a line he had no right to. But damn it, she'd let some assholes rob what she'd worked so hard for. He knew she'd had a softball scholarship, so if she never returned, she'd obviously forfeited it. Yes, her mother had passed, but Liam fully believed Macy would've gone back to school had she not been attacked.

The thought still sickened him.

"Move," she whispered. "I need to get out of here."

She was upset. Keeping her here was only making things worse. "I want to be your friend, Macy. I want you to know you can talk to me. I just can't do anything else."

A humorless laugh escaped her lips as she swiped her damp cheeks. "A one-way friendship? I tell you everything and you keep your secrets locked tight inside? I can admit I have feelings for you and you can ignore yours? No thanks. I have enough friends."

When she put it in those terms and shoved his words back in his face, he had to admit she was right. He didn't know much about relationships. He'd barely had any to refer to, but he knew that whatever was happening with Macy wasn't over.

"You can walk out of here, but we're going to have to talk sometime."

Macy stepped back out of his hold. "If you want to talk, then do it. Otherwise we're done. I'm not playing games with you."

Raking his hands through his hair, Liam wanted to get back to that punching bag. "I don't know what to do here. I have no idea and it scares the hell out of me. Is that what you want to hear?"

Macy jumped as his voice echoed in the room. "I just want you to be honest with me, with yourself."

"You don't want honesty," he countered. "Maybe you should go. Because if I open up with all the mess that's in my head, you'll wish you'd left when you had the chance."

A soft smile tipped up the corners of her mouth. "Or maybe you'll find the freedom you've needed by letting someone else in."

When he said nothing, Macy tucked her stray hair behind her ears and eased past him. Liam shifted aside to let her through and waited until the door leading to the back steps opened and closed.

Shutting his eyes and leaning against the wall, Liam pulled in a deep breath. Macy was going to shatter the little bit of sanity he had left. If he let her in, they'd form a bond he wasn't ready for. Bonds led to relationships and he sure as hell wasn't looking for another.

Tomorrow he'd follow up on that call about Magnolias. Liam needed to get out of Haven and forget all about Macy. Though that kiss and the feel of her body beneath his hands might very well be permanently embedded in his mind.

Chapter Six

Cora stepped into the kitchen, led by her seeing-eye dog, Heidi. "Please tell me that glorious smell is something I can sample."

As if he could make the guests food and not have extras. Liam pulled the quiche from the oven and set it next to the fresh baked bread he'd gotten out only moments ago.

"I'm sure I can scrounge you up a plate," he told her, removing his pot holders and setting them aside. "Busy day planned?"

Holding on to Heidi with one hand and reaching out with her other, Cora encountered the bar stool and easily slid on. Liam was always amazed at how well she adapted to being blind. She rarely ever asked for help and had gotten the layout of the resort down rather quickly before they ever opened.

Braxton was quite protective of her, but with him back to teaching at the local university, he had to let her have her space. Cora was definitely an independent woman, reminding Liam of another extremely independent woman who'd walked out of his room the other night because he'd all but pushed her away.

"This is the last day for the ladies from the church group

in Charleston. I've got them all down for a full-body massage before they leave this afternoon."

Liam went to the sideboard and pulled out a plate with a floral pattern around the scalloped edges, a design Sophie had chosen. Everything about this place screamed feminine . . . which was the entire point, but still. Between the florals, the chatty, giggly ladies, and the overabundance of perfume mixtures filling the place, Liam was getting crankier by the day.

Or maybe he was just cranky because he was so torn from too many different angles. He hadn't seen or even heard a sound from Macy in four days.

"Then you better eat up," he told her as he scooped out a healthy portion of bacon and feta quiche. After he slathered herb butter on the whole grain bread, he sat her plate in front of her. "Juice or coffee?"

"Both," she said, laughing.

Liam gave her all she needed before placing the individual quiches on a platter and taking them into the dining room. He made sure to keep this room just as perfect as his kitchen. Sophie had ordered cloth napkins and found some antique silverware at an estate sale. The room had tall, narrow windows adorned with bright yellow curtains tied back with a matching cloth. The old windows were the originals from the Civil War period. Zach had actually done a stellar job of restoring this home to the true value and charm it once had without sacrificing too much.

He'd managed to salvage the hardwood floors with a sander and stain, and unsalvageable spots were easily covered with decorative rugs. Sophie had worked extra hard to find deals during home sales when people were downsizing. Braxton had even taken a semester off to aid in the renovations. Even Brock had been on board from day one.

A tug of remorse kicked in when Liam thought of how this was a family affair. Chelsea would absolutely love how this had all fallen into place, from the home itself to the guys all working together. Another reason Liam had guilt for wanting to leave. But he couldn't stay. This wasn't his home and he didn't feel like he fit in.

After taking a bowl of fresh berries along with the butters and jams into the dining room, he filled the coffee carafes and made sure everything was in place before eight when breakfast was scheduled.

By the time he went back into the kitchen to start planning the lunch menu, Cora was finishing her last bite of bread.

"You are amazing," she stated, taking her napkin and wiping her mouth. "I'm pretty sure I can get through my day now."

When she came to her feet and grabbed her plate, Liam reached across and took it. "I've got it."

"I can clean up after myself, you know."

Yeah. Stubborn woman. Apparently that's what attracted the Monroe men. "I realize that," he stated. "But I would've cleaned up after anyone in my kitchen. Besides, you need to get to your room and get ready for the masses."

"I'm going to need a really good dessert from you later," she warned as she grabbed onto Heidi's collar. "Something with plenty of chocolate or those strawberry macaroons you made the other day. Dip those in chocolate, okay? I should be done about four today."

Liam laughed and nodded, though she couldn't see him. "I'll see what I can do for you. I know some people who ship me the best chocolate."

Cora was one of the world-renowned Buchanans who dominated the chocolate importing business. They kept Liam fully supplied in anything he needed, from dark chocolate to white to even chocolate wine, which they'd just recently added to their roster.

When Cora reached the doorway, she turned. "Have you talked to Braxton since yesterday?"

"No, why?"

A wide smile spread across her face. "Ask him. Just make sure you keep your calendar clear for the next little bit."

Confused, Liam rested his hands on the island. "For how long?"

"Just talk to your brother."

And then she was gone, her soft shoes and Heidi's nails echoing down the hallway. What was going on? Now Liam wouldn't be able to concentrate until he spoke with Braxton, who most likely was in class.

Liam pulled out his phone and shot off a quick text to Braxton to call when he was done with class. Considering Cora's sweet smile, nothing was wrong, but still Liam would have liked to know why he needed to keep his calendar clear for the next little bit. How long did a "little bit" actually entail?

In no time, the chatter from the dining room filled the kitchen. So far every group that had passed through had been great. The feedback they'd gotten was more than they could've hoped for. Everyone was thrilled with their stay and a few had already made reservations to return in the fall.

He had even survived the bachelorette party that left last night. They'd definitely been the most interesting group. They'd requested Wind Down with Wine to be their breakfast. Liam's mind ran together all the guests that had come and gone. They'd only been open a few months, but the revolving door hadn't stopped spinning. They were taking in guests and filing them out like an assembly line.

So he shouldn't feel guilty about his need to go back to where he was happiest. He'd filled in when the resort had been in a bind. Finding a replacement wouldn't be a problem . . . he hoped. He'd never wanted anything more than for all of this to work out, for his plans to fall into place and the move to be smooth for everyone. That is, if he actually managed to get the restaurant.

Liam started working on the potpie he was going to serve for lunch. No frozen food here. He knew his clients at the resort just as well as his patrons at Magnolias. An older church group would love something down-home and simple like a homemade potpie. And his crust was pure perfection, thank you very much.

His mother had stressed the importance of doing all things from scratch. She'd always said, "When we have our restaurant, people aren't going to want processed foods. They want fresh." He'd lived by her standards, making him exactly who he was today.

Liam mixed up the dough and rolled it out, using his mother's old rolling pin. So many pieces of her life carried over into his. Nobody knew the old mixer he kept in his apartment had been hers, just like this rolling pin. He wanted to keep those memories of his mother, of happier times, locked inside where he could treasure them forever. He didn't want to share her.

Even though he'd been young when she passed, Liam had kept a box of a few of her items. No matter where he went, that box had gone with him.

Liam's phone vibrated on the counter. With hands full of gooey dough, he glanced at the screen.

I'll swing by your apartment later.

Braxton was a man of many words. Couldn't he just text him what this big hush-hush secret was?

Seconds later his cell vibrated once again.

Change of plans. Meet at Zach's at seven.

Liam blew out a breath and shook his head. Whatever was going on, there was a family meeting being called. Staring at his phone for another moment, Liam willed the damn thing to ring. If he hadn't heard back from Mark by the time he left work today, Liam was calling back. Friction and bad terms weren't going to keep Liam from pursuing his dream of owning his own restaurant. Surely his brothers would understand.

Maybe he would know if the place was indeed for sale by the time the family meeting was called. Having Zach and Braxton together at the same time would make it easier to drop a hint and lay some groundwork, so that way when Liam left, it wouldn't be so shocking.

"Excuse me?"

Liam jerked, his gaze landing on the doorway where a guest stood with a smile. Her eyes immediately went to the left side of his face. Instinct had him shifting slightly.

"I'm sorry to bother you." The sixty-ish lady with short, silvery hair smiled. "My friends and I just wanted to tell you how wonderful the food has been while we've been here. Whatever you did to that quiche was absolutely amazing."

Liam gave a brief nod and attempted to return the smile. "I'm glad you enjoyed it."

He stayed in the kitchen to avoid people, but he couldn't be rude or standoffish when this was his family's business and Chelsea's vision. They all had to work together to make this a success. Stepping out of his comfort zone was something he knew he'd have to do when back in Haven, but that didn't mean he had to like it or embrace it.

"There will be a midmorning snack around ten and lunch at one," he added, focusing back on his dough. "Cora said you're all up for massages, so I'll make sure to leave everything out in the dining room so you can come and go as you please."

"Sounds great. This is quite an amazing place you guys have."

Unease settled in his stomach. "Thank you."

Where was Zach? Wasn't he supposed to be here this morning? Braxton only came by in the evenings because of his teaching schedule, but Liam really didn't want to be left on his own. Sophie had a closing on a home this morning, but Zach should be here, damn it.

"I'll let you get back to work. I just wanted to say thanks and we plan on coming back."

Liam glanced her way once more, more than happy to be drawing this social time to a close. "We're glad to hear it. Let me know if you need anything before you go."

That was hard. He wasn't used to being this . . . helpful. Wasn't he hired to cook? There was a reason he was a behind the scenes guy. Another point he'd bring up when he saw his brothers later today. Cora was always around, but she was clearly busy, and this resort was supposed to be Zach and Braxton's baby. Liam had only reluctantly come on board as a financial backer at first, then at the last minute he was talked into being the chef.

As much as Liam loved being part of this endeavor, he agreed to join in on the business with the hope he'd only be a silent partner.

Nothing was going to plan since he'd moved back. Every day that passed, he was more torn up than ever. Without even trying, Macy was relentless in getting under his skin. The woman had him in knots and there wasn't a damn thing he could do about it except get the hell out of Haven. Now he just needed to set the plan and execute it before he lost what was left of his sanity.

His need to save those around him had narrowed drastically. Now he was in dire need of saving himself.

* * *

Liam pulled up in front of the house where he'd spent his teen years. The home now belonged to Zach, Sophie, Brock, and a whole host of dogs. Zach had taken in a pregnant stray a year ago, and once the puppies came, he ended up keeping them because he didn't want to separate the siblings.

He never came out and said it, but Liam knew Zach's upbringing influenced how he treated the pups. The Monroe boys were all softhearted when it came to vulnerability in people, and apparently animals, too.

Braxton's car was already in the drive. Liam let himself in the front door and braced himself for the slew of barks and excitement. Maybe he should get a dog, he thought. Dogs were always happy to see you, dogs didn't judge, and dogs were loyal. So long as you fed them, they'd be your best friend. That was one relationship Liam could totally get behind.

He reached down to pat each one as they jumped, vying for attention.

"Welcome to the zoo." Zach stepped into the foyer with a bottle of water in his hand. "We're all out back on the patio. You want something to drink?"

Liam stood straight and shook his head. "I'm fine. More interested in what's going on."

"Then you'd better follow me," Zach stated, and headed toward the back of the house.

Zach slid the glass door open and gestured for Liam to go ahead. All the sturdy wicker couches and chairs were new, as was the concrete patio with a faux stone design. Zach had made quite a few changes to their old home once he decided to keep it and stay in Haven.

Zach had also wanted out, but ended up falling in love with Sophie. Those two were meant to be. It had just taken a decade of hurt and recovery for them to fall back together.

"Nice fence," Liam snorted as he took a seat on the end of the outdoor sofa.

Zach flipped him the finger before taking a seat next to Sophie on another sofa. "We need privacy."

"Your neighbor still an issue?" Braxton asked, resting his hand on Cora's knee.

Sophie laughed. "Mrs. Barclay has had to deal with me when she makes surprise visits. I think she's growing tired of seeing my face."

Zach's neighbor, who was a good fifteen years older than him, never made it a secret which Monroe brother she'd set her sights on when she moved to town. Zach had dodged her multiple times, and less than a year ago, Braxton had admitted he'd had a moment of weakness and ended up spending some time in her home—as in her bedroom.

But Braxton had definitely changed his outgoing ways since meeting Cora. The two complimented each other, looked out for each other, and made a great team. The tug on Liam's heart as he observed their closeness wasn't welcome. Liam didn't want to find love—such a thing didn't exist for him. He'd let himself believe once before, but all that had done was leave him alone and hurting once again. So that tug could just go away.

While Liam was happy for his brothers, he was also content to go on just the way he was, so long as he could get out of Haven.

Which had him thinking back to the phone call he'd gotten earlier. Magnolias was indeed for sale and Liam knew the price Mark was asking. He needed to do some budgeting of numbers and think of a reasonable offer to make, but he wanted that restaurant and was confident he could make everything work out. On paper, anyway. Dealing with family and emotions was a whole other ball game.

"I'd rather not discuss our neighbor," Zach chimed in. "What's going on, Brax?"

Cora slid her hand over Braxton's and smiled. "We were hoping to close the resort the second weekend in May since we have no bookings."

"Okay," Zach said slowly. "Why?"

"We want to get married there," Braxton declared.

Sophie leaned across the sofa, wrapping her arms around Cora. Zach shook his head and laughed. "No problem. It's a great idea."

Braxton glanced over to Liam. "You okay with this?"

"Of course." Why wouldn't he be? The resort would make the perfect backdrop for a wedding, and Braxton and Cora deserved everything they wanted.

"Good." Braxton's smile widened. "We were hoping you'd do the cake."

Liam grunted. "Am I invited if I refuse?"

"Maybe."

"I'll do the damn cake," Liam said, then slid his gaze to Cora, who was still beaming. "Cora, let me know what you'd like. I'll do anything for you."

"Why not what I like?" Braxton asked.

"Because she's prettier and everyone knows the wedding is about the bride."

Zach quirked a brow. "Really? And you know a lot about weddings?"

With a shrug, Liam defended himself. "Magnolias hosted plenty of weddings in my time there. People rented it out fairly often and I did my share of cakes."

"I don't really know what I want," Cora stated, reaching down to stroke Heidi's neck. "Let me think about it and get back to you. I know I want a simple white cake, but other than that I'm clueless about the decorations."

"No chocolate?" he asked.

Cora shook her head. "Maybe a chocolate fountain, but my favorite cake has always been a basic white."

"Just think of the icing flavor you'd like, or fondant is an option, too. We can talk later," Liam agreed.

And another talk that would have to come later was the fact he was planning on leaving. He didn't want to ruin this moment with his own selfish needs. He wouldn't be going anywhere in the next three weeks anyway. After the wedding, though, he couldn't guarantee he'd be around much longer.

"There's more," Cora said. "Sophie has something to add."

Zach jerked his gaze to his fiancée. "There is?"

Settling back into her seat, Sophie looped her arm through Zach's and smiled. The way those two looked at each other would be sickening to some, but Liam knew they'd both overcome hell to get where they were today. Liam almost felt like maybe whatever was about to happen should be done in private. But whatever.

"I know we kept putting our wedding plans off because of the resort. Then we were focused on the custody issues with Brock. But Cora and I talked and a double wedding only makes sense."

Silence filled the patio and Liam held his breath. Cora and Braxton seemed to shift in their seats as well.

Zach rubbed the back of his neck. "Are you sure you want to do it at the resort?"

Sophie's face fell slightly. "If you do."

"I only want you happy." Clearly Zach had noticed her slip in excitement. "If you guys want a double wedding, Braxton and I will be there. Just tell us what time."

Liam sank back against the cushions. "Does this mean a bigger cake?"

Sophie laughed. "I'm sure the guest list won't be too large. Cora and I both want something small."

"My parents are coming for sure," Cora added, biting

her lip. Heidi sat obediently at her owner's side. "Maybe you should do a chocolate cake."

"I thought you wanted white," Braxton said.

Cora's family's name was in nearly every household, every kitchen, including his own. He also knew her parents had high standards and wanted the absolute best for their daughter, so she worried about disappointing them.

"I can do both to keep all parties happy," Liam supplied. "Just leave it up to me."

Sophie stood back up. "I need to head back to the resort. I left Brock there to answer phones and finish washing all the sheets since our guests left. A new crew is coming in the morning."

"Don't say anything to Brock about the wedding," Zach requested. "I want to tell him together when you guys come home."

Sophie kissed Zach on the cheek. "I won't say a word."

Once Sophie was gone, Braxton and Cora said their good-byes, leaving Liam and Zach.

"I need to let the hounds out. Brace yourself."

Zach slid the patio door open, unleashing seven awkward pups, who were still growing into their long legs, and their mother, who trailed behind them. Their gorgeous yellow coats seemed to shine in the moonlight. Heidi didn't even budge from Cora's side. Not only was she used to the chaos, but she was a well-trained service dog and faithful to Cora.

Darkness had settled in. The outside lights had clicked on and the moon shimmered off the pond. The resort was exactly what Chelsea had envisioned in outlines and binders full of pictures and notes. Liam knew she had to be looking down and smiling at how she'd ultimately brought all of them together.

The lump of guilt in his throat threatened to choke him. They may all be together now, but circumstances would be changing soon. He only hoped his brothers understood why he couldn't be here long term.

Liam hadn't realized how late it had gotten, but he didn't really have anywhere else to be except maybe another date with his punching bag. With all the thoughts flooding his mind, he could definitely use a stress reliever.

One of the pups, Hulk if Liam was guessing right, jumped up onto his lap.

"Don't let Sophie know he's up there." As soon as Zach sat back down, Thor jumped up beside him, which triggered Hawk to do the same. "She just replaced the patio furniture last week and she didn't want them on the new stuff."

"You have to train them," Liam replied, rubbing Hulk's neck.

Zach shrugged. "I think they're trained. They don't get on it when she's out here. They're pretty smart."

Hulk lay down, resting his paws over the side of the cushion and his head in Liam's lap. "Where were you today?" Liam asked.

Zach crossed his ankle over his knee. "I had a bid to finish up. Why?"

"Nobody was at the resort except me."

"And?"

"That's not the deal."

Between the moonlight and the antique lights hanging from the perimeter of the pergola, Liam could make out Zach's face perfectly. Zach's gaze narrowed as he tipped his head.

"The deal?" Zach repeated, his hand stilling on Hawk's head. "The deal was we were all doing this together. I assumed you could keep things going for a bit while I handled my other job. Sophie was only gone a few hours for her closing."

"Interacting with guests isn't what I wanted when I agreed to come here."

Zach's jaw clenched and Liam was working up a good bit of mad himself. "We're all in this together, just like Chelsea would've wanted. I can't help it if you're so hung up on your looks that you are afraid to talk to people."

Rage coursed through Liam. "My looks? You think that's all I care about? I never wanted to come back to begin with. I was more than happy staying in Savannah, sending money to keep this place running until we started seeing an income. I'm not supposed to be front and center here, Zach. This was your idea to get this going."

"So, because you had to talk to people, you're getting cranky?"

Liam gently shifted the dog and came to his feet. Hulk lay on the sofa, oblivious to the turmoil. "I'm done here. Just make sure someone is at the resort because I have a job there and it's not to do meet and greets."

As Liam turned to go, Zach's low, angry voice stopped him. "If you want to leave, then go. We were getting along before you decided to jump on board and we'll get along without you. Chelsea wouldn't want you here out of pity or duty, and I don't either. You either want to help your family or you don't."

Liam kept his back to his brother, but couldn't form a single response. He wanted out of this town, back to the place where he was comfortable, to fulfill his own dream. But he couldn't find the words to tell Zach exactly what he wanted, so he opened the door and went inside. He was done here for the night. Anything he said at this point would only cause more of an argument and he didn't think this family needed any more hurt.

As Liam climbed into his SUV, he realized he was growing, changing. At one time he'd been all too happy to take verbal jabs at Zach. Right now, though, he didn't have the heart for it.

Maybe there was hope for him after all, or maybe he was just done. Either way, Liam had a plan and nothing would stop him from moving forward.

Chapter Seven

Girls' night at Macy's house was exactly what she needed. Tomorrow she'd be going to the softball game and she was still unsure how she even felt about that. She hadn't seen Liam, and the fact she kept replaying their kiss over and over in her mind only ticked her off. He was avoiding her, which only led her to believe their encounter had hit him just as fiercely.

So, some wine, some pointless gossip, and a carefree evening was exactly what she needed to relax and unwind . . . and not think of Liam. Or his lips. Or the way her body still tingled because he'd left a permanent imprint on her.

"Did you hear the news?" Cora asked, crossing her legs and easing back on the bar stool. Heidi lay on the floor beside the stool, eyes open, but relaxed.

Macy refilled Sophie's wineglass. "What news?"

"Cora and I are getting married," Sophie squealed.

A laugh escaped Macy as she stared back at her beaming friend. "You two will be very happy together."

Cora swatted in the direction of Sophie, but missed by quite a bit. "Shut up. We're having a double ceremony at the resort on May fourteenth. You're invited."

A double wedding. It sounded so perfect and romantic.

And the resort would be absolutely breathtaking. The old Civil War–era home with the pond, the patio, the lush landscaping intermixed with the centuries old mossy oaks. It would look like something from a magazine, Macy was sure.

Brothers who found love inadvertently due to the dream of their late sister. Didn't the greatest pieces of literature have romance stemming from tragedies? If so, Macy was long overdue for her proverbial white knight.

A May wedding would be stunning and another milestone in pointing the Monroe family in the right direction. After so many years of heartache and tension, maybe they were finally due for their happily ever after.

"I couldn't be happier for you guys."

Macy truly meant it. But she couldn't ignore the tingle that crept up her spine. One day she would marry, have a family. But for now, her friends were deliriously happy and Macy was thrilled for them. Not to mention Zach and Braxton deserved this. Those boys had been through quite a bit before coming to Haven and being adopted.

"Can I do anything for you?" she asked. "I mean, clearly not cook, but something else to help you get things ready?"

Sophie smiled and reached across the sofa to squeeze Macy's hand. "We'd like you to stand up and be our maid of honor."

Shocked, Macy blinked. "Me?"

"Of course," Cora agreed. "You've been a great friend to me since I came and I just feel like you guys were the sisters I never had. To marry Braxton with both of you by my side would be the perfect day."

Macy glanced from Cora to Sophie. Both women had seriously come to mean so much to her. Sophie had always been a friend, but Cora had slid right into their world as if she weren't a millionaire heiress. She fit effortlessly into the small town lifestyle, a perfect addition into their world.

"I'd love to," Macy stated. "But, please, tell me the dress isn't pink."

Both women laughed. "Actually, you're the only one we want up with us, so you can pick your own dress. We're having flowers of all colors, so I'd say you'll be safe with anything."

If she was the only one standing up with the women, Macy had a pretty good idea who the only man standing up with Braxton and Zach would be.

Wonderful. If she saw Liam in a tux, she might be forced to ravage him against his will and ignore every speech she'd ever given herself about how she wouldn't throw herself at him ever again.

"Can I wear my boots?" she asked.

"Honestly, you can do whatever you want," Sophie replied, sipping her wine. "The wedding will be in the evening, out by the pond. We're hoping for a gorgeous sunset to send us off."

A gorgeous sunset, a double wedding, and Macy would be walking the aisle with Liam. Didn't this just kick her straight in the gut of all the feels?

"I know this is short notice," Cora went on. "But we saw the resort wasn't booked that weekend and I wanted a spring wedding anyway. There's just been so much going on that Sophie and I kept putting everything off. We figured the guys could care less if we did it together or separately."

"With the resort being a family affair anyway, it only makes sense," Sophie added. "And if we keep putting it off, we'll be in a nursing home before we actually find time to do this."

Macy smiled and reached for her Chardonnay. "I think it will be perfect."

"Now that all of that is settled, spill the scoop on what's happening with Liam." Sophie curled her feet beside her on the sofa and swirled her wine around in her glass. "And don't say nothing."

Macy cringed. What was there to say? They drove each other crazy, they fought, they kissed, and the cycle repeated. One of these days they were going to snap and most likely end up naked . . . hopefully together. Because if that didn't happen soon, she was going to need to invest in her own punching bag.

"She's quiet," Cora whispered. "What's her face look like? That will tell you everything."

"I can't tell if she's smiling or sneering," Sophie replied.

Macy couldn't help but laugh as she finished off her wine. "I don't even know what face I was making. I have too many emotions when it comes to Liam."

"Really?" Cora asked, her brows raised. "Why don't you share them and we can help you sort them all out."

Part of Macy wanted to spill everything, but the other part of her wanted to keep whatever was going on with Liam to herself. She'd never been one to gossip about her dates, but Liam was different. They weren't dating, or even having sex. They were simply driving each other crazy.

"There's not much to tell," Macy explained. She glanced to her empty wineglass and figured she'd better stop now. Even though she was at her own house, she might get too chatty if she had much more. "He's quiet and easily irritated. I'm more outgoing and happy. We couldn't be more opposite."

"Yet you spent the night in his apartment," Sophie added with a smirk.

Macy groaned, setting her glass on the old trunk she used as a coffee table. "That statement sounds extremely interesting, but the migraine I was nursing killed the evening."

"I heard you were there because you weren't feeling well." Cora stretched her legs out onto the ottoman and crossed her ankles. Heidi slept obediently beside her chair. "I was hoping that wasn't true. But still, Liam took care of you, right?"

Macy nodded, then remembered. "He did. He carried me upstairs when I—"

"Wait." Cora held up a hand. "He carried you? Like an over the shoulder fireman's carry or I'm the man in charge and taking you to my bedroom carry?"

Blowing out a sigh, and realizing she shouldn't have even gone into details, Macy sank back against the couch cushions. Might as well get comfortable because she had a feeling this was going to be a long conversation.

"I was nauseous and he carefully took me upstairs." No way was she about to admit she'd found herself in his bed. "He wouldn't let me drive, so after I took my medicine I ended up falling asleep. When I woke up, he was already gone for work."

Sophie's eyes narrowed as she pursed her lips. "This may explain why he's so irritable, then. He wants you, you want him, and nothing has been done. Or has it?"

"No," Macy exclaimed, throwing her arms in the air. "We kissed once. That's all."

"A kiss?" Cora perked up. "When did this happen?"

"Wait." Sophie held up a hand. "Why don't you start from the day he moved in above Knobs and Knockers and give us a detailed timeline. I'm going to need more buffalo chicken dip and wine first. Can I get you guys anything?"

Macy groaned. "Maybe I should have another glass after all."

Why not? At this point she wasn't going to get out of this girls' night without spilling her Liam secrets and she might as well finish off the bottle Cora had brought. Who knows, maybe the girls could offer some insight as to what move to make next, because she was at a loss when it came to Liam. He had her so confused and the only consolation she had was that he was just as messed up as she was when it came to what was going on.

"When you're done grilling me I'd like to talk to you about a surprise party I want to throw for my dad," Macy said when Sophie came back with a plate and full glass. "I need some quickie invitations printed and help spreading the word."

Sophie eased back into her spot on the sofa and smiled. "Happy to help. Now, start at the beginning of life with Liam and leave nothing out. Be sure to use plenty of adjectives during the kissing part of the story."

Five o'clock. Macy nearly wept as she checked the clock. Just as she rounded the counter to lock up, the bell over the door chimed and Tanner Roark stepped inside.

"Hey, Macy."

Tanner's smile spread across his face. The man was drop dead gorgeous in that southern boy charmer type of way. They'd gone out once, kissed twice, and that had been the beginning and end of their story. While Tanner was a great guy, she just didn't feel anything toward him. Although she'd seen him in his uniform, since he was a new member of the police force, she still didn't get any fluttering when she was with him.

"What brings you by, Tanner?" she asked, returning his smile.

"Hadn't heard from you and was curious if you wanted to grab dinner this evening. I'm off and I know it's short notice, but I thought I'd see if you were busy."

Why couldn't she like him in that way? Tanner had everything going for him—a great job, looks, his own home. Still, there was no spark. They were good friends, nothing more. He and his cousins were as close as brothers, all bachelors. Seriously, why couldn't she be drawn to one of them?

"I actually already have plans tonight," she told him. Not a complete lie.

With a tip of his head, he narrowed his eyes. "Everything okay?"

"Fine. Just busy."

"Why don't you let me know when you're free? I still owe you a payback for that last poker hand when you cheated me out of fifty bucks."

Macy couldn't help but laugh. "I have no idea what you're talking about."

Tanner flashed that high wattage smile. "I'll text you and give you more of a heads-up next time," he joked as he turned toward the door. "And be sure to bring your wallet."

Once he was gone, Macy locked the door and clicked the OPEN sign off. She smoothed the stray wisps back from her face. Her ponytail was sliding, but she didn't care at this point. She was ready to get her closing chores done and go home.

Today had been one for the record books. With spring in full swing, people were shopping for yard items to get their lawns and flower beds ready. She'd nearly sold out of topsoil, and would have to remember to get an order in tonight so it would be here by Monday. She'd also sold a record number of hedge trimmers. Fine by her, but she was exhausted.

And a load of bright colored pots in various sizes was due in tomorrow. That was a display she'd have to come in early and make room for. She'd also have to save one of the largest ones to use just outside her shop door to entice people with how beautiful the new items were. She'd definitely have to put her seed packets by the pots somewhere just inside the front door.

How had her dad done it by himself at times? There were

always slow seasons and slammed seasons, but everything balanced in the end. Right now, though, Macy was ready to keel over. Her feet were killing her and she just wanted to take her bra off and relax.

There was no way she could coach and run the store. It wasn't realistically possible, even if she wanted to step back onto the field again, which she wasn't sure she had the mental capacity to handle.

Macy pulled out all the credit receipts for the people who kept running accounts with the store. In a small town, where everybody knew everybody, in-house accounts were common.

As she divided the slips out, she thought about the softball game she'd gone to. She'd only stayed for twenty minutes. That had been long enough for her to realize the sport had never left her. She loved every bit of it. The smells, the calls from the dugout, the teammates cheering each other on, the coaches giving silent hand gestures as to the next play. Everything came rushing back to her and Macy had felt a tug on her heart. This was what she'd been missing, but she honestly didn't know if moving into this position was a possibility. Not only that, but shouldn't she move on? Shouldn't she put all of that dark night behind her?

Even the demons from her past blanketed the happiest time of her life.

Pushing beyond the obvious reason to say no, she had another glaring reason . . . an even better one and definitely more positive. She hoped to be fostering soon. Not that she wanted any child to have to enter the system, but Macy was eager to fill her home, her heart with a child who needed nurturing.

"Just grabbing some packaging tape."

Macy jerked around, holding a hand to her chest. "Liam. You scared me."

He stood at the base of the steps, not moving any closer.

"Just put it on my tab and I'll settle up when I give Zach my check. I didn't mean to bother you."

Without waiting on her reply, he moved to the aisle where the tape was located. Macy kept her eyes on him, wondering what he needed with tape, but it was none of her business. They weren't anything more than landlord/tenant at this point . . . except in her dreams, where he kept showing up and monopolizing every moment of her restless nights.

Wait. Was he boxing things up? Was he moving again? That would be her business if it were the case. He hadn't actually unpacked, if all those stacked boxes she'd seen were any indicator.

"Are you moving?" she asked.

His shoulders stiffened as he threw her a glance. "Are you asking me to?"

Swallowing, Macy stepped closer. She was just going to the counter to start closing out the register. That's all. She certainly wasn't closing this gap between them so she could look into his eyes while they spoke or so she could inhale that woodsy, masculine scent she associated with him.

"No, I'm not."

"I'm not having Sophie find another place for me."

Stunned, Macy jerked. "Why?"

"I'm working on something else."

Wow. A man of many words. What did that mean? He was working on finding a place all on his own? He was working on moving to California? Alaska? Or he was working on driving her out of her ever-loving mind?

Liam stared for another moment before turning his attention back to the selection. He grabbed a roll of tape off the hook and started back toward the steps. Macy's gut clenched in disappointment. What had she expected? He'd made it clear they were to have nothing more than a business relationship, but that wasn't working for her and she was tired of living like this, uncomfortable in her own element.

"Are you going to ignore me the entire time you live here?" she called to his retreating back.

Liam glanced toward the ceiling before spinning around. "Are you going to make this difficult the entire time I live here?"

Oh, he had a smart mouth. Macy crossed the old checkered linoleum, keeping her eyes on his the entire time. That dark, intense stare could have anyone stopping in their tracks, but she refused to back down. This was her territory, damn it. He had come back and infiltrated *her* life. Not the other way around.

"I'm not the one being difficult," she countered. "You're the one giving mixed signals. Being standoffish, kissing me, pushing me away."

The muscle in his jaw clenched as his eyes narrowed on her. "I'm doing this for you. Trust me, it's not easy."

A kernel of information she could use. "I can take care of myself, you know. If there were no consequences, what would you do?"

"Don't ask me that," he commanded, his lips thinning.

"Too late. Answer the question."

Liam took the tape, placed it on a shelf beside him, and took two steps forward to come within a breath of her. Macy instantly tipped her head up to keep her eyes locked onto his. Her heart pounded in her chest as silence settled heavy around them.

"What would I do?" he repeated in that low, throaty tone that sent shivers down her spine. "I'd forget the fact that we want completely different things. I'd take what you're offering with that look in your eyes. And I damn well wouldn't stand by and listen as yet another man asks you out on a date."

So, he'd heard Tanner earlier and jealousy was now rearing its ugly head. Finally, they were getting somewhere. Now probably wasn't the time to state that she and Tanner were just good friends. That murderous look in Liam's eye told her he wouldn't believe her.

"Maybe you should ignore the what-ifs and do what you want," she suggested, feeling bolder than usual. Swallowing, she added, "What we both want."

His gaze dropped to her mouth, then back up to her eyes. "Is that why you turned down a date for tonight? You waiting on me to let my guard down with you?"

Something about that ego of his was so damn sexy. Probably because she rarely saw him show that side.

"Maybe," she replied. In a risky move, she ran her palms up over his chest, pleased when he sucked in a breath and froze. "Maybe I'm tired of playing games, of dancing around the tension. Maybe I want to know what would happen if we pretended nothing else mattered, nothing existed but what we're feeling."

"But everything does exist."

She was breaking him down. She could tell by his tone, by the way he stared at her mouth.

"For two minutes, let's pretend it doesn't," she challenged. "For the next two minutes we're going to be honest with each other. Nothing leaves this place. Deal?"

He dropped his forehead to hers. "You make a man want to forget everything except tasting you, pleasing you."

Arousal swirled around in her stomach. She'd asked for honesty and he delivered. His lips slid back and forth across hers.

"I shouldn't want you like this," he muttered, as if reprimanding himself. "But I can't focus on anything else when you're right here."

Macy slid her hands up around his neck and threaded

her fingers through his hair. She closed her eyes, silently begging him to kiss her, to touch her. Why was he constantly pushing her away when he was so transparent about what he wanted?

"You want two minutes of honesty?" he asked, skimming those lips along her jawline. "If I thought for a second I could have you and there would be no consequences or feelings involved, I'd have you laid out on that counter before you could draw your next breath."

The image his words construed were gloriously beautiful. Although the large windows on the front doors would provide outsiders with quite a different view of her family's small-town hardware store and bring a whole new meaning to the name Knobs and Knockers.

Liam's hand spanned her waist, gliding up her sides as his thumbs teased the undersides of her breasts. Macy arched into him, craving so much more than these light touches.

"You're the only one holding us back," she whispered.

"I am," he agreed. "Neither one of us is in a place for this. Just . . . give me one more minute."

She'd give him all the minutes he wanted if he'd just keep caressing her. Macy couldn't handle his mouth being so close, teasing her so intensely. She turned her head, catching his heavy-lidded gaze before he slammed his lips onto hers. Wrapping his arms around her, he flattened his hands on her backside and pulled her body flush with his.

Yes. This is exactly what she was talking about. They were finally getting somewhere.

His tongue tangled with hers as he walked her back toward the stairwell. For privacy? How far was he taking this? She silently pleaded for him not to put on the brakes, to take her upstairs where they could continue to explore. And why had she said two minutes? Why didn't she say an hour? The entire evening?

When her back hit the wall, Liam's mouth traveled down her jaw, over her neck, and toward her ear. Macy shifted her head and sighed as wave after wave of arousal pummeled her.

Macy slid her fingers through his hair as his breath tickled the side of her neck. When his hands slid around her waist, jerking her tank from her jeans, Macy's belly clenched with both shock and anticipation.

The jerk on the snap of her jeans had her moaning, then biting her lip to keep from begging. The zipper slowly eased down and a half second later Liam's large palm settled across her lower abdomen.

"I can't stop myself." His tortured tone growled into her ear. "I need to touch you."

Then they were definitely on the same page because she was about one breath away from pleading with him. The second his hand started roaming lower, she stepped wider, cursing her jeans and the restriction.

Macy wanted to feel him, too. Needed to have his taut skin beneath her hands. She slid her fingertips beneath his shirt, pulling the material up as she explored.

But then Liam touched her exactly where she ached for him and Macy suddenly forgot about everything else as she dug her nails into his back. Dropping her head back against the wall, she let out another moan, not even caring what she sounded like.

"You're so damn sexy," he muttered as he used his lips on her collarbone. "Don't hold back."

As if that was an option?

Macy jerked her hips, needing more. She couldn't believe this was happening, but she wasn't about to ques-

hips harder. Still digging her nails into his back, she let the emotions wash over her, let Liam give her pleasure.

When he pumped faster, Macy couldn't hold back another second. Her entire body seemed to let go, shattering in his arms as the climax slammed into her. She heard him muttering something, but she couldn't focus on anything other than how amazing her body felt, how perfect this moment was, and how she couldn't wait to go upstairs and finish.

When her body stopped trembling, Liam slowly pulled his hand away and eased back. His eyes remained on hers, but suddenly he wasn't touching any part of her. A burst of cold air swept over her heated skin.

Macy didn't like that look she saw on his face. Didn't like the fact he seemed to be sliding up some invisible wall between them.

Something between torture, pain, and sorrow all mixed in and stared back at her as the cold, harsh reality came crashing back.

"I guess the two minutes are up," she muttered.

The muscle in his jaw clenched and Macy took his blaring silence as her answer. Jerking her clothes back in place, she kept her gaze on his. No way was he taking the easy way out of this. If he wanted to stop, he'd have to look her in the eye and tell her what the hell was going on.

"So, what was this?" she asked once she was covered. Throwing her arms wide, she dared him to answer her honestly. "Was this you staking your claim because you heard someone else ask me out?"

"I didn't mean to touch you," he murmured, glancing away as if he was ashamed of what just happened.

Now they were getting somewhere. Those demons of his had come out to play at the most inopportune time. But she wasn't backing down, not when he was struggling. She was feeling frustrated, but he clearly needed someone, and if he was attempting to open that door even the slightest bit, then Macy was going to barge her way in.

"Who hurt you?" she asked, suddenly not as concerned with getting upstairs, but more concerned with digging deeper into his life and figuring out what, or who, had done so much damage.

His dark eyes hardened. Gone was the passionate, giving man of a few moments ago. "Nobody. I'm sorry I let this get out of hand, but I'm human and I lost it."

"I wish we could lose a little more control," she stated, crossing her arms over her chest. "Because I was having a good time and I know you would too if you'd let yourself."

"I'm not in town for a good time," he retorted. "I take responsibility for what just happened—"

"Well, I'm so glad. Here I was worried I was responsible for my own orgasm."

Liam's eyes narrowed. "Stop being snarky. I'm serious, Macy. I don't want you hurt."

She pushed off the wall and closed the space between them. Ignoring his tense posture, she placed her hands on his shoulders. "I don't want anyone hurt. Why can't we explore what's between us?"

"Because there's nothing between us."

He pulled away, went to the shelf, grabbed his discarded tape, and threw her a glance over his shoulder. "I'll be sure to stay away from now on. It would be best if you did the same."

"Best for whom?"

He faced the other way, only offering his back when he replied, "Everyone."

Maneuvering around her without touching or even

looking at her, Liam went upstairs and closed the door. Macy sank to the floor, wrapped her arms around her drawn knees, and dropped her forehead. What she should do was leave him alone, but wasn't that the problem? Hadn't everyone left him? She wasn't sure of his entire backstory, but she was slowly piecing things together. Liam was such a mess of emotions that even he didn't know what to do with them.

Macy might be a pain in his ass, but she was going to prove to him that he wasn't alone, that someone actually cared, and that he had a chance at so much more if he'd just let his guard down.

Chapter Eight

"Please, tell me you're not serious."

Liam wasn't in the mood to discuss weddings, cakes, or anything remotely involving happy couples. But with Cora and Sophie sitting at the kitchen island, he could hardly turn them away. Now, if this were Zach and Braxton, he'd have no trouble telling them to get out of his kitchen.

"You think that's a bad idea?" Cora asked.

Liam looked down at the picture of the bright yellow wedding cake with purple butterflies and pink flowers all over it and attempted to form words that weren't too harsh. And that was just the exterior. The actual cake was marble. Marble. What was this? 1980?

"It's hideous."

Okay, that came out a little uglier than intended, but he wasn't putting his stamp on this heinous cake and he sure as hell wanted something better for his family.

Sophie burst out laughing. "We're teasing you."

Cora's fingertips felt along the counter until she came in contact with the notebook. Carefully, she flipped the page over and pointed to another picture. "I believe this is the real one. Did I turn to the three-layer cake?"

"You did," he informed her. Liam studied the simple, cake with fresh blue hydrangeas between each cream-colored layer. "Better. What flavor cake do you guys want?"

"Can you do different flavors?" Cora asked. "I was thinking one classic white, one chocolate, and one raspberry. Your raspberry cake is amazing. But my favorite is still white and my parents would die if there was no chocolate."

Liam nodded. "Of course. No problem. What flavor do you want the icing?"

As they went on to tell him what they wanted, Liam made notes on the page beside the picture. The two women were both in agreement on everything, which made his job easier. He'd only attempted one other double wedding and it had been two Bridezillas facing off and he'd landed in the middle. Weddings were definitely not his favorite event to come up with some grand, elaborate menu or cake. But he would go all out for his soon-to-be sisters-in-law.

"Oh, and can you do some of those strawberry macaroons like you had the other evening?" Sophie piped up. "Those things are amazing. Feel free to have those at the resort anytime. The guests raved about them."

Liam nodded. "I'll make sure to have them for every Wind Down with Wine when guests arrive and I'll have them at your wedding."

"We can use the outdoor patio and the sunroom for the reception, but we should keep the cake inside in case it's hot out," Sophie went on, glancing to Cora. "We already have the seating and tablecloths, so we won't have to do much other than centerpieces."

Cora nodded. "And since this will be a fairly small wedding, we won't need to add any extra tables or chairs."

As the women went back and forth, totally forgetting they were here to go over the menu, Liam's cell vibrated in his pocket. He pulled it out and read the screen. His heart sped up as he swallowed and excused himself. He answered as he stepped out the back door and stood on the porch.

"Hello."

"Liam." Mark's familiar voice boomed through the line. "Is this a bad time?"

"Not at all." Liam glanced over his shoulder through the screen door. The ladies were still chatting, oblivious he'd even walked away. "I appreciate you returning my call."

"I know we parted with some heated words, but you were still the best chef I've ever had."

A bit of pride swelled inside Liam as his ex-boss cut to the chase. "I'm ready to discuss a price for Magnolias," Liam prompted.

Mark chuckled. "I knew you'd be on board with this. I'm actually glad to be passing it to someone I trust. But I'm a little surprised you're ready to come back. I thought you'd stay in Haven."

Liam headed further out onto the porch and took a seat on the top step. "Is that so?"

"Yes, but I was hoping you were up for this. I wasn't sure how you were doing back in your hometown and I know you loved it here. Besides, the customers all miss you and this place would be in good hands if you decided to come back, especially as the owner."

Intrigued, Liam rested his arm on his bent knee. "May I ask why you're selling?"

"I'm getting tired. When you own a business, you're essentially married to it."

Well, this was one marriage Liam wouldn't mind having one bit. A restaurant of his own, fulfilling his life-long dream, coming full circle to the vision his mother had for herself. Bittersweet emotions tightened in his chest as he thought of how proud his mother would've been at the idea of Liam having his own restaurant, and one as successful as Magnolias.

"I was hoping you could come in sometime soon so we could discuss specifics and then we can negotiate a price," Mark went on. "That is, if you're serious about this. I know you'd mentioned a few times over the years that you'd love to have your own place."

Liam had dropped some hints. And why not try to get an established business as lucrative as Magnolias? He already knew the staff, the customers, how everything ran. The business side of owning a restaurant would be new to him, but he'd seen enough with Bella Vous to know a bit more than he did a few months ago.

This was a big risk, but everything he'd ever wanted was practically being handed to him. If he could get a loan for the place, everything else would be a non-issue. . . . Well, except for telling his family that he was moving back to Savannah to pursue his own dream.

Zach and Braxton wouldn't like this. Most likely they'd be furious, but Liam had to do what was best for him. He wouldn't just leave them hanging. He'd personally find a chef to take his place and make sure the resort was taken care of. The transition wouldn't be smooth, emotionally or physically, but there was no way Liam could walk away from this opportunity.

"I can meet with you," he replied, gazing out onto the pond. A few of the guests were taking a walk toward the dock, where they could feed the ducks. "It would have to be an evening."

The second the date and time were set, Liam knew he'd placed a ball into motion that would continue to roll for the rest of his life. This was the moment he'd been waiting for, a chance to make his own dreams come true. After years of cooking being just a hobby he shared with his mother, then as a way to continue to hold her memory alive, Liam didn't know anything else. This was his skill, his livelihood. And in a short time, he might be the owner of one of the hottest restaurants in Savannah and the surrounding areas.

Once he disconnected the call, it took a moment for him to remember Cora and Sophie were still in the kitchen. Female chatter sounded through the screen door. Liam came to his feet and stretched, placing the phone back into his pocket. For now, he was keeping all of this to himself. If by some chance this business didn't come to fruition, nobody would ever know he'd thought of leaving Haven.

Years ago he'd wanted out because of all the heartache and tension after the accident. Now he wanted out because he craved being back in his comfort zone, in the lifestyle he'd grown accustomed to for the past ten years. And if getting his own restaurant and fully being his own boss came along with moving, then he was ready to pack his bags.

Nearly all of his savings was tied up in Bella Vous, though, but he had some retirement he could cash in, if he wanted to pay a penalty. There were just so many variables to think on, to plan out, and everything was going to come down to timing and funds. Liam had to be patient and wait, praying everything would fall into place.

As he stepped back inside, Sophie stopped midsentence and looked his way. "Everything okay?"

Liam nodded. "Yeah. Just a friend from Savannah." Not a complete lie.

Cora came to her feet, reaching for Heidi's collar. "I need to get back. I have an appointment coming in shortly. As far as the cake, I'm fine with anything and trust your judgment."

"I promise you'll love it," Liam assured her.

Sophie pushed off the counter and stood as well, reaching over to close the binder. "I need to get moving, too. I told Macy I'd make some calls and draw up a simple invitation to her father's surprise party."

Just the mention of Macy's name had Liam's entire body

on alert. Granted, the frustrating woman was never far from his mind, but especially after last night. He could still feel her trembling against him, still feel her warm pants against the side of his face. It had taken every bit of his willpower to walk away, but her words would haunt him forever. The look on her face after he'd denied her more had kept him awake nearly all night. Somehow, he needed to fix this. . . . But how did he approach her again without seeing a look of hatred or rage looking back at him?

"Hey," Sophie said, her brows drawn together. "Something wrong?"

Liam shook away the thoughts as much as he could and offered her a smile. "Just thinking ahead to your wedding cake."

Though worry was still etched in the slight wrinkles between her brows, Sophie tipped her head and grinned. "I can't wait. I know you'll do an amazing job. Macy mentioned asking you for some help with her father's party. I'm sure that's a lot on your plate with our wedding, too. I'll see what I can do to help Macy. Surely I can throw something simple together."

"No." Liam reached out, touching Sophie's arm before he could stop his actions or his mouth. "I'll help her. It's not too much. The party is before your wedding, so we're good."

And he hadn't realized until this exact moment that he would actually help Macy. Perhaps that was a way to call a truce while he was here. She clearly needed someone to pull the party off and he needed to apologize in a major way. As much as he feared spending more time with her, there was no way around this. Macy needed people to band together, to show her and her father that she was cared for and appreciated. He wasn't a complete jerk— just when he couldn't control his hormones.

And from now on, he'd be in total control with Macy. He couldn't afford not to be.

Sophie's smile widened. "I was hoping you'd help her. But seriously, if you need me to do anything at all, please just tell me."

Liam closed the space between them and wrapped his arms around her shoulders. "You're too good for my brother."

"I don't know about that." She laughed as she patted his back and rested her head against his chest. "I think he's pretty great."

The back screen door slammed shut. "Do you always hit on my fiancée when I'm not around?"

Not letting go of Sophie, Liam glanced over his shoulder and shrugged. "Every chance I get."

Zach grunted and reached for a banana out of the decorative bowl on the counter near the back door. "Get your own woman."

Liam smacked a kiss on Sophie's forehead and released her. "All the good ones are taken."

Sophie clutched the notebook to her chest. "Your amazing brother is all set to make us the best wedding cake ever."

"I'd rather have a slab of ribs," Zach muttered around the bite. Sophie shot him a glare. "But whatever you want is fine."

Her smile beamed. "That's what I thought."

"How about I plan on a meal with smoked meat and some killer sides?" Liam suggested. "I have a new recipe I've been wanting to try, but I wasn't sure what venue to use it at."

Sophie leaned against the center island and shook her head. "No. You're doing enough. Between the cake and then helping Macy—"

"Helping Macy?" Zach chimed in. "With what?"

Liam resisted the urge to groan, but before he could answer, Sophie continued. "She's throwing a surprise birthday party for Phil and Liam is helping with the food."

Zach quirked a brow, instantly turning his attention to Liam. "Is that so? Sounds like more sleepovers are in your future."

Scratching his cheek with his middle finger, Liam returned the glare.

"I'm glad you're helping Macy," Zach went on with a slight grin.

"Helping Macy with what?" Braxton asked, stepping into the kitchen from the hallway.

Liam rolled his eyes and stared up at the ceiling. "Why is everyone in my kitchen? Don't you have classes to teach?"

"This is my short day," Braxton replied as he moved further into the room and took a seat on one of the bar stools. "So what's up with Macy?"

Could a guy not just get his work done and go home without all the gossiping and the people putting their noses into his business? Even if they were family, Liam didn't want to discuss Macy with them. Hell, he couldn't even wrap his own mind around what was going on between them. All of this up in the air chaos was seriously wreaking havoc on his sanity.

"Liam is helping Macy throw a surprise party for Phil," Zach stated.

"I'm not helping her throw the damn party," Liam yelled. "I'm doing the food. That's all."

Braxton's eyes crinkled behind his glasses as he grinned. "Sounds to me like you're helping her throw the party. Don't forget to send me an invitation."

Gritting his teeth, Liam shoved his way past Zach and ~~ed on the fridge door. "I'm not doing the invitations.

Right now, I'm starting on dinner for the guests, who actually appreciate me. Now, the rest of you get out."

"Why am I being shunned?" Sophie asked.

Liam threw her a glance. "You're guilty by association with your fiancé. Besides, you're helping, too, and nobody is giving you grief."

Liam pulled out the chicken and the seasoning mix he'd prepared earlier. The three stooges continued to stand around and stare at him. Damn it. He didn't want them to get in his business, but he knew they did because they cared—even if they had an annoying way of showing it.

Guilt slithered through him, making him question if he should keep pursuing the Magnolias option. But how could he give up a chance at having everything he wanted? His mother had instilled that in him, and the Monroes had as well. Now that they'd all forged together for Chelsea's dream, wasn't it time for him?

His selfish thoughts had him swallowing back a lump of emotions. When was it okay to be selfish? When was he allowed to put his needs ahead of others? And did they actually need him here? If he found another chef, what would it hurt if he moved on?

"He's trying to ignore us," Braxton whispered.

Sophie laughed. "Come on, guys. Let's leave him alone and let him work. I don't want him taking out his revenge on our wedding cake."

"And he promised smoked meat," Zach chimed in.

Braxton scooted the stool back and came to his feet. "Say no more. Smoked meat and cake for my wedding? I'll do whatever he wants."

As much as he hated to, Liam laughed and shook his head as he took the seasoning and sprinkled it on the chicken. "Get out," he chuckled. "Let me work so our guests are kept happy."

Braxton turned and headed out, back down the hallway

where he'd entered. Zach slid his arm around Sophie's waist and she leaned a little into his side. Liam refused to be jealous of his brothers' relationships with such amazing women. They deserved happiness. Not that Liam didn't, but it would take a special woman to be able to put up with the ugliness of his past and the baggage of his present.

"Oh, I need to let you know about the new guests we have coming next week." Sophie straightened, smoothing her hair behind her ears. "You know Livie Daniels?"

The name was familiar, but Liam was drawing a blank. "Not really."

"Didn't she graduate with Braxton?" Zach asked, glancing to Sophie.

"She did. Her dad ran the small airport in Haven and he recently passed away."

"I remember her now," Liam stated. "She was quiet in school, ran around with that one girl who was annoying. Forget her name, too, but she was obnoxious."

"Jade McKenzie. She wasn't obnoxious," Sophie corrected with that soft tone of hers. "She just didn't take crap from people. I actually really liked her. But we're getting off track. Livie, Jade, and another of their friends are staying with us for three days next week."

Liam nodded. "Fine."

"They didn't request anything in particular," Sophie went on. She stepped forward and touched Liam's arm to get his attention. "But with Livie's father just passing a few weeks ago, I figure this is a getaway for the girls to just relax and be there for each other. I know Livie and Jade are living in Atlanta, but the other girl isn't from this area. At least, I didn't recognize the name on the registration."

"Why are you telling me all of this?" Liam asked.

"I think maybe we should go all out for them," Sophie suggested with a little shrug. "You know, chocolate everything, wine always at the ready, even in their rooms."

Liam nodded. "I'll make sure to cater to emotional women. Now, can I get back to work?"

"You're all heart," Zach growled.

Sophie and Zach finally left him to his preparations, and as Liam was stuffing the seasoned chicken, he realized how quiet things had gotten in his large kitchen. The kitchen at Magnolias had always been bustling, people coming at him from all directions. He'd been in his element there. Comfortable, happy.

Now, though, he felt like he was only here out of obligation and duty. He loved Chelsea, missed her every single day. He would've done anything for her, but he also knew she wouldn't want him here if this wasn't where his heart was.

Damn it. His loyalty wasn't just to his brothers, but to his late sister. There was no clear answer as to what he should do. The list of pros and cons was too lengthy. All he could do was wait and see how his meeting went with Mark and go from there.

Until then, though, he had dinner to make, and after he got off work he had some damage control to take care of. Chelsea was somewhere laughing at him over the fact he was going to go grovel to Macy and extend his services for the party. His sister would be proud of him stepping outside his comfort zone and taking an interest in something.

Unfortunately, Liam was far more interested than he should be. And he knew the moment he offered his help, he'd be starting something he might never be able to finish . . . which would only leave one or both of them hurt.

Chapter Nine

Dinner with her dad had been great. He'd picked up a pizza and their favorite beer and had everything ready when Macy got home from the store. The paper plates were full and at the island bar just waiting for her.

Though they lived separately now, they still looked out for each other. Macy's dad knew how tired she'd been lately, but he had no clue the whole softball coach thing was keeping her up at night—mostly because she was going to have to tell one of the most influential people in her life no.

Well, that wasn't all that was keeping her awake. A certain chef who'd had her in knots for the past few months plagued her thoughts and starred in every fantasy.

She'd just pulled on her favorite pair of shorts and an oversized, off-the-shoulder T-shirt when her doorbell rang. She wasn't expecting company, but in a small town like Haven, random visitors weren't unheard of.

As she bound down the steps, she pulled her hair up and notted it with the band from her wrist.

The sun was starting to set, but the warm glow coming front windows and door highlighted her visitor in all tiful, grouchy glory. Despite how they'd left things last night, her body still reacted to seeing him on her doorstep.

Liam had never come to her house before. Dare she hope he was taking a step she'd been waiting on? Because she refused to give an inch—not anymore. She would've considered tossing all her warnings out the proverbial window had Liam not been so hell-bent on fighting the feelings between them.

Macy pulled in a deep breath before she flicked the lock and opened the door. His hair curled a bit on the ends, his stubble indicated he hadn't shaved today, and this rough exterior made him seem a bit more like his reckless brother, Zach. But Liam was much more intriguing, much sexier. He had that whole brooding complex down, but there was that underlying vulnerability that kept pulling her back in. Well, that and the fact the man could touch her and make her knees go weak in less than a second.

"Can I come in?" he asked.

As much as she wanted to tell him no and slam the door in his face, she couldn't deny those dark eyes looking back at her. She couldn't deny him anything and that's exactly how she found herself on this roller-coaster ride of frustrating emotions and raging hormones.

Without a word, she stepped back and gestured for him to enter. Once he was inside, she closed the door, then turned to face him. She crossed her arms, waiting on him to state why he was here in her personal space. Now that he stood in her home, she realized just how small its entryway was. Every time she was near Liam he monopolized everything else and all her surroundings seemed to vanish. She should've told Tanner she'd go out with him yesterday when he'd stopped in. Maybe if she'd spent the time with someone else, she'd exorcise Liam right out of her mind.

Not likely, but at this point she needed to try something besides beating her head against the proverbial wall.

"Are you busy?" he asked, shoving his hands in the pockets of his jeans as if he were uncertain.

"No."

She wasn't adding anything, wasn't giving him anymore than what she had to. She'd already given enough last night.

"I'm sorry." He stepped forward, close enough to touch, but he kept his hands confined. "What happened was—"

"Nothing," she replied, lying through her teeth. "Is that all you came by for? You could've texted or called."

She started by him, but stopped short when his hand gripped her elbow. Pulling in a deep breath of courage, she was also gifted with that familiar masculine smell that could only be associated with Liam. The nerves in her belly expanded as they did when he was near. Why this man? Why did she have to be all torn up over the most infuriating man she'd ever met?

"I needed to tell you in person." His grip remained firm, but gentle. "I don't want this between us."

She tipped her head, enough to look into his eyes. "What don't you want between us? The tension or the fact that you now know my body better than I know yours? Or maybe you want to continue to run and totally ignore everything including the fact you want me."

The muscle in his jaw ticked, his lips thinned as he closed his eyes. She waited, wondering if she'd gone too far, but she didn't think so. She'd come apart against him, so what else did she have to hold back?

"I came to help with your father's party," he told her, focusing those mesmerizing eyes back on her. "I want to call a truce. We can't keep going on like this and I can't help you if we're constantly fighting each other. I just . . . want to help."

And then he went and said things like this and she was a puddle of emotions. Damn it, this was why she found him so perfect. But he couldn't be perfect, not for her anyway.

"You don't have to help with Dad's party." She stepped away from his grip before she did something insane like grab him back—by his mouth. "I can handle it."

"Really?" He turned now, raising a brow as if to call her bluff. Clearly she was amusing to him. "And what are you making?"

Macy shrugged. "No idea, but I don't want you helping me out of guilt."

"Oh, I feel guilty for letting things go too far last night and for how I treated you, but that's not why I'm here."

Liam turned, glanced around, and set off toward the back of her house. "Kitchen back here?" he called over his shoulder.

Seriously? Was he just going to come in and take over? "You're not staying here," she demanded as she followed. Damn him. He had long strides. "I don't want your help."

Ignoring her, he started opening cabinets, moving down the line of her wall. He threw her a look, keeping the left side of his face tipped. "Of course you do. Unless you plan on serving your guests Pop-Tarts and microwave popcorn with an overdose of chemically enhanced butter."

"Don't barge into my house and start picking apart my delicacies."

Liam snorted as he kept searching. The muttering under his breath would probably be offensive if she could hear him. Macy waited, wondering exactly what his plans were now that he was here. As much as she wanted to believe he wasn't here out of guilt, she couldn't help but feel his emotions over last night played some part. But she was in a bind. She wanted the best surprise party for her father, and if that meant she had to deal with the tension and chemistry with Liam, then she would.

Besides, watching Liam move around her house sent a jolt through her she hadn't known she'd been missing. He looked good—too good. Those faded jeans hugging his narrow hips, that dark T-shirt stretched across his broad shoulders, and the wisps of hair that seemed to need trimming. The man exuded sex appeal . . . as if she needed more fuel for her inner fire.

Blowing out a frustrated sigh, Liam turned to face her and crossed his arms over his chest. "You need to go to the store."

Macy jerked. "I just went two days ago. Were you planning on cooking right now? The party isn't for two weeks."

"I'm not doing everything," he told her. "You're going to help, and in order to do that you're going to learn some basics."

Macy blinked, sure she'd heard him wrong, but when he remained fixed in place, face void of emotions, she burst out laughing. "You've got to be kidding me. I don't want to learn to cook. I'm terrible at it, in fact. If you want to help with the party, great. But if you're going to torture both of us by making me play along, I'll find another way."

Liam uncrossed his arms, slowly stepping toward her, all the while keeping those dark eyes focused on her. "Torture? I think we've tortured each other enough for a while, don't you? This is us calling a truce, for real this time. I'm going to teach you simple things and you're going to learn. That way when your dad is impressed with this party, you can tell him you did some of the baking."

Macy narrowed her eyes. "You're not playing fair using my dad like that. You know I can't resist now."

He leaned in closer, his breath warm against her face. "You're going to have to stop resisting. That's your first lesson."

Macy swallowed. She had a feeling he wasn't talking about the party any longer. But she needed to focus, and if they were indeed calling a truce, she wanted to learn something. She wanted her father to be proud of her. Of course he already was proud of how she ran the store, but she wanted to show him just how much she appreciated everything he'd ever done for her, the sacrifices he'd made to give her the best childhood ever.

"Fine," Macy relented. "You can teach me basics, but keep in mind when I say I'm terrible in the kitchen, I'm not exaggerating."

Liam tipped his head. "Nobody is that bad. You can read, can't you?"

"Of course."

"Then you can follow a recipe."

Macy shrugged. He'd find out soon enough that she wasn't joking. Perhaps now wasn't the best time to mention the time she left eggs out of a birthday cake, or the time she cooked the pecan pie for four hours because it still looked gooey in the middle. Oh, also best not to bring up the time the biscuits caught fire in the oven because she'd forgotten them and had been in the shower. She quickly remembered when the smoke alarm had started going off and then she slipped, nearly breaking her neck, buck naked covered with shampoo.

Since moving into her new home, Macy hadn't attempted any cooking, so the smoke alarm hadn't been tested yet. Weren't they supposed to be tested monthly?

"First, we need to go over this junk in your refrigerator."

Macy moved around him and jerked the double doors open. Standing back, she surveyed the contents. "I see nothing wrong with my stock."

Reaching around her, Liam pulled out a container. "This is what you're trying to call butter? It's oil and processed garbage. I wouldn't let Zach's dogs have this."

Macy lifted her chin and glared over her shoulder. "I've never used anything else."

Liam groaned. "You're a walking heart attack waiting to happen."

Rolling her eyes, Macy turned back toward the fridge.

"I'll take my chances. What else is wrong in here, oh grand food snob?"

By the time Liam finished, all that was left in her fridge was the baking soda and bottles of water. Macy glanced at all of her food on the center island.

"I don't see how criticizing my groceries is going to make my dad's party a success."

Leaning against the counter, Liam shrugged. "If you have terrible ingredients, such as processed nonsense, then the end result will be a disaster. You don't want that, do you?"

Macy threw her arms out. "Give up the guilt trip, all right? I'm going to let you teach me basics. You're purging my fridge, and now you're educating me on how unhealthy I'm eating. Don't keep throwing my dad into the mix."

The uninjured side of Liam's mouth quirked into a grin. That lopsided smile did so much to her insides that she worried this "truce" would be a short-lived one. He was too appealing, too much of an enigma that she wanted to get closer to.

"You can either restock or come to my place," he told her. "I can't work here like this."

Macy laughed. "I had no idea my kitchen was so appalling. I've never had a problem here. Let's just go to your place, because I'm more than fine with my stuff and I'm not changing simply because you don't like my stock."

He jerked his head. "Let's go then. I'll drive."

"I can follow you."

"I'll bring you back."

He left the house as if there was no room for argument. Well, okay then. Clearly he wanted control and a part of her found that sexy as hell, though she normally found an overbearing man to be a total turnoff. For some reason that whole dominant, alpha male thing worked well with Liam.

Everything about Liam worked for her, actually. Well, except for that whole truce thing. She could seriously do without that because she was ready for him to take charge, rip her clothes off, and show more of that side she'd seen last night.

Because when that man let loose, he seriously could make a woman fall at his feet and beg.

No, she couldn't fall. That would mean he had all the power and she refused to let that happen again. She'd said some ugly things last night, hurtful things. Liam was nothing like the guy who'd hurt her. To even compare the two was like comparing good and evil, and it wasn't fair to Liam.

As she followed him, she grabbed her house keys off the side table by the door, shoved her feet into her favorite cowgirl boots, and locked up. Night had settled in and she couldn't believe she was actually going to his apartment, her old childhood home, for a cooking lesson of all things. How the hell had she managed to find herself in this predicament?

Oh, yeah. She wanted her father to have the best surprise party ever and she couldn't say no to Liam Monroe.

Maybe she'd end up begging after all before the night was over.

Clearly all common sense had flown out the window. What was he thinking bringing her back to his apartment? Not only that, he'd been adamant about driving her. Yes, he wanted to get to know her more, away from the sexual tension and more on friendly terms, but he should've let her drive herself.

Liam led the way up the back steps and unlocked the door. After reaching in and flicking on the light, he gestured for her to enter ahead of him.

"I feel ridiculous inviting you into your own place," he told her as he hung his keys on the hook by the door.

Macy's smile instantly warmed him. "It's your place now."

"This will always be yours," he countered. "I won't be here forever."

Liam was glad he'd picked up the place earlier. Not that he was a slob, and it wasn't as if he had unpacked all of his belongings. But the occasional shirt or shoes were left out, or glasses on the end table. Typical guy living, but he was meticulous when it came to his kitchen. And this apartment, for being a small space, was pretty amazing.

Phil Hayward had outdone himself on the renovating, and even though Liam was used to top of the line, the appliances and countertops weren't too far from the best. Of course Phil most likely was able to get all of this at cost, so upgrades were more affordable.

"You've not really done much with the place," Macy commented, running her hand along the back of the leather sofa. "I mean, it's the same, but a little different. Definitely more masculine, like a bachelor pad. My mother would want to add some throw pillows or a few pictures if she were here."

The wistfulness in her tone had him wanting to move toward her, but if she was feeling emotional, the last thing either of them needed was him trying to comfort her. Comfort led to touching, which led to hugging, which led to kissing, and the last time he'd kissed her he'd ended up with his hand in her pants and she'd been trembling in his arms.

So, no comforting. At all.

"Do you like your new house?" he asked, hoping to steer the topic toward something positive and more upbeat.

"I love it." Macy walked toward the open kitchen and smiled at the marks on the wall. "I always got so excited when Dad would measure me. I wanted to be grown up so bad."

Liam remained near the door, just letting her talk through her memories. He had his own that he replayed through his head. It was those childhood memories, from the good years, that kept him going on the tough days. Maybe he and Macy did have something in common after all.

"Being an adult is the dumbest thing I've ever done." She laughed as she turned back to face him. "I think I'd rather go back to the days of fort building and finger painting."

"If you can pay the bills that way, let me know how," he replied.

Macy pulled in a deep breath and sighed. Smoothing her stray strands away from her face, she glanced toward the kitchen. "So, what are we starting with?"

He hadn't thought that far ahead, actually. He'd watched her take in the apartment. He'd tried to look at anything other than those long, bare legs between the hem of her shorts and her boots . . . failing miserably. The shoulder peeking from her shirt practically begged him to reach out and see if her skin was as soft as it looked.

If he hadn't known better, he'd swear she'd put this outfit on to torture him. But she hadn't known he'd show up at her house.

Glancing at his watch, he shrugged. "Do you have any-where to be in the morning?"

With a burst of laughter, she shook her head. "Am I going to be here all night?"

The possibilities were endless. He stepped closer, keeping his eyes locked on hers. "Depends on how obedient you are as a student."

Her eyes widened and he ignored the flare of desire in them as he passed her and rounded the center island. He seriously needed to watch his vocabulary where she was concerned. Everything took on a different meaning when trying to dance around sexual tension.

Liam quickly racked his brain to think of what he should tackle that wouldn't be too overwhelming for her. Resting his palms on the granite island top, he leaned forward. "What are your thoughts for your dad's party?"

Macy wrinkled her nose. "Finger sandwiches and cake?"

He couldn't suppress the groan. "Do you love your dad or not? You can't serve that."

With a defiant tilt of her chin, Macy crossed her arms over her chest. "Fine. Then what are we going to make?"

"Since you want the party in the evening, people will expect more than finger foods."

Her eyes widened in fear. "I'll change the time."

Liam laughed and pushed off the counter. "Sophie already has a mock-up of the invitations you asked for. We can make this work and keep it fairly pain free for you."

"Fine, then. Let's get started."

As he began pulling out ingredients, his mind was working overtime. Keeping things simple and staying on task would be easy. Once he started cooking, his mind instantly zoned out to everything else around him.

Perhaps she could do some simple macaroni and cheese bites baked with a seasoned bread crumb topping. Maybe some steak kabobs on the grill since she was doing the party at her house. That was certainly simple enough. But he also had a great BLT pasta salad that would work really well, especially with summer on the horizon. Liam transitioned his menus from season to season like some people did their clothing.

"This cookbook is really old."

Liam jerked around to see Macy holding his mother's cookbook. The red and white checkered cover was as familiar to him as his scarred face in the mirror.

He reached for it, carefully snatching it from her hands, and holding the loose binding onto the back. Macy startled and fisted the hand that had been holding on to the book.

"Sorry," she muttered.

Cursing, Liam set the book on the island. "No, I'm sorry. That was my mother's."

He swallowed at the pain that threatened to creep up. He'd never spoken of his mother to anyone. He'd only shared his childhood memories with Chelsea when she'd pester him in the kitchen. She'd feign that she was there to sample the goods, but he knew her tactics went deeper. She wanted him to open up, to share some of the hurt, and she'd been the only one to get him to do so.

Until now, when he wanted to share everything with Macy. For some reason being one vulnerable person to another was the key to getting him to want to rip open the wounds and reveal his pain.

"I'm still sorry," she muttered. "I didn't think."

"You didn't know," he countered, trailing a finger over the worn title. "My mother and I used to bake all the time. It was our thing. She was single and we really only had each other. She passed of a brain aneurism, so I never felt like I had any closure. I wasn't there when she died."

Macy's feet shuffled over the wood floor. From the corner of his eye he saw her delicate hand reach for his. She flattened his hand over the book, holding him there as she stood way too close to his side. Liam didn't move, barely breathed as he waited for her to say something. The silent comfort she offered was almost too much. Emotions clutched his chest as he struggled to pull in much needed air. Thinking of his mother always hurt, but sharing memories out loud was flat-out crippling.

"I'm sorry, Liam. I can tell she was a special lady," Macy commented. "She'd be proud of you."

"Probably," he agreed. The warmth of Macy's hand over his seemed to provide some type of courage he didn't even know he needed. "I learned how to make a pie when I was five. I made Thanksgiving dinner when I was eight. She let me do absolutely everything from the turkey to the stuffing and the cranberry salad. Even though it was just the two of us, I made a huge spread."

Macy's thumb stroked across the back of his hand. "I bet it was amazing."

"The turkey was dry, the pie was gooey, and the stuffing was a bit crisper than it should've been, but my mom went on and on about how wonderful it was." He smiled as he recalled how pleased his mother had been. "I knew she was lying. I mean, I tasted the food and instantly knew I'd messed up. But that's how she was. Always encouraging me to do better, try again and learn from my mistakes."

"What did she look like?"

Jerking his eyes to Macy, he tried to figure out how he could describe the most beautiful woman in both spirit and looks. "She had long dark hair, blue eyes, and a soft smile. She was always smiling. I can't imagine how hard it must've been for her to work and raise me on her own, but she managed for the first twelve years of my life."

"What happened when she died?"

Liam pulled his hand from beneath hers and turned away. "I'm not getting into that."

"I know the pain, Liam. I lost my mother, too. You don't have to say anything."

He couldn't, not when talking about the good memories gutted him. To delve into the fact his mother had been taken from him was more than he could handle right now. And Macy did get him, in more ways than he ever wanted to admit.

Macy moved around to stand in front of him. Slender

arms circled his waist as she rested her head against his chest. She didn't back down, wasn't taking his rejection for an answer.

Liam closed his eyes as a new onslaught of emotions threatened to overtake him. There was more to Macy than he wanted to admit, even to himself. She cared. She might be flirty and make offers, but that was to cover up her own hurt. Deep down, she cared for him and he couldn't help but care for her.

Still, what good would come of the two of them taking the next step? What then?

"What happened to the truce?" he asked, cursing his husky voice.

"We agreed to be friends," she murmured. "And right now my friend needs a hug."

Damn it. He wrapped his arms around her and rested his chin atop her head. She was right. He did need this comfort, this connection from someone who cared. Having Macy as a friend was something he longed for, but he didn't know if he could handle stopping there. No matter how much he tried to tell himself to leave her be, he was having a hard time. Because right now, holding her in his arms after he'd appeared so weak was exactly what calmed him. She knew him, she *got* him. He'd ripped open one of his wounds and exposed more than he wanted and Macy merely opened her arms and welcomed him in.

What would she say if she knew what he'd put up with? After his mother died, when he couldn't save her and then went on to endure hell, what would Macy say? Would she see him as weak?

Liam didn't want to dwell on his past, didn't want to waste this time he had with Macy, and he couldn't keep holding her like this when his heart was starting to get all entangled with her. There were things he couldn't afford to do, and making more ties in Haven was one of them.

Liam pulled back slightly, glancing down to her beautiful face. "Let's focus on what we came here for."

She opened her mouth as if she wanted to say something, but finally nodded with a smile. "Just remember, I evaporate water when I boil it. I also burn frozen waffles."

Liam groaned as he released her. "Frozen waffles shouldn't even be a thing."

"Actually, they're pretty good. Especially if you put some peanut butter and syrup on them."

Holding up a hand, Liam shook his head. "Stop it. We will not speak of this again."

Macy's soft laughter washed over him, filling the normally dark space with a happiness he hadn't experienced in a long time. She was good for him. As a friend, he couldn't ask for better. So long as he remembered that, this truce would be simple.

Chapter Ten

Macy stared at the cast iron skillet full of one giant, round, chocolate chip cookie. Her mouth watered and she felt a swell of pride at the fact she'd made this colossal cookie and the thing hadn't been scorched.

She turned to Liam, who was wiping off the center island. "Now what?"

He threw her a grin over his shoulder. "Now comes the good part. We're making chocolate sauce."

Just when she thought her mouth couldn't water anymore. "Please, tell me you have ice cream."

"I know how to do a sundae," he retorted, giving the counter one last swipe with the wet cloth. "I also have whip cream—the real kind, not the junk. Now, get a saucepan out of the bottom cabinet. It's the smaller—"

"I know what a damn saucepan is," she muttered as she jerked on the cabinet door. This was the same space her mother had kept their pans in. It was a bit odd to see such expensive cookware in this place now, but she was glad her childhood home was being well cared for.

As he led her into mixing the sauce, he stood back and observed. Macy only felt a little nervous being under his eye, but the prospect of eating a warm, gooey dessert took precedence over her fear of messing up.

"Use the whisk in a figure eight pattern," he explained, taking hold of her hand and showing her.

With his body behind hers, his forearm lining up perfectly along hers, and the warmth of his breath on the side of her neck, making the whisk do anything was a bit difficult for Macy. It was all she could do not to slide onto the floor at his feet. Her shaky knees were working overtime and Liam seemed to be oblivious as he continued to move her hand in the pattern.

The chocolate started to thicken up and Macy turned her head slightly. "Is it done?" she murmured.

Liam's gaze dropped to her lips, his hand tightening on hers. For a half second, Macy froze. She couldn't breathe, couldn't blink. The stubble running along Liam's firm jawline begged for her to run her lips across it to see if it was as coarse as it looked.

Before she lost her mind and stepped over their friend boundary line, Liam stepped back and cleared his throat.

"Yeah, it's done." He turned, muttered something under his breath, and jerked on the freezer door. "The bowls are in the cabinet above you and to the right."

Macy left the whisk in the pan and grabbed the bowls. It was a wonder she didn't drop them with her shaky hands, but she held strong. Now all she needed to do was ignore the fluttering in her belly and the way her body literally ached for his and concentrate on eating her dessert. Simple as that.

"Turn off your burner," he told her as he pried the lid off the ice cream. "You don't want the bottom of your chocolate to burn and I don't want my good pan ruined."

After he cut the cookie and gave them each a warm piece, he scooped chocolate-swirl ice cream on top and Macy drizzled the syrup over all of it.

"I can honestly say my new kitchen has never smelled like this," she told him, eyeing her bowl of calories. "And I'm pretty sure this kitchen hasn't smelled this good since my mother was alive."

Liam pulled out two spoons and handed her one. "Let's take these to the couch. You've worked hard and deserve to take a break."

Macy settled into the corner of the leather sofa, tucking her feet beneath her. She cut into the cookie and made sure to have a healthy amount of ice cream and syrup on her spoon before she took her first bite. The groan that escaped her couldn't be helped. This was seriously the best dessert ever.

"Damn, I'm a good cook."

Taking a seat at the opposite end of the couch, Liam laughed. "You are. Cookies in the cast iron pan are my absolute favorite."

"So you started me with your favorite instead of the basics?"

Liam eyed her. "Chocolate chip cookies *are* the basics."

Macy slid her spoon through another bite. "I figured basics would be something like canned green beans."

"Stop it," he said, scooping up another bite. "Quit talking about all of your canned and processed foods. It makes me nauseous to think people eat like that."

Macy merely shrugged and concentrated on her decadent dessert. "I'm really glad I have on my baggy shorts. I can feel the pounds clinging to my waist."

"Your waist is perfectly fine," he muttered.

There was no comment she could add to that, so she finished off her gooey treat and took her bowl to the sink. After she rinsed it out, she placed it in the dishwasher and started cleaning up the kitchen.

"I'll get it." Liam came over and put his empty bowl in the sink. "It's getting late."

"I'm not leaving you with this mess."

Macy reached past him and grabbed the cast iron skillet. The instant burn to her hand had her dropping it back onto the stove. With a hiss, she clutched her hand to her chest.

"Damn it." Liam moved lightning fast and grabbed her arm. "Let me see."

The palm of her skin and her two middle fingers were already turning a shade of purple. Macy bit down on her lip and tried to pull her arm back.

"Get cold water on this." Liam urged her toward the sink, turned on the faucet, and thrust her hand beneath the refreshing spray. "Don't move."

Without another word, he rushed out of the room and headed toward the bathroom. Macy leaned forward and let the water take away some of the sting. Stupid, stupid mistake. Of course the cast iron handle was hot. She'd used a pot holder for it earlier and they hadn't taken that long to eat.

Embarrassment overrode any pain and she cursed herself for being such a moron. This rookie kitchen mistake would no doubt make Liam think of her as . . . what? Someone who didn't have common sense? Clearly she wasn't fit for this and she was proving to him just how inept she was.

"Here." Liam turned the water off and grabbed a paper towel. "Gently dab the area dry and let me put some ointment on it."

Macy dried around the wound and barely dabbed the actual burn. Thankfully her entire hand wasn't hurt, but the throb seemed to extend far beyond the wounded area.

"Lucky it was your left hand," Liam muttered, opening the tube of ointment.

"I'm a lefty."

He squirted some cream onto a clean cotton swab and shook his head. "Of course you are. I forgot."

When he came at her with the cotton, Macy flinched.

"I haven't touched you yet." His eyes held hers. "Relax."

"I'm just preparing myself for more pain."

Gently, he held her wrist. "I promise, this stuff doesn't hurt. It actually takes the sting away and it's an antibiotic cream, too. You'll feel better in seconds."

Macy held her breath, turned her head, and waited for him to work this miracle he claimed would cure her. The delicate touch of his fingers wrapped around her wrist comforted her. Those strong hands soothed her nerves in a way that she hadn't known before. Liam had quite the bedside manner.

"I need to wrap this."

When he let go, Macy realized the pain had indeed subsided. She glanced down to her hand, which was now greasy from the ointment.

Liam unwrapped a bandage and laid it on her hand before grabbing the tape. He carefully wound the cloth-type tape around her hand. Macy stared at the top of his head as he leaned down and studied his work. He was so intent on helping her, he hadn't tried to turn away his scarred side. When he lifted his head, she realized how close they were. His hands still held onto hers and Macy didn't even resist. She lifted her good hand and rested her palm on his scar.

When he started to pull away, Macy lifted her brows and held his gaze. "Don't."

The muscle in his jaw clenched beneath her hand. The slight stubble tickled her palm. He didn't look away, didn't let go of her. For once, Liam wasn't trying to hide himself.

"You know you're attractive with or without a scar, right?" she asked, well aware that this conversation could turn against her in seconds. But she wanted him to know exactly what she thought.

Liam grunted and glanced down to her bandaged hand, then back up. "I'm sorry you're hurt."

So, he was going to spin this back to her? Macy ran her

fingertip over the jagged skin on his cheek. "I'll be fine. I'm sorry I dropped your skillet."

He reached up and pulled her hand away from his face. "I can replace a skillet. I was more concerned with you."

That low, throaty tone of his combined with that dark gaze sent this intense moment into another level of intimacy. Macy inched a bit closer, her heart quickening when his eyes grew wider.

"You have a need to save people," she whispered. "But it'll be fine."

His thumb stroked the inside of her wrist. "I don't want you hurt."

The raw conviction in his tone tore her heart in two. She wasn't so sure she was the one who needed saving at all. Maybe this strong, determined man needed someone to ride to his rescue. She knew telling him that wouldn't go over very well, so she'd just have to show him with her actions.

"You must think I'm a complete idiot to grab that without even thinking," she murmured.

"Why do you think I have all this first-aid stuff?" he countered with a slight grin. "I've done it a time or two."

His words eased her embarrassment somewhat.

"Maybe I should get you back home," he told her, his eyes darting to her lips. "It's well after midnight."

"I'm not really tired," she countered, needing him to fulfill that silent promise in his eyes. "Are you?"

"Not at all."

Heat flooded her. She wanted Liam to make a move because she would not be the one to break their truce. She was more than willing to give him the upper hand here. She never thought this would happen, but with Liam she wasn't scared. If anything, she felt safe, which turned her on even more than her physical attraction to him.

His thumb continued to run over the sensitive skin on

the inside of her wrist. There was no way she could prevent the tremble from taking over and there was no way he missed the effect he had on her.

"How do you do this to me?" he whispered. "I've been here before. I swore I'd never do this again."

That was the second time he'd mentioned being "here" before, but Macy had no clue what he referred to. Was he meaning her or someone in his past? Macy didn't want to think about anything other than this moment. There was something about the middle of the night that brought out even more intimacy. There was something to be said for knowing there would be no interruptions and that the only two people who mattered right now were Liam and her.

"Who hurt you?" she whispered, resting her forehead against his, reaching up to stroke his hair.

He pulled in a ragged breath. "She doesn't matter, but I can't do this, Macy. Damn it. I want to. I just . . . I can't."

The angst in his voice, the pain lacing each word, almost had her feeling guilty, but why shouldn't they act on their emotions? Perhaps what she'd told him had put him off. Maybe knowing she'd been a victim of sexual assault had scared him away, adding to the demons he already faced.

Or maybe he'd believed the old rumors of her being promiscuous because she liked to date. Nobody knew of her assault in college. Well, nobody but Liam. If they did, maybe they would see how she'd used each and every date to get over that fateful night that changed her forever. That she'd accepted every man who asked her out because that put the control in her corner and she needed to hold the upper hand.

A slice of pain hit Macy deep as she eased away. She stepped far enough back to be out of reaching distance. Swallowing all of her emotions, she pushed back a stray strand of hair that had escaped her ponytail.

"I'm ready for you to take me home now."

Liam tipped his head. The man who hid the scarred side of his face had returned. They were right back to where they'd started.

"I'm not rejecting you," he told her, stepping forward.

Macy rounded the island and held up her hands. "No, you're rejecting any chance of happiness. But I understand if this has anything to do with my past, what I told you. I get it if you think I'm—"

He moved so fast and gripped her shoulders so intensely, Macy let out a yelp as she was hauled against his chest. "Never think I'm turning you away because of what you've been through or what other people may say about you. The outside world has nothing to do with what is happening here."

Well, that answered her question, but brought up a whole host of new ones.

Placing her uninjured palm on his chest, she stared up at him. "And what's happening in here, Liam? Because my heart goes like crazy when I'm around you. I can't lie about this any longer. I want you to make a move, to stop worrying about tomorrow or what I'd expect in the end. I have no expectations. I know I like spending time with you. Even when we bicker I'm having a blast because you challenge me. Can't we—"

Liam's mouth covered hers. Instantly shutting down any more thoughts she might add to her ramblings. He kissed her as he did everything else, with passion and determination. His hands slid over her jaw, his fingers threaded through her hair as he shifted their angle. His tongue tangled with hers as his body perfectly lined up with every part of her from chest to knee. He moaned slightly, giving away that he wasn't in as much control as he probably thought.

Macy brought her hands up to his shoulders, but hissed and pulled away when the pressure hit her burnt palm.

Liam raked a hand through his hair and cursed. "I'm sorry. I wasn't thinking."

Macy held her hand to her chest, hating that she'd been the one to pull back when he finally relaxed and took what he wanted. She needed him to do that more often because that was the only way he'd see what they could be . . . and she desperately wanted to know how far this could go.

"Don't apologize," she told him. "You kissed me and I forgot all about my hand."

The corner of his mouth tipped up. "Maybe I didn't need to use that ointment after all."

"I like when you smile. When you laugh. But I especially like when you kiss me like you don't care about anything else."

His smile vanished and she figured she'd said the wrong thing. Too bad. She was done dancing around this, around them.

"You should know something," she warned, poking him in the chest with her index finger. "I don't plan on ignoring this attraction. You can try, but I'll fight you and we both know I'll win. Let that sink in as long as you need, but I'm ready."

She expected him to look a little alarmed, a little nervous, but if anything, his eyes darkened, his lids lowered, and he appeared to be . . . turned on? Well, hell yeah. About time her words started sinking in to that brain of his.

"You're ready for what?" he asked, his voice husky.

She leaned in close and whispered, "Anything you want to give me."

Knowing she was well ahead in the game here, she sauntered away, an extra spring in her step. But before she could get too cocky, an arm snaked around her waist and hauled her back against a hard, broad chest.

"Don't flash those eyes at me, taunt me like that, and walk away," he growled in her ear. "You want a battle. It's on.

But, honey, you'd better be able to back up what you're saying because I'm bringing my A game and you've never seen anything like it."

Macy shivered and prayed he was telling the truth. Because she wanted Liam . . . and this promised A game.

Chapter Eleven

With spring showing off beautiful days, each one more perfect than the last, women were calling and booking their getaways at Bella Vous. Some were coming just for a quick overnight stay and a day of pampering, others were seeking weekend retreats. The last report Sophie had given Liam was that they were booked through the next two months. Of course they were closed during the wedding weekend, but other than that, they had names for each room and the money would continue to flow in.

Liam still hadn't made a decision regarding Magnolias, but he did feel a bit less guilty about leaving. Mark had ended up having to cancel their meeting, but he'd called and settled on a price with Liam and discussed specifics. Liam was informed on what all was included with the price as far as equipment and inventory.

Now more than ever Liam wanted his own place. The price was reasonable because Mark wanted out, which made it perfect for Liam because he wanted in.

But making that final decision, that huge leap of faith, was proving to be harder than he thought it would be. He wasn't so much afraid of the responsibility of being married to the business—that part actually thrilled him. The problem was over the past year he'd actually grown closer with Zach and Braxton. The experiences of running the resort and the death of their sister had forced them to communicate in ways they never would've done on their own.

Well, maybe Braxton would've continued to be the mediator, but Liam never would've gone to Zach on his own. From the time they all started living together as pre-teens and teens, Braxton had been the peacemaker. Now that they were adults, not much had changed.

Liam could admit how stubborn he was, how the chip on his shoulder had kept him away for years. What initially had started out as hiding from the pain of the accident had turned into pain from a broken relationship.

Gritting his teeth, Liam snapped the lid on the BLT pasta salad for tomorrow's lunch crowd. He'd finished all of his prep and was ready to head home. To a home that wasn't really his home. Macy had grown up there and had slept in the same room he was using now.

Macy. There was another factor in his decision to go or stay. He hadn't wanted any more layers of guilt, but now he was finding himself wondering how Macy would react if he left. Would she care? Was this just a fun little flirty thing for her? Or was she feeling more than just . . . what? Sexual? When she'd thrown down the gauntlet two nights ago, was that her sole purpose?

As much as he hated to think anything bad about Macy, he had to wonder where she wanted to go with this. And not that he was looking for a ring on his finger—far from it—but he'd like to know what she was thinking. He was a guy, so sex wasn't something he wanted to turn away from, but he also felt with the shaky ground they'd been walking on lately, that maybe some guidelines should be laid out.

Or he could just take everything day by day and enjoy the time here in Haven. That's what Chelsea would've wanted. His late sister rarely made plans. The only time she thought ahead was when she was planning her next excursion and even those tended to be last minute. She'd start daydreaming of a place to visit and the next thing they knew, she'd pack a bag and be gone.

With Liam living in Savannah for the past decade, she'd often call him from the road, text him when she arrived, or she'd simply swing in through his restaurant to give him a farewell hug. She hadn't stopped in on her final trip, though, and Liam wished like hell he would've had a chance to say good-bye. To hug her one last time. But he also knew even if he'd been able to tell her he loved her and wrap his arms around her, he'd still be wishing for one more day. She was a rare gem in life. There had always been a smile on her face, and she was always looking forward to each day because she had the ability to find one positive thing in any given situation. Liam wondered if he could adapt to that mind-set, if he could try to find one positive thing each day to perk him up.

As he wiped off all the counters in the kitchen he cursed himself. What the hell was he trying to give himself a damn pep talk for? He was nothing like his gorgeous, free-spirited sister. All the things that worked for her were what made her so special. He wasn't looking to change himself. He was happy just the way he was, thank you very much. Changing for anyone because his life wasn't going to plan was no way to live.

Clearly the stars were all lining up for him with the prospect of Magnolias, Macy challenging him in that sexy, not-so-subtle way, and he and his brothers getting along as well as they ever had. Perhaps things were working out exactly the way they should be, just not the way he'd planned.

"Are you coming out for pictures?"

Liam jerked around to the back door, where Sophie stood poking her head inside.

"Pictures?" he repeated, clutching his damp rag.

"Brock's prom." Her sigh of frustration told him she was not pleased he'd forgotten. "His date will be here soon and we wanted to get some family pictures by the pond."

Family pictures. Such simple words for such a complex group of people. Liam glanced down to the black apron he wore over his jeans and black T-shirt. With a shrug, he tossed the rag on the counter by the sink and jerked the apron from around his waist. After hanging it on the peg by the back door, he followed Sophie out to the pond.

Passing through one of the pergolas covered with hanging wisteria, Liam glanced up and saw Brock standing next to the pond. A little catch in Liam's throat had him pausing. This was a boy who only a year ago was living a much different life. He hadn't been sure where he would be safe to lay his head down at night, much less thinking of going to a dance with a date.

But here he stood, fidgeting with the white flower on his lapel while he waited for a girl to arrive. Brock was living the life every teen should have, yet there were so many in the world who were living a life of hell. Thanks to people like the Monroes and Zach and Sophie, they were offering hope to one life at a time. Brock couldn't have landed in a better family. Zach would be stern but gentle, and Sophie would be motherly and make sure he had everything he ever needed. Like the perfect tux and flowers for a prom.

Liam remembered those days. The first dates, the date that truly mattered because he wanted to impress a girl. Brock had grown so much in the past year and these nerves were normal, healthy. He was hitting another adolescent milestone.

But now that Liam had experienced life a little more, had been jaded by trying to impress a girl, he was done. For some asinine reason, Macy was impressed with him and he hadn't even been trying.

Brock glanced up, caught Liam's eye, and smiled. The boy had barely smiled when he'd first come to live with Zach and Sophie, but now that he'd relaxed and realized he was safe and had a support team, Brock was a regular teenager. He smiled, he back-talked, he loved his beat-up car and was saving for the next, and asked for advice on girls. Liam was so damn proud of the way Brock was growing into a young man and that he'd gotten so comfortable here. He was truly one of their own.

"Just one picture."

Liam laughed as he stepped closer to the small crowd around Brock. Zach, Sophie, Braxton, Cora, and Heidi all stood waiting.

"I want more than one," Sophie retorted. "And you'll stand there and smile like you're having a good time."

Brock gave the typical teenage groan, but Liam knew from the glint in the young man's eyes that he was thrilled to have all of this positive attention devoted to him.

"Let's do one of the guys first."

Sophie corralled everyone in front of the picturesque pond. Liam and Braxton stood on one side of Brock and Zach stood on the other.

"Can you put your arms around each other or something?" Sophie asked, waving her arm in the air. She clutched the camera in the other and shot a glare to Zach. "You all love each other—let me see it."

In typical guy fashion, they looped their arms over shoulders and stared back at Sophie.

"A smile is too much to ask, isn't it?" Sophie asked.

"Take the damn picture," Zach growled.

Sophie snapped several, more than just a few. By the end, Liam was holding the camera and getting a picture of Brock with Sophie and Zach, then Cora and Braxton, with Heidi, of course, and then with just the ladies. Surely Sophie would be pleased with one of these.

By the time Brock's date arrived, Liam was hoping to remove himself from the gathering. He wanted to get back inside and work on preparing the meals for tomorrow, but Brock needed his family's support. Liam watched as the teen smiled at his date—Alli, if Liam recalled correctly. A genuine smile lit up Brock's face and Alli seemed to be just as taken, if the tilt of her head and lowered lashes revealed anything.

Good for Brock. The boy deserved some excitement, some fun and an evening with friends. He'd worked hard around the resort and with keeping his grades up. Zach and Sophie had done an impressive job in the short time Brock had been with them.

Liam wished Chelsea were here to see all of this. To see how they'd all come together, not only for the resort, but for Brock.

Guilt crept up fast and fierce. Liam was leaving. He hadn't made final plans, but in his heart he knew the end result would be the same. Haven wasn't home for him anymore and his dream of having a restaurant of his own hinged on Magnolias.

Shoving his hands in his pockets, he turned and headed back to the house. Voices carried, laughter surrounded him. He loved his family, loved this place, but how could he stay knowing this wasn't what he wanted for his life? Wouldn't Chelsea have wanted him to follow his dreams? She had been such a dreamer, she would understand.

Damn it, he missed her. As he let himself back into the kitchen, he thought back to the time he'd shown her how to bake bread. She'd just been dumped by some jerk and Liam figured pounding out some dough would be a great relief, plus he had to bake loaves anyway for one of the neighbors, so it was a win-win.

Chelsea had loved the entire process. She'd gotten so wrapped up in learning, she'd forgotten what's-his-name, and by the time they were finished they were both coated in flour, fingers sticky with dough, and laughing. He typically thrived on a neat, orderly kitchen even when he was younger, but seeing her so happy had been worth the disaster.

The screen door slammed shut, but Liam didn't turn.

"Running from the family fun?"

Zach's judging tone didn't help the guilt Liam already struggled with. "Just getting back to work."

"You're not happy here."

Liam jerked his gaze toward his brother, who leaned against the island, arms crossed over his chest. What could he say? Zach was right, but Liam wasn't quite ready to have this argument.

"I never said that."

Zach grunted. "You don't have to say anything. You're sending out glaring signals."

Liam ignored the jab.

"If you're leaving, we need to know."

The back door slammed once more. "Who's leaving?" Braxton asked.

Well, hell. Might as well do this now since they were all here. They'd given him the opening he needed and he might not get another easy chance like this.

Liam held Zach's gaze. "I'm leaving."

The muscle in Zach's jaw clenched as he gave a clipped nod. "When?"

Pushing off the counter, Liam shrugged. "I'm not sure. Magnolias is for sale and I'm trying to buy it. I've been in contact with the owner, but this process could take a while."

He'd been wondering when he should tell his brothers and make things more official. Looks like he'd done just that.

"All right."

Liam narrowed his eyes at Zach. "All right? You're not going to fight me on this?"

Even Braxton stared at their brother like he couldn't believe the response.

"Would it matter?" Zach retorted. "If we fought, you'd still want to go and I'm honestly tired of fighting with you. I think a decade is long enough, don't you?"

A year ago this scene would've been entirely different. And the fact that Zach had given in so easily, letting Liam off the hook, free to pursue his passion, only added to the guilt. Should he want to stay to help his family? Should he put his own needs aside like they had done?

"Will you find a replacement or are we supposed to?" Braxton asked, still standing in the doorway. Surprisingly, he looked pissed whereas Zach seemed detached. Apparently his brothers had reversed roles.

"I'll find someone." He wasn't that big of a jerk to leave without taking responsibility. "I won't leave until I know you're in good hands. I want this business to succeed as much as you guys do."

Cora's and Sophie's laughter spilled in through the screen door. Liam didn't want to tell them, didn't want to see the disappointment on their faces.

"Don't tell Sophie just yet," Zach stated. "She's too happy right now."

Braxton nodded. "Same with Cora."

Telling both women wasn't something Liam wanted to do, but they needed to hear the news from him. Granted, now was definitely not the right time.

"I'll still help financially," Liam added. "I'm not quitting this family."

"If I even thought you were, this conversation would've already taken a different turn," Zach stated.

Liam didn't say anything more as the back door opened and Cora and Sophie came in, still chatting about the couple who had just left for their prom. Liam turned to the fridge and attempted to get back into his work.

Still, something wasn't sitting right in his chest. Actually saying the words that he was leaving made things seem so much more real. And while this was ultimately what he wanted, he wondered how Macy would take the news.

Damn it. Why did he care what Macy thought? They didn't have a relationship. Unresolved emotions, then a truce, then an understanding that they'd both crossed a line they weren't sorry for.

He had no idea what would happen with her when he saw her again, but he needed to tell her he was leaving. Surprise settled into Liam as he realized this conversation might be more difficult than the one with his brothers.

Macy hung up her phone and clutched the cell to her chest. With a smile, she blew out the breath she'd been holding the entire time she'd been on the phone.

When she'd first started the process of foster care, she hadn't thought she'd be a viable candidate because she was single, but she was chosen. She'd passed the home inspection, passed the background check, and her case worker said everything was lined up and good to go. They had a ten-year-old girl right now, but Macy had requested a younger child. She worried if she had one in school that she wouldn't be able to run back and forth, plus attend to homework. A younger girl where she could give the child more one-on-one time, which is what any child needed. Macy could bring her into the store for a bit. As a kid, Macy didn't know any different than growing up around PVC pipe and bolts.

She didn't want to get her hopes up, but she couldn't help it. This was just the first step in what she hoped would lead to full adoption. Maybe that family she'd always dreamed of would happen, just not in the traditional sense she'd thought. Regardless, she was going to change a baby's life forever . . . and Macy knew her life would forever be changed as well.

The store had closed ten minutes ago and she'd yet to do anything with the receipts or the computer. But that would have to wait. The gutter on the back side of the building was coming loose and she needed to get up there and repair it while it was still daylight.

Suddenly fixing a gutter didn't seem so daunting. The idea of having a little one in her home excited her. Macy knew the child she was getting would be a little girl no older than five.

She'd already ordered a crib, but she needed to get a toddler bed as well. Or maybe a twin bed against the wall with one of those side protectors.

Macy knew her online shopping tonight would be over the top. She didn't care. She had been raised by a loving set of parents and she felt every child deserved to have that love and security. There was nothing she wouldn't do to create a family, to bring in a child who didn't have a home.

Oh, books. She'd definitely need to get a bookcase and fill it with colorful, fun books. Story time with her mother was one thing she remembered fondly. Night after night her mother would read to her while rocking her in a big, oversized rocking chair.

Which meant she'd need to order a chair, too.

Yeah, her credit card was about to take a major hit.

Macy went to the shed out back and found the extension ladder. With her tool belt in place, she propped the ladder against the side of the building and started to climb. She'd gotten about halfway when Liam's SUV pulled in.

Considering she didn't know what to say to him after their last encounter, Macy concentrated on the task at hand. As she reached the top and zeroed in on the loose section of the gutter, she spotted Liam from the corner of her eye climbing the steps to his apartment. She didn't miss the way he kept glancing her way and the beat of her heart kicked up. That man's vibe was potent and she wasn't even close.

When Macy reached for the gutter to hold it in position, a rusty nail she'd missed caught her palm. Cursing, she jerked her hand back. Damn. It was the same hand she'd burned the other day. Thankfully she still had a Band-Aid on, but the nail had torn through it and gotten to her wound. The nail hadn't gone deep, but deep enough to cause a sting and have Macy climbing back down. She couldn't continue working with an open area on her skin. She needed antibiotic ointment and a new bandage.

Once she reached the ground, she attempted to undo her tool belt. Instantly, strong hands covered hers and jerked the belt off.

"What the hell happened? If you need help up there just ask for it."

Stunned, Macy glanced up to Liam. "I don't need help and if you're already going to start with an attitude, go on upstairs and leave me be."

"You need a tetanus shot," he growled.

"I had one at my last checkup. I do know how to take care of myself."

She brushed by him, heading for the back entrance to the store.

"Damn it, Macy." Liam grabbed her shoulder and spun her around. "Let me see your hand."

Still holding it against her chest, Macy shook her head. "It's not bad. I just need to change the bandage. I have a first-aid kit in my office."

In an instant he stood in her path, blocking her from getting inside. "Do not dismiss me."

"Then don't be an ass."

Liam took hold of her elbow and led her toward the staircase. "Come up here and let me fix this."

"It's a Band-Aid, Liam. I can handle it myself."

His eyes turned to her. "Let me do this."

And here was his white knight side. The side she didn't want to find so appealing, yet she did. The side he brought out after he'd been a jerk, and she realized when he was a jerk, it was because he was afraid. He may have yelled at her moments ago, but he didn't know what she'd done and he'd been worried.

Why did he have to have so many redeeming qualities? Couldn't she just find his excellent muscle tone enough? Couldn't she just be happy with the visual turn-on instead of getting inside that head of his and dissecting every move, every word he said?

Macy stepped from his grasp and gestured silently toward the stairs, giving him the green light to go on. The man really did need to learn that she'd been an adult for quite some time and could do this herself.

Liam unlocked the door and pushed it wide so she could enter. Strange having someone else let her in, but this was the new normal.

"Have a seat."

He motioned to the couch and stalked off toward the bathroom. Macy remained standing.

When he came back with his first-aid box, he took one look at her and shook his head. "Do you have to be so defiant all the time?"

"Do you have to be so bossy?" she threw back.

With a growl, Liam sat the box on the coffee table and took her arm and jerked her toward the couch. Okay, maybe he didn't jerk her, Macy thought, but he didn't leave her much option. Stubborn man.

He took a seat on the coffee table, leaving her no choice but to put her legs on either side of his. The scenario was much too intimate for her comfort level.

When it came to Liam, she was a mess. He occupied

way too much of her mind, way too much of her life. And the last time she'd been near him he'd issued an ultimatum that she was still trembling with need from. Would he follow through or had he been just matching her words?

Liam reached for her hand and carefully pulled off the old, torn Band-Aid. The burn was healing nicely, but the nail had scratched the surface pretty good.

With a clean swab, he applied more antibiotic ointment, then placed a new bandage on her palm. His face lifted to hers, the left side still turned so she couldn't look at him straight on.

"I hate seeing your skin marked," he muttered, still holding on to her hand. "I know this wasn't a big deal, but I can't stand the thought of you hurt."

Her heart clenched. "Is this your way of apologizing for yelling at me?"

Those dark eyes briefly met hers, held, then shifted back down to focus on her hand. "No. I'm not sorry, because you could've been hurt worse and you're too stubborn to ask for help."

Macy wanted to snap back, to throw a defense in his face, but the fear lacing his words had her biting her own retort back. He'd legitimately been worried.

He continued staring down at her hand like he was lost or confused . . . or didn't want to let go.

"What are you doing?" he whispered, so low she almost questioned if she'd heard him right.

"What are you doing to me?" With his head still bent down, he raised his brows and sought her gaze. "I'm not angry with you, I'm angry with myself for wanting you, for letting things get too far out of control with us."

Her heart kicked up. "We haven't gotten too far out of control."

Heavy lids lowered, a quirky smile hinted on one side of

his mouth. "In my mind, baby, we've done it all, in every way you can imagine."

Macy's breath caught in her throat, and her heart clenched. For a man who pushed her away, called a truce, and then promised to bring his A game next time he saw her, he was well on his way, and she didn't know if she should be afraid or jerk off her clothes and make this happen.

"My imagination is pretty vivid," she said.

The muscle in Liam's jaw clenched. "Don't challenge me."

Macy pulled her hand away and did the only thing she could. She pulled her shirt over her head and flung it across the room.

Let the battle of the "A games" commence.

Chapter Twelve

Liam couldn't help himself. His eyes went directly to Macy's pale yellow lace bra. The scalloped edging against her skin practically begged for his fingertips—or his tongue—to trace an outline. She sat there so perfectly, so confident. And while he had talked quite a bit about taking charge, he was actually a poser, relatively inexperienced in this area. He'd only been with a few women, and since his fiancée, he'd been alone.

He knew what he wanted, though, and no way in hell was he turning Macy away. He sure as hell wasn't going to sit here and let her pretend this was just like any other sexual encounter. This was more. As much as he didn't want more, he couldn't deny there was something substantial happening between them.

Reaching out, Liam framed her face with his hands and eased forward until his face was within a breath. "You're mine."

Her eyes widened, her breath tickled his lips.

"Say it, Macy. If you're staying here, you'd better damn well know who you're with."

"I know," she whispered. "I know who I'm with, Liam."

The final thread of control snapped the second his name

slid through her lips. He crashed his mouth to hers and jerked her body to his. Wrapping his arms around her waist, he stood, pulling her with him. He lifted her off the floor, keeping his mouth locked onto hers. Macy's legs instantly wrapped around his waist.

Liam's hand ran up her back, clutched the back of her head, and tipped her in the other direction to dive in deeper. He couldn't get enough of her, couldn't get to his bedroom fast enough. But he also wanted to make this last because in the end, he had no clue where this would take their relationship.

Shoving that thought out of his mind, Liam started heading toward the bedroom.

"No," she panted against his lips. "Not the bed."

"I want you in my bed."

Looping her arms around his neck, she pulled her head back farther. "It's not negotiable."

Fine. Whatever her thing was, he'd go with it, but he was retaining control here. Liam turned around, heading back toward the couch.

"Any other demands?" he muttered against her lips.

"Stop talking."

"Yes, ma'am."

He stared down at her, fully committing her body to memory.

"What are you doing?" she whispered.

"I always feast with my eyes first." He let his eyes travel slowly up until he caught her heavy-lidded gaze. "Occupational hazard."

Liam followed her down to the couch. He straddled her legs and eased up to get a full visual sample. Macy's bright blue eyes held his, her dark hair falling all around her bare shoulders. That bra continued to mock him, but those jeans had to go. He reached down and jerked the button, slowly pulling the zipper down, all the while keeping his eyes locked on hers.

Her breath came in pants and Liam was nearly shaking in an attempt to keep his emotions in check. He didn't remember having this ache in him, this all-consuming need inside that pulled him toward a woman. Why Macy? Why couldn't this be just sex?

He scooted off the couch, yanking her jeans as he went. "Damn boots," he muttered when the denim got caught.

Macy laughed. "Easy there, Trigger. I'm not going anywhere."

Quickly he removed the boots, socks, and jeans. Glancing back up her curves, he appreciated the matching bra and panty set. Of course she could've had anything at all beneath her clothes and he would've still found her perfect.

"Do you always wear sexy things under your jeans and flannels?"

Her smile had his heart flipping. He didn't have room for his heart in the mix . . . not tonight, not with Macy.

"I have a thing for lingerie."

Liam swallowed at the instant image of what her collection might contain. "Mercy."

Macy reached for the hem of his T-shirt. "I'm done looking at this, and I want to know what you have underneath."

No reason to make the lady wait. He reached behind his neck and jerked his T-shirt off, tossing it across the room. Macy's eyes widened, then roamed over his chest.

"Better. You're still wearing more clothes."

Liam quirked a brow. "And the second these jeans come off, this night will escalate quicker than I intend."

Macy's fingertips walked over his abs, moving up as high as she could reach. "Then what did you have in mind?"

Tracing the edge of her yellow bra, Liam smiled when she trembled beneath his touch. "More of you. As much as

I'm ready to finish stripping you, I want to take my time and remember this."

"Oh, I'll make sure you remember it," she vowed.

Liam slid his hand up, tracing her lips with the tip of his thumb. "And I guarantee to ruin you for any other man. Don't rush me."

Why the hell had he just promised that? Why did he want to ruin her? Because he hated the thought of her with anyone else. The mere idea of another man pleasuring her, making her smile, making her tremble, was unimaginable.

"Liam."

The whisper of his name settled heavy between them. He didn't know if she was silently pleading for him to do more or trying to find answers to his statement. Regardless, Liam was done talking.

His lips replaced his thumb as he slowly claimed her. Macy would know his touch, his kiss; she'd crave it when they were apart and she'd dream of him when she was alone.

When he ran his hands down her bare sides, she arched against him. All of that smooth skin trembling beneath his touch was nearly his undoing, but he held strong. Hooking his thumbs inside her panties, Liam started sliding them down her legs. He eased up enough so she could assist. Once she was freed, he lifted her to unhook her bra and quickly jerked it out of his way.

Finally, she was completely bare to him. How long had he dreamed of this? Fantasized about this moment? He'd never let himself fully believe this was a possibility, but since he'd been back, the images of her beneath him had been stronger and stronger.

He slid his hands all across her heated skin, feeling that he couldn't get enough of her. The soft sighs coming from her made him want to speed things up, but he'd promised to ruin her for other men and he intended to keep that promise.

Holding her hips tight between his hands, Liam kissed his way across her shoulders, down the valley between her breasts and toward her stomach. Now she wasn't only trembling, she was also squirming.

She gripped his hair, tugging slightly until he lifted his eyes to hers.

"Problem?" he asked.

"You're killing me."

Liam smirked. "I'm pleasuring you. There's a difference."

He'd purposely kissed around all the parts he knew she was aching for him to touch. Heightening her arousal was his top priority right now. He'd always cared about a woman's pleasure before, but never to this extent. Seeing Macy this vulnerable, exposed, and turned on all because of him was more arousing than damn near anything he'd ever experienced.

"Then pleasure faster," she demanded.

Liam placed a kiss on her belly button, keeping his eyes on her the entire time. "Are you always this impatient?"

"I'll get you back," she threatened, narrowing her eyes.

"Looking forward to it, sweetheart."

Taking his time, he ran his hands down her hips, her legs, and back up. Sliding over the dip in her waist, Liam finally cupped her breasts, earning him a groan and a catlike arch. The way she bit her lip, tightened her eyes, and tossed her head to the side was all the proof he needed that she was relinquishing control. He never thought she'd give up such power, but for now, she trusted him. The thought humbled him, made him want to please her even more.

One thing was for sure—this night would be memorable for both of them.

In an instant, Macy sat up and shoved his chest until he

fell backward on the couch. She grabbed the button on his jeans, ripped it open and carefully tugged his zipper down.

"I'm done playing games," she told him, a serious gleam in her eyes.

Okay, maybe she wasn't giving up control like he'd thought. But she trusted him because she'd let her guard down. Even for just a few moments, she'd let him take over.

Liam clasped his hands behind his head. "Can't keep your hands off me?"

In record time, she had him stripped. He was rather impressed, but didn't want to think how she'd perfected such a skill . . . and with a bandage on her hand.

"Maybe I can't," she agreed, her eyes roaming over his naked body. "Maybe I've been waiting for this too long and I'm ready to take what's mine."

"Am I yours?"

Damn it. Why did things keep slipping out of his mouth without his permission? He wasn't asking for more than right here, right now . . . was he?

No. Absolutely not. This was all he and Macy could be.

She lifted one perfectly arched brow in a silent reply. Clearly she didn't want to get into this debate, either. Fine by him.

"I hope you have protection," she stated as she climbed back up his body. Nipping along his neck, his jawline, she whispered in his ear, "Because I don't."

Protection. Right.

"In my bedroom."

Something came over her face, but she shifted back away. "Go get it."

Clearly the bedroom was absolutely off limits. He'd figure out why later, though he had a sickening feeling he wouldn't like the answer. Right now, he needed to make record time in getting there and back because he wasn't letting this moment with Macy get away.

Liam grabbed a condom from his bedside table and headed back down the hall. Macy stood at the end, hands on her hips, the soft glow of the evening sun coming in the windows illuminating every sultry curve. Her dark hair hung over her shoulders, her blue eyes drew him in.

"What took you so long?" she asked with a smirk.

Like a panther, she started toward him, but Liam was done with her taking charge. He closed the gap, lifted her around the waist and backed her into the wall. Wedging her in place, he quickly protected himself.

"You're too impatient," he muttered against her lips as he slid into her.

Macy's fingertips dug into his shoulders as she gasped. Her head fell back against the wall and Liam didn't waste another second. He started to move, to hold her hips still as he completely set the pace and demanded she remain in place. His lips found her exposed neck as her hips attempted to rock against his.

"No," he panted against her. "You're mine."

She cried out when his mouth found her breast and before he knew it, her entire body tightened as she let go. He wasn't far behind.

Liam captured her mouth, riding out the last of her climax as his body started to tremble, to fall over the edge. Macy looped her arms around his neck and held on even tighter. As his entire body lit up, he concentrated on keeping both of them upright.

Bracing his hands on the wall on either side of her face, Liam lifted his head and worked hard to keep his breathing steady and not sound like he'd just run a race.

"Do you need help with the gutter now?" he asked.

Macy's eyes widened, then she burst out laughing. "Not what I thought you'd say after sex."

"Great sex," he corrected.

She bit the side of her lip. "Great sex. Um, you can help if you want, but I really don't need it."

Yeah, well, he wasn't quite ready to let her go and he had no clue of any other way to keep her here.

"I'd say we need to get on some pants first," he suggested.

Macy's legs fell to the floor and Liam pulled away from her. "I'll get dressed."

She turned and went back to the living room and Liam seriously had no clue how he should feel, how he should act. Raking a hand through his hair, he headed for the bathroom. Apparently he was about to repair a gutter . . . which sounded a hell of a lot easier than figuring out what had just happened between Macy and him.

One thing was for sure, though. They'd crossed a boundary whether they were ready for it or not. He didn't do casual sex and he knew she did. She was about to find out when he said "mine" he meant it.

But then what? Yes, he wanted her for more than sex, but he wasn't staying. He'd already made that clear to his brothers.

Nothing had been set in stone, so there was no reason to tell her anything right now. Anything going on with his future in Savannah could wait. He wasn't about to ruin this night.

Macy had no clue how she held her balance on the ladder with her shaky legs. She'd come to fix a gutter and ended up having amazing sex against the wall right outside her old bedroom. When Liam said he'd bring his A game, he hadn't been kidding. But the longer he'd tortured her on the sofa, the more she realized just how quickly she could lose herself to him.

And she vowed never to let that happen again. So she'd

taken the reins and still ended up beneath his power hold. Oh, but what a glorious place to be.

Macy examined her work on the gutter. Pleased, she gripped the rungs on the ladder and climbed back down. She'd barely gotten both feet planted on the concrete before Liam gripped her shoulders and pulled her against his chest.

"For the record, your ass looks amazing from down here." He nipped at her lips. "And as long as you're sleeping with me, you're not sleeping with anyone else."

Macy's heart kicked up as she held on to his biceps to steady herself. "You're implying we're going to sleep together again."

The side smirk that turned her heart over in her chest spread across his face. "I'm not implying. I'm promising."

With a quick kiss, he released her, nearly sending her backward right on that rear end he'd just complimented. Before she could even grasp the fact he'd assured her another romp, he was pulling the ladder down and carting it off to her storage shed behind the store.

Macy touched her lips and resisted the urge to smile. She would not give him the satisfaction of knowing that his ordering her around was a bit . . . thrilling. She'd never thought she wanted that before. Then again, she'd never been with anyone like Liam before. Any man she'd been with in the past had been easy to control, to manipulate. Perhaps that was the turn-on where Liam was concerned. He was a man of power, quiet, mysterious, yet still able to pack a punch when he chose.

When he came back out, she hadn't moved. Liam stood in front of her, crossed his arms over that impressive chest, ink peeking from beneath his taut shirt sleeve. She knew full well just how potent that muscular body could be. She may very well have been ruined for any other man.

"Hungry?" he asked. "I'm still working on this recipe and I need a guinea pig."

Macy shook her head. "I can't keep up with you. One minute you're yelling at me, then putting a Band-Aid on my hand. The next thing I know we're having sex in your hallway. And then you want to help fix the gutter and now you want to make me dinner?"

Liam kept his head turned slightly just so the scar faced away from her. She could see his entire body, but he still tried to shield the imperfection.

"You've summed up the evening quite well," he mocked. "Do you want to come up or not?"

Okay, maybe that attitude was sexy when they were naked, but she was back in control. "This isn't a date."

With a shrug, Liam started up the back steps leading to his apartment. Seriously? He had a habit of walking away when he didn't want to answer her. What was with him?

"What's the recipe?" she called before he reached the top. His laugh carried down to her, but he kept his back turned. "If you want to know, you'll have to come up."

Fine. She would come up, but not because she wanted to spend more time with him, but because . . .

Damn it. She wanted to spend more time with him. She couldn't even lie to herself at this point. After what they'd just shared, she didn't want to cheapen it by leaving like the experience meant nothing at all.

Resigned to the fact she had clearly lost her mind, Macy started up the steps and let herself into Liam's apartment. When she closed the door at her back, he didn't turn. From across the room she watched as he pulled out ingredients, poured random things into bowls, whipped up something, and then set it aside. He made no move to even glance her way. Obviously he was in his zone.

Who knew watching a man cook could be so sexy? Liam was definitely a rare find. He had that whole mysterious, sexy, gentleman thing down pat and she was sliding deeper and deeper into uncharted waters with him.

"Are you going to come on in or just stand over there and stare?" he asked without looking up from the sauce he was stirring in a pot.

"I'm perfectly content with staring."

With a slight grin, he shook his head and gestured toward one of the bar stools. "Take a seat and keep me company."

"How's the leaky sink in the bathroom?" she asked, sliding onto one of the saddle-style stools. "All fixed now?"

"Just needed a little putty." Liam pulled a baggie full of chopped meat from the refrigerator and dumped it into the sauce. "I hope you like Italian."

Macy's stomach growled. "I'd be happy with a bowl of cereal."

Throwing her a glance over his shoulder, he quirked a brow. "Don't insult me in my kitchen."

Unable to stop herself, Macy smiled as her stomach did more of those ridiculous flutters whenever Liam threw her that sultry stare. She'd just slept with him and he was still able to make her flutter without even touching her. What did that say about her? More importantly, what did that say about the level they'd taken their relationship to?

"I've been doing some thinking about your dad's party." Liam pulled out another pan and put water on to boil. "I think a heavy meal is too over the top, but we need substantial finger foods. I have a good recipe for mac 'n cheese bites and if we pair that with some little slammers, that's a good start. Any objections?"

Crossing her arms on the counter, Macy leaned forward and shook her head. "None from me. Is there something I'm going to actually be able to make?"

"You're going to do all of it."

Macy waited for him to laugh or clue her in on the punch

line of the joke. But he kept cooking, not grasping at all that she sat in utter shock.

"You do recall that I can't boil water properly, right?" she reminded him.

Still unfazed, he kept working on dinner with his back to her. "I'll be with you, but you're going to put in just as much work as I am. You can also help me with the wedding cake."

Macy sat straight up. "Excuse me?"

Liam's laugh filled the open space. He grabbed a towel, wiped his hands, and flung it over his shoulder. Turning to face her now, he rested his hands on the island and leaned toward her.

"I'm making the wedding cake for my brothers. Double ceremony, you know."

Macy's nerves went into overdrive. "A wedding cake? I'll ruin it. I'm not helping with something that important. Forget it."

Easing around the island, he came to stand right in front of her. His hands covered her shoulders as he turned her to face him fully. "We're working on this together because you're going to stop being afraid of things that scare you. You're going to face those fears. We'll start with the kitchen and move from there."

Then he leaned in within a breath of her lips and whispered, "And you're going to sleep with me again. In my bed."

Macy stiffened. "No."

His eyes held hers, but he didn't back away. "Facing your fears, Macy. Whatever stranglehold you're in, I'm going to break it."

Yeah, but at what cost? She didn't know if she could handle being in a bed with a man. A man powerful and persuasive. A man who made her want things she knew were likely impossible with him. They both had their own issues to deal with and she didn't want to face hers with an audience.

What if he got her to the bedroom and she flipped out? Humiliation wasn't something she welcomed in her life, wasn't something she cared to have rear its ugly head during an intimate moment.

"Whatever is in your head, stop," he demanded, taking her face between his strong hands. "Don't let your past ruin what you want."

Macy lifted a brow. "And what are you doing? You're still running, too."

His eyes closed for the briefest of seconds, as if he needed to gather his thoughts or push aside the demons he didn't want to face. "I'm not running. I'm just trying to get back to where I need to be."

A little piece of her heart cracked. This was precisely why she didn't want to feel anything for him. She could tell he wasn't staying, didn't want to be here. But she'd slept with him and any feelings she'd had before that moment were now intensified and there wasn't a damn thing she could do to stop it.

Macy swallowed. "And that's in Savannah."

"I have a life there," he defended as he dropped his hands and stood straight up. "I have an opportunity to own the restaurant I've been at and I have to try."

Macy understood all about dreams. Wasn't she pursuing her own right now in trying to adopt? How could she be selfish in wanting him to stick around simply because her feelings had grown for him? The emotions she'd had as a teen were nothing compared to what she felt now, but telling him would only put him in a position that wasn't fair. If he wanted to stay or go, ultimately he had to make that call.

"So, while you're here, we're what? Friends? Lovers?"

Liam held her in place with his sultry gaze. "Both."

Okay, well. She could go with that, couldn't she? Yes, it would hurt when he left, but she had already come this far. Why shouldn't she enjoy their time together?

"Have you told your brothers?" she asked.

"I have." Liam went back around to the stove, stirring the pots and then pulling down two plates. "They were supportive. I don't know what I expected, but knowing I have their approval makes my decision easier."

Macy didn't want to discuss this any further. She had no hold on him. She had no right to even ask him to stay to see where this led. But at the same time, when they'd been together, he'd called her "mine." What did he mean by that? That she was his for now? She was his until he left and was finished with her?

As he sat their plates on the counter and joined her in the empty stool next to her, suddenly Macy had more questions than ever . . . and she feared she didn't want to know the answers.

Chapter Thirteen

The customer load this week was light, for which Liam was slightly thankful. He could handle the three women in the dining room. The one woman he couldn't handle was the one who'd gotten inside his head and had him all torn up in knots.

Liam placed the caprese salad on the glass plate and headed toward the sideboard in the dining room.

Now that they'd arrived, Liam remembered Livie and her friend, Jade. The other lady, Melanie, was from Atlanta, and Liam knew that's where Livie and Jade lived now.

The ladies were drinking their tea, and as much as Liam hated to interact with people outside his comfort zone, he couldn't ignore the reason they were here, either.

"Livie, I'm sorry about your dad."

Paul Daniels had owned and operated the small airport strip in Haven. Liam had the impression Livie was set to follow in his footsteps, from what he'd heard during their school days, but then she graduated and left. Liam didn't keep up with the hows or whys, but Paul had run the airport until his death two weeks ago. Now, to Liam's knowledge, the mechanic who worked for Paul for years was running the place, but for how long was anyone's guess.

With a tight smile, Livie nodded. "Thank you. It's hard being back, but this resort is absolutely amazing and exactly the escape I needed."

Liam returned her smile. "We're here to honor Chelsea."

"She would be proud of what you guys have done."

"I've already texted some of my friends back in Atlanta," Jade chimed in. "They'll be calling soon to book a weekend."

That's what Liam liked to hear. They needed to keep this momentum going, to keep the business buzz thriving and spreading all over the state and beyond. He also needed to get on the ball in finding a new chef.

"I'll let you get back to your meal. I just wanted to offer my condolences."

Feeling better about stepping from his little box of comfort and speaking to Livie, Liam headed back toward the kitchen, where Cora and Heidi were waiting.

"Liam?"

"It's me," he told her. "Everything okay?"

"I'm done for the day and Braxton isn't here to take me home. Have you heard from him?"

"I haven't. I'll try his cell."

Cora reached for the island, feeling along the edge, then down to where a stool was. "He had class until four and then he was supposed to come straight here," she said, taking a seat.

"Maybe he got held up by a student," Liam offered as he pulled his cell from his pocket. The call went to voice mail, but Liam wasn't too concerned. Braxton would be here.

"How about you have a glass of wine?" he offered. "Your parents just shipped us an insane amount. I need to figure out a way to thank them for always being so gracious with the chocolates and now the wine."

Cora waved her hand and shook her head. "We're all family. I'm glad they're helping the resort. I think they know how much this life means to me."

Liam pulled out a sweet red and poured Cora a glass. Her parents had given her a hard time about not taking over the family business, but Cora had held her ground. She was definitely someone he admired for not backing down and for going after what she wanted in life. So he shouldn't feel any guilt about wanting to do the same. But he'd seen the look in Macy's eyes. She'd wanted to voice her opinion, but she'd kept it to herself.

Part of him wanted to know exactly what she'd thought, but the other part was afraid he wouldn't like her answer.

"So, the ladies staying this week, are they from here originally?" Cora asked, taking a sip of the wine.

"Two of them are. The other one is from Atlanta. Livie's father just passed, so she's been in town for that and her friends decided to pamper her."

Cora sat her glass down and tipped her head. "That's nice—to have friends who can be there for you. Family means so much, though. There's a void when they're gone."

Liam knew that void all too well. He never wanted for anything when his mother was alive. She may have been a single mom, but he never felt like he suffered in any area. She was a remarkable woman. But once she was gone, he'd gone into spiral mode, never knowing what would happen next, and he'd honestly never fully settled down.

He loved the family he had now, not so much the path that the last decade had led them down, but they'd come together, and he was still ready to walk away.

His cell vibrated in his pocket. Liam jerked it out, saw Braxton's name on the screen, and quickly answered. "Hey, man. Cora was just curious where you were."

Instant relief spread across Cora's face. Her shoulders relaxed, her lips tipped into a smile.

"I was in a slight accident."

Liam gripped the phone tighter, thankful Cora couldn't

see him, because he was sure his face showed a slight bit of fear. "Go on," he said, not wanting to alarm Cora.

"I'm okay. I'm actually in the ambulance getting checked over."

Ambulance? How was that okay?

"Don't scare Cora, but I need someone to come pick me up. I'm pretty sure they're wanting me to go to the hospital because of a possible concussion."

"I'll be there," Liam confirmed.

"Thanks, man. I know you have to tell Cora, but I didn't want to call and get her all worried."

"Understood." Liam glanced to Cora, who had tensed back up. "See you soon."

Liam disconnected the call and pulled up Sophie's number. He was pretty sure she had a showing today, but hopefully she was finished and could come to the resort.

"Something's wrong," Cora stated, gripping the edge of the counter. "You were very veiled with your answers."

"He was in an accident, but sounded fine on the phone." With a panic-stricken face, Cora started to stand. Liam reached across the island and squeezed her hand. "He called, so we know he's not in bad shape. Right? He was adamant that you not be scared."

"Not be scared?" she repeated with a laugh. "If he was in any accident, I'm scared. Where is he now?"

"He said he was going to the hospital to get checked out. I'm calling Sophie to see if she can come here and then I'll take you to the hospital."

Cora closed her eyes and rubbed her head. "I hate depending on other people at times like this."

Liam admired her independence, but there were times she was limited due to her blindness. "Braxton wouldn't want you to be upset over this and I promise this is not you depending on me. I'd be going anyway, so don't go there in your mind."

Cora nodded, smoothing her hair away from her face. Liam was a bit nervous for his brother, too, but Braxton hadn't sounded shaken on the phone and assured them that he was okay. Still, he could have a gash on his head and broken bones and Braxton the Peacemaker wouldn't say a word about it.

The back door opened and closed. Brock came in carrying grocery bags.

"Is Sophie with you?" Liam asked.

"Yeah, she's getting the rest of the bags." Brock sat his load on the island. "Something wrong?"

"Braxton was in a slight accident and Cora and I are going to pick him up."

"What?" Sophie stood inside the back door, her arms loaded with bags. "Is he okay?"

"He called and talked with Liam," Cora chimed in, grabbing Heidi's collar. "We're heading to the hospital now, but we need someone to stay here."

"Of course," Sophie stated, handing her bags to Brock. "Was he injured?"

"He sounded fine," Liam said. He didn't want to mention the possible concussion at this point. No need to worry anyone more than necessary. "He just needs a ride, so I assume his truck is totaled or at least immobile."

"Keep us posted." Sophie gave Liam a hug and kissed his unmarred cheek. "I'll let Zach know when he gets here."

Liam led Cora and Heidi out to his vehicle and prayed Braxton was actually fine and not just saying he was. Liam would feel much better once he saw for himself.

As Liam pulled out of the drive, Cora reached for his hand and squeezed. Liam wasn't used to consoling people, wasn't used to having anyone lean on him, but he knew Cora was scared.

"He'll be fine," Liam assured her, giving her hand a reassuring squeeze. "Braxton doesn't want you to worry."

"I'll stop worrying when I can hear his voice and hear from the doctor that everything is fine."

Liam's cell vibrated from the console. Glancing down, he saw a text from Macy. He'd have to read it later. Right now, his family was his top priority.

"And remember, it's a surprise."

Macy handed the invitation to one of her father's long-time customers. So far she'd passed out around fifty, hoping people would come to show her father how much he was appreciated. She also hoped she could pull this off without him hearing about it. The town was notorious for small talk and gossip.

Which is how she'd heard about Braxton's wreck a few hours ago. She'd texted Liam and Zach, then when those went unanswered, she'd texted Sophie. Finally, Macy found out that Braxton was going to be okay, but the family was understandably shaken up.

And it wasn't the fact that Braxton was in an accident that had the town talking. Apparently the mayor, who had dated Braxton's former fiancée some time back, had T-boned Braxton's SUV. The rumor mill was flying with conspiracies on whether he'd been drinking or texting while driving, or Macy's favorite, checking out his hair in the mirror. Rand was quite vain and tended to look more like a sleazy used car salesman than the leader of their picturesque town.

Macy was anxious to talk to Liam and hear how Braxton was doing and get the actual story. Even though Braxton had clearly moved on and was marrying Cora, there was no love lost between him and Rand. The two were the epitome of oil and water. Since Rand and Braxton's ex teamed up, leaving Braxton broken and betrayed, the Monroe boys really had no use for the mayor.

In the end, Braxton was better off having found the love of his life in Cora. Macy headed to the back room to get more shopping bags for the front register. One day she wanted that love. The love that Zach and Sophie, and Braxton and Cora had found. The type of love that made you smile just thinking of the other person, that gave you a reason to look forward to coming home.

Not that Macy had to have a man to complete her life, but she did harbor that dream of one day having a family with a husband and children. She was a traditionalist in some ways, and even though she may have faced some ugliness in her life, she wasn't about to let her ultimate goal fade into the background.

Macy carried the box of new bags to the front counter and glanced at the clock. Only a couple minutes until closing. Grabbing her box cutter from the shelf beneath the register, she slid the top of the box open and pulled out the stacks of bags with her family's store logo stamped in black on the front.

The front door chimed again and Macy lifted her head to greet the customer, only to find Diane. Macy had already made her decision, but letting down her old coach and friend was going to be difficult.

"I hadn't heard from you and thought I'd swing by." Diane made her way to the counter and rested her hands on the edge. "I don't want to pressure you, but if you have any questions . . ."

Macy offered a smile. "I stopped by the game like you suggested."

Diane nodded. "I saw you on the other side of the fence."

Pulling in a deep breath, Macy drew strength from realizing this was the best decision for her and she couldn't say yes to everything.

"As much as I'd love to help you and the team out, I just can't commit."

Diane tipped her head with a slight grin. "I didn't think you could, but I thought I'd ask anyway. I know you're busy with the store and I'm sure you want to have a social life. It's hard to juggle everything during the season."

"I hope you're not disappointed," Macy went on. She didn't want to bring up fostering. She wasn't quite ready to let anyone else in on that just yet. "I know the team would need someone to be there for them one hundred percent and that just couldn't be me. You're going to be tough to replace."

"I admire the fact you know your limits," Diane commented, pushing off the counter and crossing her arms over her chest. "I'm sure this decision wasn't easy for you, but I respect it. I have a couple other people I plan on talking to, but you were my top pick."

Pride swelled within Macy. Softball would always be a part of her life, the good and the bad memories, but she was done for good with the sport. From now on, she was focusing on her store and on the fostering, which she hoped would lead to adoption.

"I won't keep you." Diane started for the door, but turned back around. "Maybe the new coach could call on you sometime to show a few pointers to the players?"

Macy nodded. "I'd like that."

Once she was alone again, Macy locked up and closed out the register. Thankfully, she'd not had any more migraine episodes since the last one. Apparently that had been triggered by sexual frustration . . . or so she kept telling herself.

Once she was all closed out, she glanced around the front of the store. A new shipment of extra seed packets was due tomorrow and the snazzy display she'd ordered with it. She really should clear out a space by the front door to make accommodations for their arrival. She'd already set up the colorful pots in various sizes, but she found herself wanting to go upstairs and wait for her tenant to arrive home.

Should she take it upon herself to just go on up and wait for him to get home? Wasn't that crossing some major line they'd yet to discuss? She wasn't his girlfriend, but they'd slept together once and agreed this could be a thing while he was here.

She couldn't live her life the way she wanted without taking chances. She wanted to see Liam and she cared for him. She would just hang around the store until he came in and then she would greet him. That wasn't stalker-ish or clingy. Waiting in his living room naked might have been taking things a bit too far. But he could actually appreciate her boldness since they were going to become lovers.

The most brilliant idea popped into Macy's head. Before she could talk herself out of it, she headed for the back steps and waited for Liam.

Liam finally got Braxton, Cora, and Heidi home. Braxton was banged up with a very mild concussion and bruised ribs, as well as a cut across his forehead that a few stitches had taken care of. Cora promised to stay near him as nursemaid. Liam knew she'd worry herself sick, so he'd call and check in on them later.

Right now, he wanted to get upstairs, shower, and text Macy. He'd never returned her message and no doubt she'd heard of the accident by now. Liam was still livid over the entire situation and it was all he could do not to punch Rand in the face at the hospital. But, seeing as how the good ol' mayor had a whole host of problems, starting with his DUI today, Liam opted to focus on Braxton.

Macy's truck was still parked in the back of the store, but Liam wasn't in the mood for company. He was on edge waiting to hear if his offer on Magnolias was accepted, irritated his brother had been in an accident by a man who was drinking heavily in the afternoon, and ticked because he had no idea how the hell he was going to keep a hold on his feelings for his landlord.

His mind spun in so many different directions, he needed to relax and attempt to sort things out. Knowing Macy was his while he was here . . . he sure as hell wasn't about to turn that down. If he was lucky, he'd get her out of his system before he headed back to Savannah. Doubtful, but perhaps.

Liam stomped up the steps and let himself into his apartment. He tossed his keys on the side table, not bothering to turn on the lights. There was a soft glow coming in the window as the sun was setting.

The second he stepped into his kitchen, he stopped. Wearing only a pair of familiar cowgirl boots, an apron tied at the neck, and a smile, Macy stood there with her hand propped on the center island.

"I think I'm ready for my next lesson. That is, if you're not too tired."

The challenge in her eyes, the tilt of her head, and that naughty grin instantly reawakened him. "I didn't know we were doing lessons this late."

Mercy, her legs seemed to go on forever. From the ruffled hem of her apron to the tops of her boots, those legs mocked him and he couldn't wait to feel them around his waist again.

"I was hoping you'd make an exception." She moved toward him, like a walking fantasy. But she was real. And for now, she was his. "I have a few things I'd like to show you. I think I'm getting the hang of this."

Liam slid his hands up her bare arms, pleased when her eyes darkened. "Oh, you've got the hang of this, all right."

In one swift move, he jerked the knot at her neck until the top of her apron fell to her waist. Before she could utter a word, he yanked on the tie behind her back, sending the thin material falling silently to the floor at their feet.

"We'll continue this lesson without obstacles."

Macy bit her bottom lip and quirked a brow. "Then you better remove yours."

Liam wasted no time pulling his shirt off as Macy went to work on his jeans. In seconds he'd stripped bare and she stood before him with all that loose hair and her boots. Stilettos may be every man's fantasy, but right now, this hometown girl looked like the sexiest woman he'd ever seen.

Thrusting his fingers through her hair, Liam tipped her head to capture her lips. She leaned into him, wrapping her arms around his waist and sighing into his mouth. Everything from the day faded away and all that existed was this, was them.

Her warm body plastered to his from chest to thighs had Liam eager to get her into his bed.

No, not his bed. She wouldn't go there and he still hadn't fully uncovered the reason why. Soon, though. But not tonight. She'd come to him out of trust, and he wasn't about to sever that.

Without breaking the kiss, Liam banded his arms around her and hoisted her up onto the kitchen island. The heels of her boots banged against the side of the cabinet as she spread her legs for him.

Her lips trailed over his jaw, down his throat. Liam couldn't get enough of her as his hands roamed up her sides, over the swells of her breasts.

"Protection," he muttered. "I need to go get it."

Macy eased back. "I'm clean and on birth control."

"I've never gone without."

Lifting her brows and holding his gaze, she silently gave him the choice. The thought of nothing between them was too tempting. There was no way he could let this moment go by.

When he didn't answer, Macy scooted toward the edge of the counter, locking her ankles behind his back. He eased into her, swallowing her gasp when he covered her mouth with his. Macy's short nails bit into his shoulders, her knees tightened on his sides.

The heat running through him, the intensity of her hold on him, had Liam quickening his pace. He couldn't concentrate on anything other than Macy, on bringing her pleasure. He broke the kiss, molded her breasts in his palms, pleased when she arched back on a groan.

"Liam."

Her whispered plea did something to him. As if he'd been waiting for her to fully give herself to him, to have his name on her lips when she came apart.

Her entire body tightened as she cried out, and Liam tumbled right with her. Together. There was no other way he wanted to be.

As their bodies ceased trembling, Liam tried not to think about the path his thoughts had traveled. Right now he had Macy in his arms, in his kitchen. She'd come to him in the boldest of ways and he wasn't looking any further than right now.

"Stay with me," he whispered in her ear.

Instantly, the body that had been trembling moments ago went tense. "Liam—"

"Just tonight." Why was he begging? Damn it. He knew full well asking such things meant this was more than what they'd agreed on, but he couldn't stop himself. "We won't do anything in that bed but sleep."

She lifted her head, those bright eyes zeroed in on him as if she could see into his soul. And maybe she could. Perhaps she was one of the few people in this world who actually wanted to get that deep.

"I've never slept in a man's bed before," she whispered. Shaking her head, she pressed her palms against his chest and gently pushed him away. "I can't. I just . . . I can't."

Fear. He knew she spoke from fear. Her voice shook and she couldn't meet his eyes any longer. Some men might see her rejection as a personal jab, but he knew her better. He stepped back, helping her off the counter without another word.

Silently, they gathered their clothes and dressed. She'd had a little sundress in the living room he hadn't spotted before. Now with her flushed face, her tousled hair around her shoulders, and that simple yellow dress with boots, she looked so wholesome, so vulnerable.

She smoothed her hands down the front of her dress as she faced away from him. Liam came into the living room, stopping just short of touching her.

"I want to know what happened to you."

Macy stilled, but didn't turn. "No, you don't."

Liam curled his fingers around her bare arm, gently so she didn't feel trapped. Because that's what all of this boiled down to.

"If we're going to keep seeing each other, I deserve to know. I won't be like your other guys, Macy."

Throwing him a glance over her shoulder, she drew her

brows in. "You've never been like any other guy. Before . . .
before my incident I was infatuated with you. You've
always been different for me."

The soft curtain of her dark hair covered part of her face,
but he could make out her eyes and she was serious. She'd
had feelings for him for a long time, longer than he'd ever
thought. A viselike grip tightened around his chest. He had
no clue what to do with this information. Whatever was going
on here was something more than he'd ever anticipated.
He'd tried to avoid it, had fought himself, fought her, but the
reality was they had crossed a line both physically and
emotionally.

Liam stepped around to stand directly in front of her.
Cupping her face, he directed her gaze into his.

"I won't force you to do anything." She started to look
away, but he gave her a slight jerk. "But you can't keep
hiding. I won't let you."

Moisture gathered in her eyes. "And what about you?
When are you going to stop hiding?"

Liam clenched his jaw. "I'm here, aren't I? Hard to hide
from this family."

"They love you," she told him with a slight smile. "They
won't let you run, either."

No, they were giving him free rein to do what he wanted.
Stay, go . . .

He stared into Macy's bright blue eyes and ignored the
slam of regret. How could he feel this strong and want to
leave at the same time? He had goals, damn it. But right
now, seeing this pain in her eyes, this determination to push
through to get him to open up, his goals seemed to fade
away.

"I need to get home."

She pushed around him and he let her go. He watched as
she went to the door, then stopped and turned back around.

"I didn't even ask about Braxton."

Liam shoved his hands in his pockets. So were they just moving on like nothing had happened? Like she hadn't just exposed herself by coming here, by allowing their intimacy without protection, and then showing just how vulnerable she was by not staying? He would play this game, but only for so long.

No matter how shallow a relationship they'd agreed upon, he would figure out what was holding her back. Had anyone ever attempted to heal her? Doubtful she'd let them, but he wasn't giving up.

"He was a little banged up, but otherwise fine."

"I heard Rand hit him."

Liam couldn't help but laugh. "Yeah. Asshole was drinking and driving. I imagine his days as mayor are over."

He'd been a thorn in Braxton's side for years, and so damn arrogant. Liam wasn't sorry the mayor would be out of a job. Though Liam wished Braxton hadn't gotten hurt or a mangled truck out of the ordeal.

When Macy turned back to the door to go, Liam didn't want her to leave feeling unsure or as if this was complicated. Granted they had complication stamped all over their relationship. He wanted her to feel at ease because that was the only way he'd truly earn her trust and she damn well needed someone to talk to about this.

"Come back tomorrow," he told her. "You're going to start working on party experiments."

She flashed a smile back at him as she opened the door. "I'd like that."

And then she was gone. As if she hadn't come in here, rocked his world with that greeting she'd given him. He hadn't even known he had a fetish for a girl in an apron, but he sure as hell wouldn't look at those things the same ever again.

Liam vowed to give her the space she needed, but he wasn't backing down. Now more than ever he wanted her in his bed . . . for a totally different reason than he'd started with. She said he was different for her; that gave him all the ammunition he needed to get her to fully heal.

Because, damn it, she was different for him, too, and he wasn't about to let another man show her the right way a woman should be treated.

Chapter Fourteen

How much did a teenage boy eat?

Liam slid two more pancakes onto Brock's plate. The boy had showed up at nine and Liam knew something was up. Without questioning him, he let Brock in and started breakfast. Clearly something was going on, because no teen was up that early when he didn't have to be.

"Not working at the resort today?" Liam asked as he refilled Brock's juice.

Brock shoveled in another hefty bite and shook his head. "Not until two. I have to help clean the rooms when the guests leave."

"You want more bacon?"

"Nah," he said around the pancakes. "I'm getting full."

Liam turned to clean up as he hid his smile. Brock had inhaled five pancakes and seven pieces of bacon. Obviously he was in a growth spurt, or at least that's what Sophie always said. He and Brock had bonded from the start, but it still wasn't like him to just show up for no reason, let alone on a Sunday morning.

Liam worked on cleaning the kitchen while Brock finished. Once he was done, Liam put the dishes in the dishwasher and started it up. Turning back to the island, Liam rested his palms on the granite and leaned forward.

"Ready to tell me what's wrong?"

Brock attempted a smile, but shook his head. "I don't know, man. Being a teenager sucks."

Liam laughed. "It only seems that way now. Trust me, being an adult sometimes sucks more."

Brock leaned back in the bar stool and crossed his arms. "Well, at least you can afford a nice car."

So that's the issue. "That's because I work my ass off to have nice things."

"You live in an apartment over a hardware store," Brock stated dryly.

"For now. In Savannah I had a killer condo right next to a park. My condo had a balcony off the master bedroom. I have a nice amount of savings and, yeah, I have a nice car. When you want something, you have to work for it. Nothing is just handed to you."

"I don't want things handed to me," he mumbled. "But I want a nice truck. Like Braxton's. Well . . . like the one he had before it was smashed."

Liam leaned down on his forearms and considered his words. Teenagers were touchy creatures, but he felt he could be completely honest with Brock.

"Have you thought about the fact that some teens don't have any car? That you're actually lucky you have one at all?"

Brock lifted a shoulder. "I know. I really do get it. If I still lived with my old man, I wouldn't even have a bicycle to get around with."

Liam hated the fact Brock was ever with such a worthless piece of garbage posing as a father.

"Okay, then let's look at another angle." Liam's mind started working overtime. "Why don't you look for a part-time job? Something that maybe you could do just on the weekends or a few hours after school."

Brock's eyes widened. "How would I do that and still help at the resort? They need me."

Liam knew full well they were using him at the resort to teach Brock responsibility and so he could save a little money in the process. They'd definitely get along just fine without him.

"I think Zach and Sophie would be fine with it," Liam explained. "Talk to them first, but I bet you could find a part-time job that maybe you could do in addition to the resort. Then you'd have two sets of income coming in. You're almost done with high school, so you'll be able to put in more hours in the summer."

Brock nodded. "I just don't want Sophie and Zach to think I'm trying to get out of helping."

"They'd never think that, trust me."

"Since my little fender bender last year, Zach is a bit more protective."

Liam completely understood why. There was no amount of time that would pass that would completely erase the pain and heartache of that night when Zach had been driving and wrecked, ultimately altering their lives. They'd all been younger, but the effects would last forever.

"Zach will be protective so long as he's alive, so don't expect anything else."

Brock pushed from the bar and came to his feet. "I guess I'll talk to them if you think it's a good idea."

Liam stood straight up and pulled in a deep breath. "I think they'd be upset if they knew you wanted something and were too afraid to ask."

Brock rubbed a hand through his messy hair. He'd need it cut soon, but that wasn't Liam's place.

"Are they making you wear a suit to the wedding?" Brock asked.

From the tone, Liam guessed Brock would rather go without a new set of wheels than get in a suit. "They're not making me," Liam corrected. "I'm going to put a suit on because if I don't, Cora and Sophie would be disappointed."

Brock laughed. "Yeah, I guess they would."

"You wore a tux to the prom. That wasn't so bad, was it?"

Brock lifted a shoulder. "I guess not, but that was different."

From the sheepish look on Brock's face, Liam knew the difference. "Talked to Alli since then?"

"Maybe."

Typical teenage boy. Liam didn't blame him for keeping some things private, so long as they were the right things. "You're welcome here anytime," Liam told him. "But make sure you don't close off the communication with Zach."

"I already had to tell them all about my prom date," Brock groaned. "Believe me, there's plenty of communication."

"Don't—"

The knock on his door stopped his thoughts. Macy. She'd said she'd stop by today. When Brock had knocked, Liam had thought for sure it was Macy, not that he was sorry to see Brock. He rather enjoyed the little bonding time they had. But Liam was more than ready to see Macy, to get past the intensity of last night, and continue to build on gaining her trust.

"Expecting someone?" Brock asked.

"Actually, yeah, but you don't have to go."

Liam crossed the room and pulled the door open. "Morning," he greeted Macy. She wore another little dress like the one she had on last night. With boots. Bare legs. She was truly trying to torture him and he loved every minute of it.

"Hi." Her smile widened as she stepped inside and caught sight of Brock. "Do I need to come back later?"

"I already got what I came here for," Brock stated as he headed toward the door. "I'm done."

"He means to say he pounded pancakes and finished off my bacon," Liam countered. "He's using me for my cooking."

"So am I." Macy laughed, throwing Liam a sassy grin. Damn, she was gorgeous when she wasn't so on guard. He wanted her just like this. Relaxed. Not a worry in the world.

The way she smiled at Brock and the easy banter between them warmed Liam.

The idea hit him hard. "Brock, you don't have to work until this afternoon, right?"

Brock nodded.

"Then stick around and maybe you'll learn something," Liam added.

Macy's face lit up. "Yes, stay. If nothing else, you'll get entertainment from watching me test his patience."

Oh, she tested him all right. Liam brushed past her, needing even the slightest bit of contact. But he had to keep things in perspective. Nobody knew what was going on between Macy and him. Well, maybe they suspected something, but he wasn't about to add fuel to the proverbial fire.

"I don't know," Brock muttered.

Liam rested his hands on the edge of the island. "You want to impress the girls? Then it starts right here. Trust me."

Macy lifted her brows, crossed her arms over her chest, and smiled. He didn't know what had her in this mood, but she seemed different than last night. Maybe the emotional turn they'd taken had her wanting to trust him more.

But on the coattails of her trusting him, he knew she'd want the same in return. There was too much pain in his past, too much that didn't relate to her. He didn't want to expose himself in that way. He wanted her to feel safe, to feel . . . what? Loved? That wasn't something he could venture into right now. If ever.

"So, you're staying, right?" Macy asked Brock.

Liam glanced at his nephew. No matter that the teen only came to live with Zach a year ago—he was family. They were all family with deeper bonds than most who had the same DNA. Brock fit in like the perfect puzzle piece they hadn't known they were missing.

"Sure, I'll stay."

Macy reached over and wrapped her arm around Brock. "This will be so fun."

Liam didn't know if Brock actually wanted to stick around or if he was giving in to the pressure. Either way, Liam wouldn't have this morning go any other way. He wanted Macy here to take the edge off the intensity of their relationship. Did they have a relationship?

Yeah. They did. Whether he wanted to put a label on it or not, they had a relationship. Even if they were only intimate a short time, there was a bond they were building.

"Let me clean the counter real quick." Liam shot Macy a wink, and on cue she bit that lip. Yeah, there was no forgetting what had happened here last night. He just hoped he could control himself if she put that damn apron back on.

Macy stared down at the mess that was mac 'n cheese bites. "Well, they're not burnt, so that's a plus."

Liam set another pan of freshly baked bites on the island. "And they'd be better with the bacon crumbles on top, but someone ate all the bacon I had."

Brock grabbed one of the cooled bites and popped it into his mouth. "Yeah, bacon would be amazing on these things."

Macy wrinkled her nose. "Are they good? Just tell

me they're edible because I think my dad would love something like this."

Brock reached for another. "I know I'll be at the party if you have these."

Macy picked one up, stared at the elbow noodles pressed together by various kinds of melted cheeses and butter and some seasonings Liam swore would make this the best appetizer she'd ever tasted. But he'd let her do it all. She'd seriously done this.

"If you're not going to eat that, I will." Brock started to reach across the island, but Macy pulled his hand back.

"You've eaten the entire time we've been here," Macy scolded. "This one is mine."

With a shrug, Brock grabbed another. Macy took a sample bite of hers to see if it was truly edible. Going on Brock's reaction, they were amazing, but teenage boys loved food in general, so that wasn't the best judge.

"Well?" Liam asked, leaning an elbow on the counter as he waited for her response. "Pretty amazing, right?"

The cheeses literally exploded in her mouth and Macy didn't even attempt to hide the groan that escaped her, nor did she try to hide the fact she inhaled the rest. Once she finished savoring each flavor, she glanced to Liam, who had a wide smile on his face. He tipped his head, the habit she'd come to just accept where he was concerned.

"And you didn't think you could cook," he teased.

"Hey, I did the sliders," Brock stated. "Can I take some of those with me?"

"Sure, but don't take all the credit, kid. I smoked the pork yesterday. You put them together and baked them."

Macy listened to the two bantering back and forth. Liam was so good with Brock. She couldn't help but wonder if he ever wanted kids. Not a topic they needed to get into.

But did Liam have any aspirations beyond living in Savannah? She knew he wanted his old life back and couldn't fault him for the need to return to his comfort zone. After all, she'd come right back to hers when life got too hard to handle. But she wondered if he was growing used to being here. The completely selfish side of her wanted him to stay, to see where this was going, because with each day that passed, she grew more and more used to the idea of having him in her life.

And that scared the hell out of her. If Liam ended up leaving, she'd survive. She wouldn't like it, she'd nurse a broken heart for some time, but she couldn't keep him here. He had to figure out his own life and what truly made him happy.

"I'm going to go get ready for work." Brock clutched his to-go plate and grabbed his keys from the counter. "I'll talk to Zach today about that job."

Liam slapped a hand on Brock's shoulder. "I think he'll surprise you. They want you to be responsible and this is a good way of showing that. They won't think you're letting them down, I swear."

Once Brock let himself out, Liam released a sigh and raked his hands through his hair. Macy adjusted her apron and retied it.

"Everything okay?" she asked.

Liam turned and nodded. "Just teenager issues. He's such a good kid and he's so worried about upsetting Zach and Sophie. Part of me thinks he worries if he doesn't break his back pleasing them that they'll stop loving him or something."

Macy reached forward, cupping the unmarred side of Liam's face. "I'm sure you worried when the Monroes adopted you."

Liam shrugged. "Somewhat, but I was mostly concerned with watching my back around Zach and Braxton."

Macy dropped her hand and leaned against the side of the counter. "You guys started fighting off the bat?"

"No." Liam's face hardened. "I was just coming off a hellish foster system and needed to be on guard."

He'd never spoken of the time between when his mother passed and when he'd started living with the Monroes. From the telling statement he'd just delivered, Macy knew he'd endured a period that had scarred him for life.

"Let's not go backward," she told him. "For right now, let's just have fun. Unless you want to talk about it."

She knew he'd say no even before he shook his head. And that was okay, because she definitely wasn't ready to dive into her past and give him all the details. He knew enough, more than anyone else she'd ever known.

"What do you say we tackle some jalapeño dip?" Liam suggested. "It's simple and it's a nice appetizer that will go a long way."

Macy shrugged. "You're the boss. I killed those mac 'n cheese bites, so bring it on."

Liam laughed. She loved that sound, wished he'd do it more often. Perhaps he was getting accustomed to being back in Haven. He didn't seem as uptight, as angry as he had when he'd first arrived. There was something to be said about amazing sex.

"What's that look on your face for?" he asked, narrowing his eyes. "If you think you're going to use that apron and those boots on me again . . ."

"What?" she asked, laughing.

"You're absolutely right."

When he reached for her, Macy jumped out of his way and ran around the island. He swatted at her again, managing only to catch the ties on her apron, jerking it undone. She squealed when he reversed his path and caught up with her.

He had her wedged in the corner with the countertops at her back and his perfect form molding against her in the front. Not a bad place to be.

"I thought we were cooking," she murmured, trying not to get lost in those mesmerizing eyes of his, and failing.

His lips feathered softly over her cheek. "Oh, we're cooking."

Firm hands slid up her sides, lifting her dress. His fingertips dug into her hips as he tugged her closer. Macy closed her eyes, fully giving herself up to anything he wanted to do. Control was still hers to own, but she'd give him this moment . . . and maybe she was giving it to herself as well.

"You'll be in my bed, Macy," he murmured against her ear. "Maybe not today, maybe not tomorrow. But you'll be there."

She stiffened against the warning. Macy wasn't afraid of him, more like she was afraid of all the feelings he conjured up inside her. What if she let him take her to bed? What then? She'd flip out and be even more humiliated than she was now.

"I can't," she whispered. "I'll do anything else. Don't ask that of me."

Liam rested his forehead against hers. "I'm not asking, Macy. I'm telling you I'm going to be the man to get you past this."

She started to say something, but in a swift move his hands left her hips and framed her face. He forced her gaze up to his.

"Me," he reiterated. "No one else, because you *will* get beyond this fear."

Tears pricked her eyes. She wanted to give in so much. She wanted him to be the one to take away her demons, but . . .

"I don't want this burden on you."

He nipped at her lips. "And I won't let you carry it around any longer."

Macy trembled at his intense tone. He was serious about helping her, about getting her to overcome her fear. How could she not fall head first into love? How could she not want to let him do this? She never thought she'd ever find a man that she'd consider going that next step with. But Liam showed up, and after she'd pushed and pushed, he came back at her and forced her to take a look at herself.

Damn it, that wasn't at all what she'd had in mind when she'd tried getting closer to him. She never once thought he'd pull these emotions out of her.

When Liam's lips slid across hers, Macy reached to the side and gripped the edge of the countertop. Before she could fully melt at this man's words, his seductive touches, he eased back.

"Now, let's get to work, because I have so much to teach you before the party."

He turned away and started bustling about the kitchen as if he just hadn't turned her completely on, then laid down a promise that had her so anxious and terrified at the same time. How did he do that?

Macy shoved away from the counter and spotted the one and only cookbook propped against the side of the refrigerator. The fact he kept that book through the foster home hell and all the time with the Monroes really spoke volumes as to how much this man valued family, valued that personal bond. He might want to come across as not needing people, but that was a mask he wore . . . and wore quite well.

She was about to rip it off and thrust the mirror in his face for a change, because as much as she needed healing, and she couldn't deny she did, Liam needed it just as much.

Carefully, Macy picked up the cookbook. "What was your mom's favorite recipe?"

Liam had just closed the refrigerator when he saw what she was holding. Eggs in hand, he stared at her, and Macy wondered if she'd gone too far, but she didn't think so.

"Is it my turn to talk?" he asked, setting the eggs on the island.

"Only if you want to. I'm only asking about your mom. Anything beyond that is your call."

Liam let out a deep sigh and nodded. "You're going to be sorry you asked."

"I doubt it."

Macy sat the book on the counter. She wanted him to have that visual reminder of the better times. His mom was such a huge part of the man he was today. She literally shaped him and he'd carried that with him even during the worst possible moments. Macy obviously had never met the woman, but no doubt his mother would've been proud of the man he turned into.

"She liked dumplings," Liam told her. A smile flirted around his lips. "She made dumplings all the time. That was one thing that took me forever to master. I actually didn't get them down until I was out of school. After she passed, I didn't get the opportunity to cook at my foster family's house. I either avoided going home, or I locked myself in my room."

To protect himself.

"Once I came to live with the Monroes, and I felt safe, I started again. Actually, Chelsea and I would experiment in the kitchen. She would sample as I'd cook."

The wistfulness in his tone as he spoke of his mother and Chelsea clenched Macy's heart. No wonder he kept that shield of protection around himself—he'd lost every woman who mattered to him.

"Then she'd love that you're the chef at her dream resort," Macy stated. Cooking lesson forgotten, she moved around the island and took a seat on one of the stools. "There's so much irony in the fact that you and your brothers are complete opposites, but Chelsea continues to pull you all together."

Liam tipped his head, crossing his arms over his chest. "Yeah. I wish she were here to see all of this. She'd get such a kick out of Zach heading that whole project up. Not to mention the fact he and Braxton are planning a wedding at the house."

Macy reached across and gently flipped the cover open on the cookbook. "Let's do the dumplings."

"Now?"

She glanced back up at him. "Why not? You have something else to do today?"

"I'll have to go to the resort at some point and get some dishes ready for tomorrow."

Macy shrugged. "Then let's take this show on the road. We'll do dumplings at the resort and the guests will love some nice southern cooking."

Liam narrowed his eyes. "You want to come cook at the resort with me?"

The more she thought about it, the more she loved this idea. She'd not spent much time at the resort; it wasn't as if she had the time to spare.

"I would love to." She came to her feet. "And later, I'd like to talk to you about something."

She hadn't known when she'd tell him about the fostering. Actually, she wanted to make sure the child was indeed going to be in her home. The call could literally come at any time.

"Something wrong?" Liam asked. He straightened, worry etched on his face.

"Actually, something I'm pretty excited about. I've not told anyone yet. Well, my dad knows, but that's all."

Liam grabbed the eggs and put them back in the fridge,

then rounded the island. He turned her stool until she faced him, and stepped between her legs.

"Tell me now, since you're excited."

Macy wasn't sure what he'd think, or what he'd say. She had no clue what they were doing together, or how long they'd be doing "it" together, but she refused to let anything deter her from her goals. A family was the one main thing she wanted and there were too many children out there who needed good homes.

Macy clasped her hands in her lap. "I'm going to be a foster mom."

Silence. Stunned silence. Liam continued to stare at her. He didn't move, didn't speak. Was he breathing? Nerves fluttered in her stomach.

"Liam?"

"Yeah, I'm processing all of this."

Macy laughed. "There's not much for you to process. I mean, I'll be caring for a child. Dad is actually excited to help and she'll be coming to the store with me on occasion."

"She?" Liam asked. He sank back on a stool as if the conversation had knocked him for a complete loop.

"I requested a little girl under the age of five. I had my home inspection done and passed my background check. I've been evaluated over and over. I finally got the green light."

Liam ran a hand over the back of his neck, then faced her again. Well, he kept the unmarred side to her. The habit was one she fully intended to break, but he'd done this for over a decade. Hard to deprogram something that was second nature to him.

Still, as intent as he was on making her overcome her past, she was just as hell-bent on seeing him tackle his own host of issues. And she had a feeling the scar was just a minor portion of all that weighed heavy on his shoulders.

"That will be one lucky little girl," he told her. "Are you sure that's not too much with the store?"

Anticipation flooded through her. "Not at all. My parents raised me in that store. I plan on having Dad watch her a few days, then bringing her in a few hours a week. She will have fun. I even still have my old toolbox my Dad got me when I was five. She can play with it and not get hurt since it's all rubber."

Liam continued to stare at her.

"You think I'm crazy."

Instantly, he grabbed her hands and squeezed. "Not at all. I'm just surprised. Though I'm not sure why. I know you want a family. You'll be an awesome foster mom."

The unknowns still had her a bit worried, but overall she was so excited she could hardly control herself.

"I still have a few things I want to do to the spare bedroom, but I'll be ready."

"We can ditch the cooking and finish the room if you'd like."

Macy hopped down off the stool, but held on to his hands. "That's sweet, but you're not getting off the hook. I want to learn that dumpling recipe and you need to get things done at the resort. Then we can think about working on the room."

Liam came to his feet, trapping their hands between their bodies. The way he loomed over her, as if she were tiny, always made her feel so feminine. She'd never felt that way with another man. Granted, Liam made her feel different than any other man had, in many different ways. Because he cared, because he wanted her to be the best version of herself. Again, how could she not fall in love with that?

Liam leaned down, nuzzling the side of her neck. "And then you're mine."

When he nipped at her earlobe, Macy couldn't suppress the shiver. "Mine." He said the word so boldly, so matter-of-factly.

On a sigh, Macy whispered, "Yours."

Chapter Fifteen

"I'm pretty sure that's not right."

Liam peered into the boiling pot at the blob of . . . Well, they couldn't be called dumplings. Maybe one giant-ass dumpling, but, yeah. That wasn't right.

"Okay," he said. "That happens." Not to him, but she was still new at this. "We've got plenty of dough. Let's tear off some more."

Macy blew out a breath. "Why don't you do them? I'm wasting all of your ingredients."

He'd waste all of his stock to get her happy and relaxed. "It's fine," he assured her.

Heidi's nails clicked down the hallway, the only warning they had when Cora was coming.

"Whatever you are making, I want some."

Liam laughed. "I'm teaching Macy how to make dumplings."

Cora's hand slid along the countertop and stopped just before the industrial stove. "I thought I heard your voice, Macy. I'll gladly be your guinea pig."

Groaning, Macy glanced toward the boiling stock. "I'm not sure you want this."

"It's fine," Liam stated, giving Macy an elbow to the

side. "It glommed together and made one giant dumpling. That's all."

Cora gasped. "A ball of carbs? Let me take a seat and you can serve it up."

Macy started laughing, but Cora literally made her way to the bar stool and sat down. Liam glanced to Macy, who simply shrugged.

"My first customer," she stated, reaching for the ladle. "Grab a bowl."

Crossing to the cabinet, Liam pulled out a bowl. "Cora, would you like to wait until the bread is done? I have some rolls already made up. I can pop a few in the oven and they'll be done in no time."

"No, thanks." Cora waved a hand in the air. "I'm waiting on Sophie to finish upstairs. She's taking me to pick up my dress. Macy, do you want to come? Do you have your dress yet?"

"I ordered one online," Macy stated. "I hope it fits okay. I actually have things to do today, but thanks."

Liam held the bowl to Macy as she carefully scooped out the oddly-formed dumpling. The look on her face was nothing short of defeat. He didn't think she wanted to go dress shopping—that wasn't necessarily her thing—but he knew she was discouraged over the food she'd prepared. That was definitely an area he could relate to.

"Hey," he whispered. "It will taste fine. You had all the ingredients right. And I promise, this is better than the first time I made them."

"What is that smell?"

Liam glanced over as Brock came into the kitchen.

Macy blew out a sigh. "I attempted Liam's mother's recipe for dumplings," she explained. "I'm pretty sure the smell is better than the taste."

"No." Cora pushed her fork into the dumpling and scooped

up another bite. "It tastes amazing. It doesn't matter what it looks like, my taste buds are pretty happy."

Brock pulled a drawer out, grabbed another fork, and settled onto the stool next to Cora. "I'll be the judge of that. There's no way you can eat all of this."

Cora laughed. "Not if I want to fit into my wedding dress."

"Well, I'll finish this off and then you won't have to worry about it," Brock mumbled around a mouthful.

Liam went back to the island where the rest of the dough sat in the pile of flour. He motioned for Macy to come over. She shook her head. When he raised a brow, she crossed her arms over her chest and glared back.

Cora and Brock continued to argue over the dumpling as they took stabs at their bites. Liam didn't take his eyes off Macy.

What was it about this woman in her little apron? He'd worked with female chefs before, had seen plenty of them in aprons, but he'd never once thought of stripping one of them and taking her on the counter.

Clearly there was something about Macy, apron or no apron, that made him think twice about everything he ever wanted.

Sophie breezed into the room, immediately looking toward the stove. "Liam, I swear you make this house smell better than any air freshener I could put out."

Shaking his head, he pointed to Macy. "She did the work."

Sophie's eyes widened. "You're learning to cook? That's great. Liam is an awesome teacher."

Macy held her hands up. "Oh, no. I'm not a great student. There's one giant dumpling those two are fighting over."

Cora laughed. "That's because it tastes amazing. I don't care what it looks like to you all."

"It's really good, Soph," Brock agreed. "But you can't have any."

Sophie crossed the room, reached around Brock's shoulder, and grabbed his fork before he knew what she was doing. When he yelled, Heidi came to attention, but Cora quickly reached down and patted the dog.

"I just want a bite." Sophie helped herself and then ended up getting two more bites. "You're right. That does taste amazing."

Liam threw a lopsided grin to Macy, who was fighting back her own smile. After all the raves, there was no way she could deny that she'd done a great job.

"I actually do have to finish working on some things for tomorrow." Liam circled the wide island and braced his hands on the top. "Are you all about done attacking that bowl?"

"I better stop or my dress won't zip and I already paid for the alterations," Cora told him as she dropped her fork onto the counter. "But feel free to make those anytime. Better yet, let Macy assist you in the kitchen."

Macy assist him? He threw her a glance, noting her wide eyes. He couldn't help the chuckle. "I don't think she wants to make this a permanent arrangement. We were working on things for her dad's surprise party and dumplings just happened to come up, so here we are."

"Then find something else to work on and I'll be happy to test it as well," Cora added as she came to her feet and reached for Heidi's collar. "I'm ready when you are, Sophie."

The ladies ushered one another out the back door, leaving Brock scraping the bottom of the bowl.

"Do you want me to leave this stock boiling?" Macy asked.

"No. Go ahead and turn it off. I'll use it in the morning to make up the dinner."

"Are you guys dating or something?"

Liam froze at Brock's question. Macy had turned her back as she twisted the burner off. But seeing her rigid shoulders, he guessed she was just as stunned by the words hovering in the air.

"I'm going to take that silence to mean you aren't dating, but you're more than friends."

As if the one-sided conversation was completely normal, Brock got up and put his bowl and the two forks in the dishwasher. "It's cool," he went on as he turned to face Liam. "I think you're both awesome, so if you want to date, that would be—"

"We're just friends."

Damn it. Why had that come out of his mouth? He didn't mean to downplay what they had going on, but at the same time, he didn't know what to say and he didn't want Macy to feel uncomfortable. So . . . yeah. Now the words were out and she probably felt even more uncomfortable.

Macy turned, pasted a smile on her face, and nodded. "Just friends. But glad we have your blessing."

Brock looked back and forth between them, clearly not believing them, but Liam wasn't about to say anything else. Finally, he shrugged.

"I have a proposition for you." Brock glanced at Macy and shoved his hands in his pockets. "Do you need any part-time help in your store?"

"Whoa." Liam held up his hands, shaking his head. "Did you talk to Zach or Sophie?"

Brock glanced over his shoulder. "No. I thought I'd see what Macy said and then I'd talk to them."

Macy shifted the pot to the back burner. "Well, I haven't thought about needing anyone. Dad still comes in some-times and we've never had anyone other than family work there."

Brock turned back to Macy, but not before Liam saw the

teen's face fall. "Oh, okay. No big deal. Just thought you were an obvious choice to ask."

"Wait a minute." Macy held her hand up and pursed her lips as if she were doing some calculating in her mind. Knowing Macy, that's exactly what she was doing. "How many hours were you thinking?"

Brock lifted a shoulder, shifted his feet. "Not sure. The resort is a top priority for me, so maybe just a few hours. I just want to earn some extra cash."

Macy stole a look over Brock's shoulder, catching Liam's eye. Liam didn't say a word. He was rather proud the boy was taking initiative, but he wished Brock would've discussed this first with Zach.

"I'm sure I could find things for you to do." Macy shifted her attention back to Brock and smiled. "You talk to Zach and Sophie and give me a call. How's that sound?"

"Really?" Brock's voice lifted, as did his whole demeanor. "That's awesome, Macy. Thank you."

"Don't thank me just yet," she countered as she tugged the strings of her apron undone and pulled it over her head. "Let's see what they say before we go any further. You still have school and that comes first."

"I know," Brock agreed. "I'll call you later today. That work?"

Macy laughed. "Of course."

Brock practically ran out of the room, most likely to find Zach or text him or to make sure the resort was all set to go for their guests arriving in the morning. Regardless, Macy had just made his day.

"He wants a different car."

Macy nodded. "I figured it was something like that."

"I have a few more things I need to do here. Shouldn't take me more than an hour."

Liam wanted to cross to her, but he also didn't want to get caught kissing her or backing her into the counter and groping her . . . which is exactly what he'd do if he knew they wouldn't be caught.

"You want to wait or do I need to run you home?" he asked. "I know you want to work more in the room, but I can help."

"I think I'll take a walk out back, if that's okay. I never take time to just do nothing."

Liam knew that feeling all too well. In fact, coming home had given him more free time than he'd ever had when he worked in Savannah.

Was that something he was willing to give up? Was he ready to get back to that hustle and bustle? And if he thought he was busy before, going back in as an owner would be pure insanity . . . and everything he'd ever dreamed of.

"Liam?"

Blinking, he focused back on Macy. "Go ahead. I'll come find you when I'm done."

Stepping closer, she tipped her head. "Everything okay?"

"Yeah. Um, about that whole friend thing earlier—"

Waving a hand, she shook her head. "I know. It's all right."

"Really?"

Laying her apron on the counter beside her, she blew out a sigh. "I don't know what to call this—us. I know you didn't want to get into all of this with Brock, but hearing you say the words just had me thinking."

His chest clenched. "About?"

She opened her mouth, then closed it. "Nothing. Come find me when you're done. I'll probably be out by the pond watching the little duck family."

Macy let herself out the back door, the screen slamming behind her. Liam had no idea what she'd been wanting to say, but whatever had gone through her mind had involved them.

No, they weren't "just friends" as he'd indicated, but at least she understood why he hadn't said more. Seriously, what could've been said? Like he was just going to tell Brock, an impressionable eighteen-year-old, that he and Macy were having sex as often as they could, but they weren't dating. In fact, they'd never gone on a date.

And that was a smack of reality to the face. He'd been adamant that Macy not treat him like the other guys she'd seen, yet here he was making sure she did just that. He'd never taken her on a date. He'd never even attempted to actually do something romantic.

Romantic? Is that where he wanted to go with this?

He glanced around the empty kitchen. His kitchen, technically. He'd given Zach the exact specifications for the remodel, not having a clue he'd actually be the one working here. Yet, here he was. Fate was funny that way.

Liam didn't even remember what he wanted to get started on for tomorrow's prep. Shifting slightly, he stared out the back door.

The pond in the distance was always a breathtaking view, but the woman standing at the edge was captivating. The skirt of her dress blew in the breeze, swaying against her bare legs. He had no clue what expression she wore on her face, had no idea what she was thinking.

When he'd come back, he never dreamed he'd get tangled up with her. He wasn't sorry. How could he be when she was such a bright spot in his life? How could he regret being here for his family when they needed him most?

He had a serious decision to make. When the phone rang, Liam ignored it. The machine would pick up and Sophie would return the call later. He continued watching Macy. She tucked the dress against the back of her legs as she lowered herself to the grass. What was she thinking? About the child she was going to foster? The potential of adoption? What went through her mind when she thought about him? She knew he wanted to go, but they'd never fully discussed that fact.

Perhaps they were both avoiding a topic that would invite more questions than answers—and emotions neither were ready to deal with.

With an unwanted ache in his heart, Liam turned away and started working. The sooner he got done, the sooner he and Macy could leave. He wanted to know what was going on in that head of hers. And if that coincided with her heart, then he'd have to be ready to deal with those emotions as well.

"Perfect."

Macy stood back and watched as Liam adjusted the curtains on the newly hung rod in the spare room. The curtains were perfect, as was the view from her angle. When she'd sat out by the pond earlier, she'd worried about where she and Liam were headed. But then she realized she needed to keep her questions to herself because she didn't want Liam to feel pressured to stay. He owed her nothing, had promised her nothing.

Still, she deserved to know if he was for sure going back to Savannah. He'd tell her. Surely he wouldn't keep something like that all to himself. Liam had been honest with her from the start. So, for now, she'd enjoy their time together.

Liam came down off the step stool and propped his hands on his hips. "You've done a good job in here."

Macy glanced around the room. The twin bed in the corner with a bright yellow blanket and yellow and white checkered sheets. The toy chest, and the small basket overflowing with new books. The white chest of drawers she'd had as a little girl had been repainted and now held a little giraffe lamp.

"I hope she likes it." What would the little girl think? Macy only hoped she could provide some stability, some sense of security. "I'm a little nervous."

With outstretched arms, Liam crossed to her and pulled her into his embrace. "You're going to be fine. You're going to care for her—"

His cell went off, cutting through the moment. Macy stepped back and waited while he pulled the phone from his pocket.

He glanced at the screen first before answering. "Hey, Sophie."

Not wanting to seem like she was obviously listening, Macy went to gather the empty curtain containers. She threw them away in the kitchen and came back to fold up the step stool. Liam's closed eyes, his head dropped forward, shoulders slumped, put Macy on alert.

Placing a comforting hand on his arm, she couldn't help the thoughts spinning through her mind. Was someone hurt? Was it Brock? Did something happen at the resort?

"I'll think about it," he finally stated. "Yeah, um . . . that's great. I'll let you know."

When he hung up and slid the phone back into his pocket, he raked a hand through his hair and pulled in a deep breath. The fact he hadn't looked at her yet also sent warning bells off inside her head.

"What is it?" she asked.

Shaking his head, he pulled away. "Nothing."

Macy crossed her arms over her chest and watched as he picked up the ladder and left the room. Okay. So he was just going to shut her out?

Macy stood in the doorway from the kitchen and watched as he went down the hall toward the attached garage and hung the ladder back on the wall.

When he turned to face her, she merely raised her brows.

"It's just resort stuff," he told her.

"Resort stuff? That's why you look like you're torn into several pieces?"

His lips thinned, the muscle in his square jaw ticked. "Macy . . ."

"What? I wouldn't pry into your personal calls if you didn't look like you were ready to run away."

When he remained silent, Macy threw up her arms and went back into the kitchen. She wasn't begging.

Footsteps followed behind her as she headed toward the hallway. It was getting late, so whatever the call was about must've been important. Not important enough to share with her, but whatever. Hadn't she already told herself he didn't owe her anything?

She had fallen in love. Maybe she'd been fooling herself to think—

Liam's grip on her arm as he spun her around cleared all thoughts from her mind. Suddenly she was backed up against the wall of the hallway, looking up into a set of heavy-lidded eyes. She couldn't tell if it was passion or anger staring back at her. There was such a fine line between the two emotions.

"I'm not shutting you out," he claimed. Those powerful hands came up to frame her face. "Sophie threw me for a minute, that's all. I just need to think some things through."

No matter what headway she thought she was making with him, she kept finding herself slammed against the blocker he placed between them. Exhausted, Macy dropped her head back against the wall.

"You don't owe me an explanation," she murmured. "I just . . . I thought I could help."

His thumb raked over her bottom lip. "You help, Macy. Just being here helps. I wasn't looking for this and that's what makes everything so damn difficult."

She reached up, gripping his wrists as he held her face. "I wasn't looking for this, either. But I want—"

"What?" he whispered as he stepped closer, lining their bodies up together. "You want this? I told you that I wasn't going to be like other guys in your life, Macy."

The warning of those words hit her hard. Liam wasn't a man to just sit back and let her control every aspect of their intimacy. That ever-present fear coursed through her, and as much as she willed it away, she couldn't just dismiss how she'd purposely kept herself protected.

"Liam, I can't."

His thumb slid over her bottom lip. "You trust me?"

Macy couldn't look away from those eyes. How could one look make her feel so vulnerable, yet so protected at the same time? She knew in her heart he'd never physically hurt her, never force her. She'd given herself to him many times, but what he was asking was so far outside her comfort zone.

"I don't trust myself." How humiliating that was to admit aloud. "What if we get in there and I can't stand it? What if I embarrass myself and you—"

His finger covered her lips. "And what if I get you in that bedroom, *your* bedroom, and you have an experience like nothing you've ever had before?"

Macy opened her mouth, but he kept his finger in place.

"And what if you stop questioning everything that scares you and let me show you that you're worth so much more than a quickie in some random place."

Liam removed his hand and brushed her lips with his. Those strong hands came to encircle her waist as his mouth traveled along her jawline and toward the sensitive part beneath her ear.

"Say the word, Macy, and I'll make sure you're never afraid again."

How did he do that? How did he obliterate every single nightmare she'd held inside her for so long? There was something special about Liam, not that she needed this moment to prove her theory. But he wanted to crush that defense mechanism she held so firmly in place.

And to be honest, she wanted him to.

She'd never wanted to face her fears with another man, never gave it a second thought.

Clenching her fists at her side, she tipped her head to give him better access. "What if I can't do it?" she asked.

Liam lifted his head, looked her dead in the eye. "Then we'll stop. I meant it when I said you could trust me."

Could she do this? Now? With Liam?

"Stop thinking of all the things that could go wrong," he ordered. "Take what you want. Don't let those bastards control you another second. They have no place coming between us."

The way he used the word "us" clicked. Her heart turned over in her chest and Macy knew she'd been on this path for some time. Liam was the man she'd been waiting for to break this hold.

Macy looped her arms around Liam's neck and held on tight. "Take me to bed."

Chapter Sixteen

Liam lifted Macy in his arms. She hadn't expected romance.

Resting her head against his shoulder, she kept her arms around his neck as he toed open her bedroom door and let himself inside. She didn't have a clue if she had clothes everywhere or if her bed was made. Right now, she didn't care. Her heart pounded hard in her chest, and her nerves swirled around in her stomach.

The glow from the hall light filtered in through the open door. Liam gently laid her on the bed, which had been made. He eased back, keeping his eyes on her as he yanked his shirt over his head and tossed it aside.

"You good?" he asked.

Macy nodded, trying to stay in this moment and not go backward. When he reached down to take her boots off, Macy cringed.

"It's me, Macy." He kept his eyes on hers the entire time. "Just you and me. Nothing else comes in this room."

She nodded, knowing she came across as weak. She wanted to be strong for Liam, for them. The freedom he was offering by breaking her chains was the greatest gift.

She needed to overcome all the doubts and fears in her mind because this man was absolutely everything to her.

Liam came around the side of the bed and grabbed her hands, pulling her to her feet.

"Let's start here," he told her. "We'll work our way down."

Macy nodded. "I'm s—"

"Don't even apologize," he scolded. "Do I look angry?"

No. If anything he looked like a man who was determined to make this moment all about her.

"Tell me what you want me to do or not do."

Macy stilled. "Honestly, I don't even know. I've never attempted this before. I mean, not in a . . . a bed."

There was no room for humiliation, only honesty.

"Then you say the word if you feel afraid," he told her. "I mean it."

Nodding, Macy offered a smile. "I'm sure you'll know if I start freaking out."

"You won't," he assured her, sounding so confident in his answer. "I won't let it get that far."

Macy didn't want this to simply be one sided. Drawing on the strength Liam exuded, Macy reached for the hem of her dress and pulled it up over her head. Tossing her hair out of her face, she met his gaze as the dress dropped silently by her bare feet. Standing only in her matching pink bra and panty set, she pulled in a deep breath. She could do this. She *wanted* to do this. All those years she'd commanded herself to remain in control—this was no different. Liam was giving her all of the power here, he was just guiding her with a dominant yet gentle way.

Macy held her arms out, her eyes never wavering from his. The hint of a smile curved the corners of Liam's lips as he wrapped his arms around her and unfastened her bra. The warmth from his bare chest comforted her at the same time anticipation and arousal shot through her.

Once her bra was discarded, Macy left her arms out, giving him the silent go ahead to remove the final piece. As she stood before him, more exposed than with any other man in her life, Macy didn't have the fear she'd been so overwhelmed with. Maybe every moment up until now was preparing her for him. Maybe she'd waited all this time for Liam to come back into her life, to show her how she should be treated.

Macy wasted no time in assisting him out of his clothes as well. She ran her fingertips over the taut ridges on his abdomen. The trembling beneath her touch had her smiling as she glanced up.

"I thought I was the one who was supposed to be nervous."

He gripped her hands, lacing their fingers together as he tugged her to fall against his chest. "You're supposed to do nothing but relax and let me pleasure you."

Oh, the promises held within that bold, toe-curling statement.

Macy backed up a step until her legs hit the edge of the bed. Sinking down, she reached her arms out.

Liam braced his hands on either side of her hips. Without saying a word, he covered her lips with his as he eased her back. She settled into the down comforter, but when his weight landed on top of hers, she tensed.

"Easy," he murmured against her lips. "Just us, remember?"

His hand trailed down her side, over her hip, and along her thigh. Back and forth, he stroked her heated skin until she was arching against him. When he placed his hand between her legs, Macy opened, letting him in.

The way he touched her, pleasured her, loved her was so overwhelming. Macy tossed her head back as Liam made good on his promises. He nipped at her lips, her chin, down her neck to her breast. The sensations rushing through her, over her, were too much. She cried out as Liam lifted just enough, their eyes locking as she shattered.

Before she ever came down off her high, Liam pulled her with him as he rolled to his back. Instantly, she found herself straddling him, looking down into those captivating eyes. He didn't turn his scarred side away from her. Perhaps on some level he was exposing himself as well.

Macy reached out, sliding her fingertip along the edge of the jagged scar. Liam didn't tense, didn't look away. He merely gripped her hips and waited.

"You're more than I thought I'd find," she confessed. She didn't care that she'd said the words without thinking first. She meant them and she wasn't a bit sorry they were out.

As she positioned herself over him, Liam kept that firm hold on her hips. She may be in charge, but he was still holding the reins . . . so to speak.

Before Macy could move, Liam sat up. "Wrap your legs around me. I want to touch all of you."

As she shifted, they came together and Macy bit her lip, closed her eyes, and let the new onslaught of emotions take over.

"Look at me," he demanded.

She opened her eyes, not surprised to see his face a breath from hers. Their bodies touched from shoulders down. Macy tightened her hold around his waist, encircled his neck with her arms, and slid down to connect them.

Just as she started to move, Liam's fingertips dug into her hips. "No. Not yet."

Macy needed to move, she needed . . . something. He was killing her.

"You good?" he asked.

Unable to speak, she nodded.

"Keep looking at me," he demanded, his voice husky, as if he were suffering just as much. "Don't take your eyes off me."

Keeping their bodies in perfect alignment, Liam stood and turned. "Trust me?"

Macy threaded her fingers through his hair, keeping his command of eye contact. "Completely."

He turned, laying her on the bed as he came down with her. But he didn't fully press his weight into her. Macy's arms fell beside her head as he loomed above her. An inkling of fear curled low in her belly. She glanced to the canopy above her bed.

"Eyes here, Macy."

The moment she made contact again, the warmth in his eyes instantly erased the anxiety. She trailed her fingertips up his arms and over his shoulders. As he started moving, everything vanished but this moment. Not once did he look away, nor did he try to put any more of his weight on her.

Macy curled her hands around his shoulders and urged him down. She wanted to feel him against her, wanted to feel only him and no other memory or nightmare. Liam was it. Now and forever.

But that was a thought for another time. Right now, she relished the way he braced himself above her, still not fully coming down.

"I want to feel you, Liam. I'm okay."

Resting his weight on his forearms on either side of her head, Liam nipped at her lips as he quickened the pace. Macy opened her mouth, claiming his as her entire body took over. No longer was she in control, but the most glorious feeling of euphoria overcame her. Liam's delicate touch, yet passionate lovemaking was everything she'd ever needed, and everything she didn't know she needed.

When her body climbed, when she trembled with release, Liam tore his mouth from hers and whispered something in her ear. She couldn't make out what he said, all she knew was she'd never felt this way before.

Liam tensed, his jaw clenched as he arched back when

his own release hit. Macy had never seen such a beautiful sight as Liam above her, his muscles tight, the way he opened those gorgeous, expressive eyes and held her in place. Something passed between them, something Macy couldn't identify. She knew exactly, without a doubt, how she felt. But if she wasn't mistaken, love stared right back at her.

Did she dare hope that he was falling for her? Did she even want to place her heart fully on the line?

As Liam relaxed, he rolled to the side and pulled her into the crook of his arm. Macy eased her leg over his, wanting to keep the contact, *needing* to keep the contact.

Words were useless at this point. Liam had done what she'd always thought impossible. Not only had she fallen in love, she'd overcome her greatest fear.

Liam held on to Macy. Too much flooded his mind right now. The damn nerves he'd had moments ago had now exacerbated. He'd wanted everything to be perfect for her, every touch, every moment to be exactly what she needed. But he'd quickly discovered this wasn't all about her, like he'd promised.

The phone call from Sophie had him a jumbled mess. When he'd already been confused over his move back to Savannah, now he had another wrench in the plans he'd so carefully made. Those plans had started crumbling the moment he'd taken the chef position at Bella Vous. They'd been obliterated this evening.

Macy may not have expected this, but he sure as hell hadn't known what he was getting into, either. He wouldn't change a thing . . . except maybe to acquire some insight to tell him what the hell to do next.

"I was asleep in my dorm when they came in."

Macy's soft tone broke the silence. Her fingertips drew

a lazy pattern over his chest as she lay tucked against him. She was about to reveal what he'd both wondered and feared.

"You don't have to say anything," he replied, curling his arm around her a bit tighter.

"My roommate had gone home for the weekend."

She went on as if he hadn't given her the out. Liam prepared himself for the worst, but reminded himself not to get angry. She didn't need that right now.

"My team had just won a huge game against our biggest rival. We went out after for pizza with our friends. A group of guys I'd seen with my other friends were there. I'd never had a problem with any of them before. I mean, they flirted and joked, but they were eighteen years old, so it was just part of college life."

Her lashes tickled his side each time she blinked. She continued that random pattern on his skin and Liam waited for her to go on. Whatever she had to do to push forward, he'd support. And if that meant saying nothing, then that's what he'd do—though he wanted to find the bastards and show them what fear was. Liam figured if they did this to Macy, then they'd gone after other women.

"I jerked awake when one of them fell on top of me," she went on. "Or maybe he meant to land across my bed. I instantly smelled beer. It was so overpowering it was almost sickening, so I knew they were drunk. I pushed the one off my bed and he fell onto the floor. I still thought they were just being stupid, but I didn't know why they'd broken in to my room, or how they ever got beyond the dorm mom in the lobby."

None of this should've ever happened. Ever. And she'd carried this night around with her for years, not telling a soul. How did she intend to recover if she never leaned on anyone?

Not that he was one to judge, but damn it, he wanted

better for her. He wasn't about to get into all the hell in his own life, or the reasons he kept everything to himself. This was all about Macy, about making her realize she'd overcome that night and there was no reason to ever be afraid again.

"Before I could even get up, another guy ripped off my covers and started jerking on my pajama bottoms. That's when I knew if I didn't make some commotion and fight back, that I'd be their victim."

Macy pulled in a shaking breath and kept going like the fierce woman he knew her to be. "I screamed, banged on the wall next to my bed. With it being the weekend, I knew several of the girls had gone home, but I was hoping I'd wake someone. One guy put his hand over my mouth, but I managed to bite him. Then he just held me down while another taunted me about how they'd been deciding who was going to bang the star athlete. When they couldn't decide, they thought I'd want to do them all."

Moisture gathered on his side. The tears she shed pissed him off. Shifting, Liam rolled her onto her back as he lay beside her, his elbow propped by her head as he looked into her misty eyes.

"I've heard enough."

"Actually, that's almost the end," she informed him with a tight smile. "They didn't follow through. After I bit the one guy, he fell backward into the other two. I managed to get out the door. I ran down the hall in my panties and T-shirt. I hid in the basement of the building until morning. I was so afraid to come back out for fear they'd be there waiting for me."

Liam stroked her hair from her face. He wasn't sure if he was consoling her or himself by the constant touching, but he couldn't stop.

"I was a virgin then," she admitted. "I was shaking so hard

while I was hiding. All I could think was that I would not let any man take away my rights, let alone my innocence."

Liam's heart clenched. The image of a young Macy terrified gripped at him.

"I finally snuck back to my room, grabbed a bag, and shoved some of my things in it. I didn't shower, didn't do anything else, but got the hell out of there. I never went back."

"And your mother passed that day."

Macy closed her eyes. "She had a stroke that morning before I made it home."

The pain she'd endured, essentially alone, was something no person should ever have to go through. Liam framed her face, realizing she probably felt ashamed of what had happened. He was damn proud she'd fought them off and ran. The possible flip side of that story terrified him.

"You're the strongest woman I've ever known," he told her. When she lifted her lids, those bright eyes pierced his heart. "To keep all of that in—"

"Makes me a coward, Liam. You can't sugarcoat that." She blew out a sigh and wiped at her eyes. "I just . . . I couldn't tell my dad, not then. And when he mentioned me returning to school, I just told him I'd take some time off to help at the store. We settled into a nice routine, and that pretty much brings us up to date."

She smiled, as if she hadn't just opened her heart and let him inside the darkest part of her life. The trust she'd instilled in him was humbling. The fact she'd never exposed herself in such a way said so much, and Liam wished he had all the answers. Wished like hell he could see into the future as to what path he should take.

At a loss for words, he nipped at her lips. When she wrapped her arms around him and shifted her body to edge beneath his own, he found himself settled perfectly between her legs.

"Show me again," she murmured against his mouth. "Show me how perfect this is, how perfect we are."

Was the answer that simple? Were they perfect for more than just right now? Part of him wholeheartedly believed yes. The other part worried he'd be throwing away everything he'd worked so hard for.

Then there was the call from Sophie with another proposition he hadn't seen coming.

Pushing all of the doubts from his mind, Liam did as he was ordered. Being with Macy made everything else seem so insignificant, but the reality was, he had goals. He had a plan. And one woman had single-handedly turned his world upside down and made him rethink everything he'd ever wanted.

Macy stared at the directions once again. She'd done everything Liam had told her to do. Of course he'd be busy at the resort getting various things prepared for the weekend, but she was failing here. Her mac 'n cheese bites looked like burnt turds.

Well, the party was tomorrow afternoon and clearly she was going to have to pull an all-nighter to get this done. And by all-nighter, she meant Liam would just have to suck it up and help her when he got off work. She knew he'd done a few small appetizer things at his place. After much begging and a little bedroom coercing, she'd managed to get him to agree to doing more than he originally intended.

She quickly shot off an SOS text, complete with picture of the round charcoal bites spread out across the wax paper over her island and the counter by her stove. She'd put them in as long as he'd told her to, on the temperature he'd said.

How in the world had this happened to every single

batch? She kept thinking the next pan she put in would be better, but no. She'd even turned the temperature down. And actually the final two batches weren't as burnt, but they didn't look healthy. Had she not added enough cheese? Enough milk or butter? Wait, she'd totally forgotten the bacon crumbles . . . not that those would help at this point.

There was no way she could pull all of this off. What had she been thinking? She should've stuck with pizzas like she'd first thought. Who cared if it was the easy way out? She thrived on the easy way out when it came to the kitchen. And who didn't like pizza?

When her cell rang, she thought for sure it was Liam ready to make fun of her situation.

The second she saw the name on the screen, though, her heart kicked into high gear. She didn't even bother wiping off her hands as she lunged for the phone and swiped the screen.

"Hello?"

"Macy, this is Laverne with Children's Services."

Macy gripped the counter. "Yes."

"I have a little girl, age ten months, who was just placed in our care. Her mother was in a car accident and there's no father in her life. A grandmother on her father's side is the only other relative, but she's in another state and we haven't been able to reach her. Would you be willing to take this girl?"

Nerves, anticipation, worry—they all swirled around in her stomach as she frantically looked for her purse. The back door. That's where she'd hung it.

"I can meet you right now." It wasn't as if she had anything else going on. The food was ruined and she couldn't move forward without Liam. And she would've dropped everything anyway to bring home an abandoned child. "Where do you want me to go?"

Laverne gave specifics and Macy realized she was

heading toward the garage with no shoes on. She'd waited for this moment for so long, she wasn't thinking clearly. Granted, she didn't want any child to have to enter the system and be torn from parents, but that was a reality.

Laverne said she would discuss more when Macy arrived. Macy hung up, slid into her favorite pair of cowboy boots, and headed out the door.

So many scenarios raced through her mind. Would this little girl feel safe here? No matter what else was going on, Macy wanted any child she brought in to have a sense of stability and security. Macy had had a wonderful childhood and she only wanted to offer the same to kids in need.

Her cell rang again as she headed toward town. Thankfully the meeting place was only a few minutes away, because Macy didn't know if she'd be able to drive too much farther. Her hands were shaking as she pressed the SPEAKER button on her steering wheel.

"Hello."

"Where are you going?" Liam's voice boomed through her car. "I saw your taillights as I was coming down your street. Did you not need me anymore tonight?"

"You have no idea how much I need you, but right now I can't focus on cooking." She made a left turn; only one more block to go. "I'm on my way to pick up a little girl and I burnt the hell out of those macaroni bites, so I need—"

"Wait. You're picking her up now? Alone? Do you want me to meet you?"

Macy's lights cut through the darkness as she turned into the parking lot. There was one other car and she knew exactly who waited on her. A child on Christmas morning wasn't this excited. There were no words. Macy just hoped she could truly make a difference.

"No. Let yourself into my house." She gave him the code and promised to be home shortly. Hopefully he'd do something magical in her kitchen and her father's party wouldn't be a disaster.

Honestly, though. She didn't care. She knew her father wouldn't care, either. There was a little girl in need and Macy was making her top priority.

Everyone would understand.

"I have to go," she told him. "I don't know how long I'll be, but . . . just . . ."

"I'll stay," he told her. "Go get your girl."

Macy swallowed the emotions welling up in her throat. He totally got her. Since a few nights ago when she'd finally opened up to him about her past, they'd been connected in a way she couldn't explain. But she still hadn't been able to get him to open up completely. He still kept a measure of distance, which was wise on his part if he was so determined to leave. Lately, Macy was just as determined to get him to stay.

Pushing everything aside—the party, Liam, her own doubts and fears—Macy pulled next to the SUV and killed the engine. There was a little girl who needed comforting right now and Macy was more than ready to show her all the love.

Chapter Seventeen

Liam had purposely stayed away from Macy for a couple days. He needed to think, get some space so he could figure out what he truly wanted.

He'd taken a few hours away from the resort and gone to Magnolias to speak to Mark. They'd agreed on a very reasonable price and Liam wouldn't even have to finance the entire cost.

But there was still that opportunity here in Haven . . . and he didn't mean connecting with Macy. So many factors weighed on his decision. So many things he never even knew he wanted, never thought a possibility.

Since he hadn't seen her for a few days, he was anxious to get to her place. But she was out picking up a little girl and this would change the dynamics of everything. Liam hadn't thought about a family of his own; that was one of the things he'd automatically dismissed. But he was here now, and he would give Macy the support she needed.

Liam entered Macy's garage using the code, then hit the button to send the door back down. Whatever she'd killed in the kitchen had permeated the garage. How did someone destroy so many mac 'n cheese bites? The image she'd sent him had him laughing, but at the same time, how the hell?

Seriously. The recipe wasn't difficult. She'd made his mother's dumplings, for pity's sake, and she managed to murder these simple bites?

The moment he stepped into the kitchen, he groaned. Yeah. These were for the garbage. He doubted even the neighborhood dogs would want them. Hell, Zach's pups would snub their noses at the hockey pucks.

Liam cleaned up her mess. Clearly she'd been in a hurry to get out the door. She had bowls in the sink, pans with half-burnt cheese on them lying on the counter, wax paper cemeteries for the bites, and boxes of pasta all over. Just looking at the mess made him twitch. He thrived on a clean work environment. Besides the fact that professional kitchens had health codes to follow, Liam couldn't handle an untidy work space.

As he tossed the mess, wiped off her counters, and started searching for more ingredients to get the party food made up, his mind remained on Macy and the little girl she was bringing home. He remembered when he'd first been sent into foster care. The unknowns terrified him, and perhaps rightly so, considering what had happened to him.

But the system wasn't always so dark. There were wonderful families out there, amazing people who selflessly took children into their homes and loved them. The Monroes, Zach and Sophie, and now Macy.

Liam put water on to boil for more of the pasta. He couldn't even imagine the anticipation Macy must be feeling. He kept waiting to hear her garage door go up, for her to walk in with a little girl.

Should he even be here? Would seeing him scare the girl? Who knew what type of home life she came from and if she was afraid of men?

Doubts had Liam turning off the burner and tossing the water. He'd make these up at home in no time. He'd already smoked the pork for the sliders, the cupcakes only needed to be iced, and Macy had texted him to say she'd managed the nonbaking finger foods just fine. So they were on track for now.

Damn it. He was running again. There was no way of getting around the truth. He was afraid to stay here, afraid he'd scare the little girl, afraid he'd feel too much like he was waiting on a family to come home . . . *his* family.

Liam raked a hand through his hair and started toward the front door, but froze as the soft whir of the garage door started. Well, there was no leaving now.

Pulling in a deep breath, Liam attempted to shove aside his jumbled up thoughts as he waited for the door leading from the garage to the kitchen to open. He sincerely hoped the little girl didn't come from a home where she'd been mistreated by a man . . . or anyone for that matter. He just didn't want to scare her.

Especially with his scar. Damn it. When Macy had told him she was bringing a little one back, he should've gone home right then. This wasn't his place. He and Macy weren't . . .

What? They were sleeping together, she'd opened up and trusted him more than anyone, and she'd admitted to falling for him. If he were on the outside looking in, he'd damn well say this was a committed relationship. But, wait, hadn't they agreed to keep this just physical while he was here?

When had this developed into something more?

Macy's soft voice filtered in seconds before the door eased open. Liam braced himself. He didn't know what he expected, but Macy carrying in an infant in her footed pajamas wasn't it.

The little girl with short, curly blond hair clutched a stuffed dog in one hand and sucked the thumb on her other hand. Macy turned to close the door, then met his gaze over the top of the girl's messy bed head.

"Hey." She smiled. "Can you stay here for a bit? I just

want to show her to her room and get her settled. She's . . . she's had a rough night."

Macy's voice caught on the last word and there was no way in hell he was going anywhere. She couldn't do this alone. Her father was out back in his apartment, but Macy wanted Liam. Another click locked into place. Was this where he should be?

He nodded, ignoring the lump of emotion in his throat. "I'll be here."

As Macy headed down the hall, the girl's bright eyes met his. He kept his marred side turned away, but offered what he hoped was an encouraging smile.

He figured Macy would be a while and he needed to concentrate on something he could control. Cooking had always done that for him.

Once again, he started up some water to begin on the mac 'n cheese recipe. The party was still going on tomorrow, so he needed to step up and finish the food so she wouldn't have to. He could also whip up something for her so she didn't have to worry about breakfast, too. Hopefully she had the right ingredients.

Nearly an hour later, with mac 'n cheese bites in the oven, he managed to find what he needed to make some homemade cinnamon rolls. Surely a toddler would eat those, right? He knew absolutely nothing about children, but food tended to bring people together. Bonds were made in kitchens, around dining tables. He couldn't do much, but he could at least try something.

He'd just pulled one pan out of the oven and slid another one in when Macy came into the kitchen, with red-rimmed eyes and a quivering chin. Liam forgot everything he was in the midst of and crossed the wide kitchen. She fell into his arms, gripping his shirt as she sobbed. There wasn't much he could do for her. He had no idea what she was dealing with, but if she needed to lean on someone, he wasn't about to let anyone else take his place.

He rubbed his hands up and down her back, rested his chin on top of her head. Her shoulders shook as she tried to keep her crying under control, but he wished she'd just cut loose. If she needed to break, he'd gladly pick up the pieces.

"I'm sorry." She eased back, shaking her hair away from her face. "This was all more than I'd thought."

Liam used his thumbs to swipe away the moisture on her face. "Don't apologize for caring for a child, Macy. She's lucky to have you."

Macy nodded. "I'm just sorry I soaked your shirt."

"It will dry." He bent his knees, angled his head to look her in the eye. "Want to tell me about it, or do you want to go to bed and I'll finish in here?"

She blinked, peered over his shoulder to the island. "You've been busy."

"I needed to distract myself and you needed help."

She let out a laugh. "It was pretty bad in here earlier. But I'm okay. I couldn't go to bed now if I tried."

When she shifted around him, Liam crossed his arms over his chest and leaned against the counter. She was wound so tightly, she needed to relax.

"Why don't you take a seat at the counter and let me do the rest," he suggested. "I'm working on some cinnamon rolls for your breakfast so you won't have to worry about what you two will eat."

Oh, no. That chin started quivering once again. Tears filled her eyes.

"You didn't have to do that."

With a shrug, he moved to the oven to check on the bites. "I know I didn't have to, but I wanted to and I knew you'd probably open one of those nasty cans of biscuits or something. I couldn't let you do that."

"Actually, I would've done Pop-Tarts."

Liam cringed as he stood back up, resting his hand on the edge of the counter. Even with her puffy eyes, the red splotches on a face void of makeup, Macy was absolutely breathtaking. She wouldn't believe him if he told her now, but she was perfect. Beauty was seriously found on the inside, something he'd learned from his mother and the Monroes. Macy let her beauty flow freely in the way she felt so deeply for others.

"Why are you looking at me like that?" she asked, her brows drawn in.

Liam smiled. "Because I can. Now take a seat and talk to me while I work. Talk about tonight, the party tomorrow, the store. Anything."

Silence settled into the room as he wiped off the island, then sprinkled a light coating of flour onto the surface so he could roll and cut the cinnamon rolls.

"Her name is Lucy. She's precious." As she talked Macy flattened her palms on the counter in front of where he was working. Her eyes focused down on the dough he worked. "She clutched that dog and just kept saying 'Mom.'"

Liam's heart ached for that little girl. He'd been young when his mother died, but not that young.

"And all I could think of was how you must've felt," she went on. "Lucy's mom was single, no siblings. There's a grandmother who lives in Texas, but she hasn't had contact with Lucy since she was born. She has no one, Liam."

Macy pulled in a shaky breath. "Lucy's mom was killed in a car accident on her way home from a job interview while Lucy was at the neighbor's house."

Liam froze. His hands gripped the dough, his heart clenched. That feeling of isolation, of abandonment, came rushing back. The crippling emotions were always hovering, ready to surface at a moment's notice.

Liam knew this little girl was young enough to move

past the pain because she didn't fully understand, but at the same time, she'd always feel that void, the heartache.

He attempted to roll the dough again, trying to stay strong for Macy, for Lucy.

"You don't have to do all this," Macy added. "Just you staying here was enough. And helping with the party. I just couldn't be alone after I got her, and I needed you and—"

"It's okay." He quickly smoothed the dough and lathered on the cinnamon filling before making a roll to slice. "I want to be here. You can lean on me anytime."

"Do you mean that?" she whispered.

He risked a quick look in her direction and was met with her bright blue eyes. She wanted answers. Hell, she *deserved* answers.

"Is now the time to get into this?" he asked. "We're both pretty raw. Let's just get through this next week with your party and the wedding."

Macy shifted in her seat. "If you know when you're leaving, then just say it. I don't want you here out of obligation, or even pity."

Damn it. He hadn't meant to start an argument or hurt her even more, but at the same time, he knew if they started this entire conversation, more hurtful things could be said. He wasn't ready to commit to anything, and wasn't offering promises he couldn't fulfill.

"I'm not here out of pity."

He concentrated on placing the rolls on the pan, then switched out the bites in the oven for the pastries. When he turned back to face her, he propped his hands on his hips and shook his head. Looks like they were getting into this after all.

"I'm here because we're friends."

Macy laughed. "Right. Friends until you leave. But we've pushed the friendship boundary, don't you think? And I'm not just talking sex."

This is why he never did relationships. He had no idea how to communicate without sounding like a complete bastard. Rubbing the back of his neck, Liam struggled to pull words together in some pathetic attempt to smooth this issue out.

The only way to get her to understand was to come completely clean with a past that humiliated and shamed him. "After my mother died I was sent to a foster home where I was beaten." When his eyes widened, her mouth dropped. He pushed on. He had to get this out, to make her realize exactly why getting too close terrified him. "Not by the parents, though they were enablers and just as guilty. Their son decided I was an easy target, and at the time, I was."

Macy sat forward, her hands covering her face, elbows on the bar. "Please. Don't do this to yourself."

"I'm doing it for you." He came around the island, leaned against the edge, and pried her hands away from her face. "We all have our own levels of hell, Macy. You want to understand why I can't give you everything you want?"

With his fingers around her wrists, she fisted her hands and kept her eyes focused on him. Liam didn't let go, didn't give her a chance to turn away again.

"I learned to fight back," he went on, recalling the first time he'd had to defend himself. "I was punished and sent to my room for hitting their precious son. But that didn't stop me. I wasn't about to be a victim again. I was there for too long, long enough to become hardened, cold. By the time the Monroes adopted me, I was pretty bitter."

"And you were put into a house with three other kids, two being boys."

Liam nodded. "Exactly. Zach and I just didn't hit it off to begin with. We were both so angry and it was easy to take it out on each other. Braxton and Chelsea always attempted to bridge the divide, but rarely did that work. It was best that Zach and I stayed in our separate corners."

Liam hadn't recognized the fact that Zach was hurting just as much, but they'd been kids, and like most preteens and teens, they'd been self-absorbed.

"Then when our parents passed, it was just the four of us. Zach and I attempted to be civil, then the accident happened." The accident that left him scarred, Sophie with a limp, and Zach in prison for a year. "Life had dealt blow after blow and I was done. So to take control, I just left. I pushed everyone aside and got the hell out of Haven. This town, just being here, reminds me of everything I've ever had taken away."

Macy chewed on her bottom lip, the habit he knew she did when her nerves kicked in. Slowly, he released her wrists, but didn't step back.

"Do you get what I'm saying?" he asked, hoping the shortened version of his life made sense to her.

With a slight nod, she eased down from her bar stool, causing him to move out of her way. "Yeah, I get it. You're trying to prove to me that you don't do relationships, and I see why, but at this point, I'd think you'd want to take back control. You say you wanted it, that's why you left, but you're just as hell-bent on leaving now."

Was he? He was so damn confused. He wanted it all. He wanted Magnolias, he wanted Macy, he wanted to help his family and push forward with the success that was Chelsea's dream.

"I was given the opportunity to buy Magnolias," he told her. "It's the move I've always wanted to make."

Biting the inside of her cheek, Macy glanced down to her lap, then back up. "Then you should go. If that's what will make you happy. You knew you wouldn't be staying here, so . . . yeah. You should go and live your dream."

That was it? She thought he should take this chance?

Liam eased back and blew out a breath. "I haven't fully

decided yet. I told Braxton and Zach, but Cora and Sophie don't know."

With a shrug, Macy brought her eyes up to his. A soft smile formed around her mouth. "This is what you've worked so hard for. If you're waiting for a blessing from me, you have it."

She kept her voice so steady, her eyes never wavering. He wasn't sure what to say at this point. He'd expected . . . what? Did he want her to beg him to stay? Maybe. But at the same time, being passive-aggressive wasn't his style, either.

"Something is holding you back or you would've left by now," she added. Resting her elbow on the bar, she propped her head up on her fist. "You're torn over the resort, right? What Chelsea would think?"

That wasn't the only female he was concerned about.

"Honestly, I think she'd tell me to follow my dream." Too damn bad that lately his dreams had become hazy and he couldn't see them so clearly anymore. "Working at Magnolias for years only made me want more. I would leave every night knowing that one day I'd have—"

The cry booming through the baby monitor on the counter scared the hell out of him. That was definitely a noise he wasn't used to.

Macy jerked up from her seat. Liam spun around as she rushed by him. He debated for a half second if he should follow her, but he remained in the kitchen. Her soft murmurs filled the quiet space as the monitor picked up everything. The baby's cries calmed and Macy continued to speak in a soothing way. Then she began to sing and Liam had an instant flashback of his own mother singing to him.

Macy brought on so many conflicted emotions inside him. Was it any wonder he couldn't get a grip on anything in his own life lately?

Here he'd been feeling sorry for himself, ruminating and

obsessing on what the hell he should do, when there was a little girl whose entire life had just been ripped apart. Not only that, but he'd only added to Macy's stress.

"I need to settle her back in bed." Macy stood at the end of the hallway, the little girl wrapped in her arms. Poor thing still clutched her stuffed animal. "Just set the alarm on your way out."

And just like that, he'd been dismissed. Yes, she had more pressing matters, but she hadn't asked him to wait this time. Hadn't said they could talk later. Clearly their conversation, half-assed as it was, had come to an end.

There were so many other things he could be doing besides getting in Macy's way. He ended up cleaning her kitchen, wrapping up her breakfast, and putting the food for the party in her fridge. Once all was said and done, he was exhausted considering he'd started at Bella Vous at six that morning.

He started to leave her a note on the rolls, but opted not to. What would he say? He knew exactly where she stood. He'd seen the hurt in her eyes when she'd told him he should go. There had been pain, and Liam didn't think he was too far off the mark in believing she was falling for him.

But she wasn't about to ask him to stay. Why did he have to find her damn pride so attractive?

Her entire life, Macy had put the needs of others first. When her mother passed, she'd stayed at the store—though that had also been a defense mechanism. Then she'd been so assertive with her fostering, even if that meant putting her personal life on hold.

One thing was for certain. Macy may have dismissed him, but he sure as hell wasn't done with her, no matter what he decided to do. If he did leave, then he'd damn well attempt to smooth things over with her. He couldn't live with himself if he just let this pain fester between them.

Chapter Eighteen

"I think she liked the park."

Macy turned onto her street, glancing in the rearview mirror at Lucy, who still held tight to her toy puppy. The blond curls were a little more tamed today. After a rough night, Macy knew the little one needed something fun. And taking her to the park was the perfect distraction to get Macy's father out of the way, too.

Thankfully there were reinforcements at her house getting things set up. Macy didn't know what she'd do if it weren't for all her friends.

"Lucy's lucky to have someone like you," her father commented. "I'm proud of you, Macy. For fostering, for opening your home and your heart. Your mother would be proud, too."

Macy's throat clogged. This was definitely one of the many times in life when she missed her mother. On countless occasions Macy would need motherly advice, or just some girl talk, but her poor father had to fill the void.

Macy had loved seeing him pushing Lucy in the baby swings and lifting her in the air to spin around. All the same things he'd done with Macy when she was a child.

The need to take pictures had been great, but Macy

feared getting too emotionally attached. Someone would eventually adopt Lucy and Macy would have to let her go. Or CPS would get in touch with the grandmother and she'd come forward.

For now, though, Macy was just going to enjoy the moment, love on a little girl who was emotionally broken, and hope she made it into the hands of the right family.

The closer she got to her house, the more Macy's anticipation built. All the flyers and personal invitations she'd handed out would bring a nice crowd of people, guaranteeing this party would be a huge success. She wanted her father to have a memorable birthday, and doing the party a week in advance would totally catch him off guard.

When she turned onto her road, she couldn't help but smile. Cars not only filled her driveway, they were parked along the road. So many familiar faces stood out in the front yard, several holding up a long banner that read HAPPY BIRTHDAY, PHIL!

"What?" he muttered as he sat up straighter in the seat.

"Surprise," Macy squealed.

He glanced to her, to the house, then back to her again. "Macy Jayne, I never . . . This is . . ."

Macy laughed. "I take it you really had no idea."

He shook his head, a smile spread wide across his face. "A party didn't even cross my mind. I thought we were just going out to eat for my birthday."

She pulled the car in behind Zach's truck. "We can do that, too."

Her father turned, looking back at Lucy. "How will she be around all of these people?"

Something Macy had definitely already thought of. "I'm going to let you go on ahead and I'll keep her out here for a bit. I may even end up in your apartment. I don't want her to be afraid of all these unfamiliar people."

Phil leaned across the seat and kissed her cheek. "I've got the best daughter in the world."

Macy patted the side of his smooth cheek. "Only because I was raised by the best parents. Now get out there and greet your guests."

As he stepped out of the car, Macy couldn't help but look for Liam. She knew he was here somewhere. He'd texted her this morning saying he'd bring the food and set up while they were out. After she'd left him in the kitchen last night, she'd wondered if she'd been too closed off when he'd asked her opinion.

Couldn't he tell how much she cared for him? That she was falling for him? Being honest and flat-out saying she loved him wasn't a smart move at this point. She didn't want to scare him, but she seriously wanted him to face his own emotions.

Macy refused to beg him and she absolutely wouldn't tell him he should stay. If he was that torn, then he could only help himself at this point.

Lucy started to whimper in the backseat. "It's okay, sweetheart."

Macy stepped from the car, warmth instantly hitting her. Spring had come early, blessing them with gorgeous days and warmer weather. Macy saw several park days in their future. . . . Well, as long as Lucy was in her care, anyway.

Macy was unfastening Lucy's straps when she felt someone at her side. Turning her head, she saw Sophie.

"Hey, Sophie." Macy pulled Lucy out, instantly holding her to her shoulder.

Sophie smiled at the baby, then said to Macy, "Liam told us about Lucy. What a tragedy. He filled us in while we were setting up."

Macy reached in for the diaper bag. "I didn't get a chance to text any of you yet. It all happened so fast."

"Let me," Sophie offered, taking the bag. "Are you going inside?"

"I don't think she needs to be surrounded by chaos right now." Macy closed the car door with her hip. "I thought about going for a walk."

"I'll go with you. We need to talk."

The tone in her voice had Macy freezing. "What is it?"

"Don't be alarmed—"

"When you start like that how else am I supposed to feel?" Clutching Lucy, Macy tried to remain calm. "Just say it."

"Liam cut his hand with one of his knives. He didn't know it was in the sink and went to wash up the dishes we were done with." Sophie's nose scrunched up. "It's a pretty bad cut, actually. Braxton just took him to the ER."

Macy looked over to the crowd surrounding her father—all the laughter, the smiles, the pats on his back. She wanted to leave, but how could she? She not only had her father and so many people from the town at her house, she had sweet Lucy to think of.

"How bad was it?" Macy asked, turning her attention back to Sophie.

Sophie gripped the diaper bag straps on her shoulder, her diamond engagement ring sparkling in the afternoon sun. "Bad enough that he immediately asked Braxton to take him. Zach and I finished getting things set up and Cora started greeting guests in that sophisticated way, as if she were welcoming royalty into your house."

Even with the fear of what was going on with Liam, Macy couldn't help but laugh. That sounded exactly like Cora, who'd grown up in a high society world, but blended perfectly into their small town.

"I don't know what's going on with you two," Sophie went on. "But I know it's more than friends."

Lucy fussed and Macy patted her back, bouncing a little.

The poor thing was most likely ready for a much deserved nap. Between the hell of yesterday, the big day at the park, and adjusting to brand new surroundings, Macy needed to get her settled.

"It's complicated." Macy wasn't sure how to approach this. She and Liam had never talked about what was going on between them outside their little bubble. But his family wasn't naive or stupid. "And after last night, I'm pretty sure friends is where we'll stay."

Those words hurt to say, but the sooner she faced reality, the sooner she could heal . . . she hoped.

"Really?" Sophie shifted, holding her hand up to block the afternoon sun. "Because I thought for sure once I told him about the opportunity at Bella Vous, that he'd jump on opening his own place and—"

"What?" His own place? Here?

Sophie pursed her lips. "I take it he didn't tell you."

"No." More hurt seeped in. Why was she letting him hurt her when this clearly was a one-sided relationship? A relationship he'd told her up front couldn't happen and she'd readily agreed. "What opportunity?"

"I should let him tell you."

Macy kept rocking back and forth gently, and the slow breathing from Lucy indicated the baby was finally resting. "Too late, you've already told me. Now just give me the details."

More laughter echoed behind Macy as she waited. She was thrilled her father was having a wonderful party, and she'd get to it eventually, but now she had a resting child and a man to figure out.

"After Rand was removed from the mayor's office, Dax McGlone took over. He called the other day stating he's been getting calls from all over. The town is really thriving with more tourists since we opened the resort. Between the women flooding in from Savannah, and the talk of

Liam's cooking, Dax wanted to know if we'd be interested in opening a small bakery to sell to the public."

"We . . . meaning Liam?"

Sophie nodded. "He hasn't told me what he wants to do yet, but I think this is exactly what he needs. He's been so . . . I don't know, almost lost since he came back. I know his heart isn't here, but I'd hate to see him go again."

Little did Sophie know the man already had one foot out the door. He hadn't told Macy about this opportunity and clearly this was the call he'd taken the other night when he'd pushed her questions aside. He hadn't wanted to let her in, hadn't wanted to discuss the options he'd been given.

In short, he wanted to do this all alone.

Tears pricked her eyes and she was thankful for the sunglasses she still had on. "Well, I'm sure he'll let you know soon. I need to take Lucy to Dad's and let her rest more. Can you let him know I'll be back?"

Sophie patted her arm. "I'm sorry. I know you're upset. I just assumed he told you."

"It's fine. We don't share everything." Well, she did, but obviously he hadn't wanted to open up to her. "Will you come tell me the second you hear how he is?"

Sophie handed over the diaper bag. "Of course."

Adjusting the bag onto her own shoulder, without waking Lucy, Macy watched Sophie head back toward the party. Macy opted to walk on the other side of the house and then around back. Nearly everyone was inside now, so she could sneak away and into her dad's apartment without being seen. While her dad was having a great time, Macy needed to pull herself together.

Once Lucy rested for a while, she'd take her back to the house. She knew she'd be bombarded with questions about the baby, but those would be easy to answer.

It was everything else in her life at the moment that

was causing major anxiety. As Macy let herself in to the back of her father's apartment, she leaned against the door and sighed. Between the store and Lucy, she had enough on her plate. She just wished she'd listened to herself months ago when she told herself not to get emotionally attached to her new tenant.

Unfortunately, she'd fallen in love with a man who couldn't get out of town fast enough.

Punching with one arm was a bitch, but that didn't stop Liam from beating the hell out of his bag. He'd been in the ER so long, he'd missed going to Phil's party. After he was dismissed with too many stitches, a wrap, and a pissy outlook on his future as a chef, Liam had told Braxton to just drop him off at home.

Home. The second floor of an old building in the main part of town. His "home" was the property of a woman he couldn't get out of his mind, but he couldn't let her deeper inside, either.

The pounding on his back door had him freezing. He didn't want visitors. He sure as hell wasn't ready to face off with Macy again. He'd been dead set on seeing her after the party, but that was before he'd injured himself. Now he wanted to be left alone with his punching bag and his thoughts.

Unfortunately, the unwanted visitor kept pounding. It couldn't have been Macy—she would've let herself in by now.

He'd barely wrestled a glove onto his good hand earlier. Now he tucked his glove beneath his opposite arm and tugged until he was free. Tossing the glove onto the bed, he headed toward the door as the persistent knocking continued.

As soon as he jerked the door open, he was greeted with his brothers and Brock. Three sets of eyes, angry if he was reading body language correctly, stared back at him. Great. What had he possibly done now? He'd been in the damn ER for hours.

"Oh, good. My day is about to get worse."

He turned away from the door. No need to invite them in. They'd do what they wanted.

"Count on it," Zach confirmed as he closed the door behind the posse. "What the hell are you thinking stringing all of us along?"

Liam ignored the pain in his hand and sank down onto the leather sofa. "I'm not in the mood for games, so spit out whatever you really want to say."

"He wants to know when you're going to make up your mind about staying or leaving," Braxton intervened. "Because you told us you were most likely leaving to go back to Magnolias. Then Sophie tells us you have an opportunity to stay here and open your own place, branching off the resort."

"So what the hell are you doing and why are you so damn secretive?" Zach continued to glare as he practically shouted his question.

Brock stood between Zach and Braxton, his arms crossed over his chest. The anger rolled off Zach, but Brock appeared to be more hurt than anything. Anger Liam could handle, but knowing he was causing pain was a hell of a guilt trip.

"I'm still sorting shit out," Liam threw back. "Why did you all barge in here to attack?"

"Because Sophie told Macy about the offer at the resort and she said Macy seemed upset." Zach took a step forward, leaning against the chair opposite Liam. "Clearly whatever you two have going on is a mess if you didn't even tell her. She deserves more than you jerking her around."

Yeah, she did. This wasn't exactly news to him. And this

was also the main reason he'd told her they would only be together while he was here. She'd agreed.

"I'm not taking on the extra work at the resort." He hadn't known exactly what he was going to do until now. "I'm going to push through with my plans to go back to Savannah."

There. He'd made a decision. Part of him was relieved, the other part . . . Hell, he didn't know. Liam was positive no matter what decision he made, he'd have some regrets.

"So that's it?" Brock asked. "You're going to leave?"

Liam nodded, ignoring the lump in his throat. "It's what I've always wanted. I came back to help you all out of a bind. You know I never wanted to be here."

"You made that very clear from the beginning." Braxton circled the chair Zach leaned against and took a seat. "We just figured you'd have a change of heart and end up staying. Then when this opportunity opened, we thought for sure you'd make the best of it and—"

"And what?" Liam asked. "Forget everything I'd worked for? I did my part. I didn't let Chelsea down. I didn't let you guys down. I will stay until I find a proper replacement. I won't let the resort suffer."

"It's more than the resort," Brock murmured.

Damn, that was low, bringing the kid in on this, Liam thought. Not that he was a kid—he was definitely more adult than most eighteen-year-olds—but still.

"Then you can tell Sophie that you're not taking this opportunity," Zach stated. "And you can smooth things over with Macy."

"Macy is none of your concern."

Zach sneered in that typical cocky way of his. "She's my friend, and when you're gone she'll still be my friend. So looks like she's more our concern than yours at this point."

Liam fisted his good hand. "I'll take care of Macy."

"I hate to bring this up, but it needs to be addressed."

Braxton nodded to Liam's injury. "What about next weekend? I don't know what the doctor told you, and I know Cora and Sophie will be concerned about you, plus the wedding."

Liam inwardly groaned. He hadn't told anyone what the doctor actually said. Because the words "nerve damage" and "only time will tell" had crushed him.

Still, that didn't mean he couldn't go to Magnolias. Being the chef wasn't all he'd wanted. He wanted the Savannah hot spot to be his very own. And if he couldn't get back to the chef he used to be, that would be a new level of hell, but he'd still have a grand, successful restaurant.

Maybe if he came clean about his hand everyone would see this as him running again. Perhaps he was. Still, that wasn't going to stop him from going back to Savannah. At least there he could have some control over his life, because here he had none. He didn't want his family to know he might never have full use of his hand again. He didn't want them to see him as a failure.

As the new owner of Magnolias, he would handpick the best of the best to fill his place in the kitchen and no one would be the wiser.

"I'll make sure your wedding is taken care of," he assured Braxton and Zach. "Nothing to worry about."

Total lie, but he kept his tone firm and his eyes never wavered from Braxton. He'd find a way to make everything work out, no matter what he had to do or whom he had to enlist for help.

Macy was a bit surprised when Liam told her he was on his way over. Oh, she wasn't surprised at his lack of manners. Telling her instead of asking her was typical Liam fashion. He didn't want to give her the opportunity to say no.

What shocked her was the fact he was the one reaching out and wanting to talk. Or whatever he was coming over for.

Macy had just put Lucy down for a nap when the front door opened and closed. Again, just like Liam to use the code to let himself in.

As she pulled the nursery door shut, leaving a sliver cracked, Macy took a moment to take in a breath. No matter how hurt she was, no matter how angry she was at herself, she couldn't just cut him completely out. Not only did she want to see him, she wanted to know if he was okay. He'd never made it back for the party and she hadn't heard anything until he texted her. Macy had sent Sophie a message, but all she said was that Liam went home after the ER visit.

Smoothing her hair back from her face, Macy turned to head down the hallway, but Liam stood at the end. His broad shoulders took up so much space in the opening, and his eyes pinned her in place. The white wrap on his hand drew her attention.

"Are you okay?" she whispered as she tiptoed toward him.

With a shrug, he replied, "It's nothing."

Again, the fact he wasn't fully letting her in hurt. She had no one to blame but herself because she'd given him the power.

When she started to brush past him, he reached his good arm out. His hand curled around her shoulder, but Macy kept her eyes forward. Had he come to say good-bye? No, he wouldn't leave before the weddings were over next week.

"Look at me."

She jerked at his command, tipping her head to meet his intense stare. The scar on his cheek was now highlighted at the angle he faced her.

At least he no longer tried to hide that from her.

"How's Lucy?"

Standing this close, the warmth of his body blanketed her. She wanted so much from him, and being like this, touching even in the most innocent way, was only going to make all of this harder when he finally did leave.

"She's asleep. We had a pretty good day. I took her and Dad to the park before the party, then we've been home for a few hours. I just held her on the couch and sang silly songs. I rocked her. I hope she feels safe here."

Liam slid his hand up, his thumb gliding beneath her eye. "You're tired."

Macy nodded. No denying she probably looked like hell. After last night, then today, there had been so much to take in.

"Thank you for getting things to the party," she told him, still unnerved at his touch and the fact he now cupped her cheek as he continued to stroke her face. "I—"

"I didn't come here to talk about the party or my hand or anything else."

Her eyes widened. "You seriously think that—"

"I think there's still too much tension between us." He stepped in closer until their bodies lined up. "I think we need to talk. We need to discuss a whole host of things, but I also know I need you, Macy. I'm selfish, and I'm human. So if you want me to go, just say the word."

She swallowed. "You're going anyway."

"Yes."

The affirmation clenched her heart because they weren't talking about today. He was actually leaving Haven.

Macy pushed away until she went into the living room. With shaking hands, she picked up the two tiny stuffed animals. Tossing them in the basket by the sofa, she tried to remind herself that crying did absolutely no good. No matter how much she wanted him—and mercy, she did, because she was human, too—she just couldn't give him that control ever again.

"Macy."

She took extra time arranging the toys in just the right manner before standing and turning to face him again.

"I can't stay here."

For you.

He might as well have tacked that on, but deep down, beneath all the hurt and questions, she knew he was running. He feared relationships, so everything they had only drove him toward this decision.

"So you came to tell me what?" She folded her arms over her chest. "If you're waiting on me to beg, I won't do it. If you want one last quickie, I'm not your girl. Thank you for teaching me I deserve better, by the way."

"Damn it, Macy." He marched across the room, taking her shoulders and jerking her until she fell into his chest. "I didn't come here to fight."

"I know why you came here," she tossed back.

He let her go and took a step back. "I actually came to ask for your help, but when I saw you, every time I see you, I want you. It's been that way for so long, but Zach was right. You deserve better."

Macy threw her arms wide, anger rolling through her. "Oh, now Zach is deciding what's going on between us?"

When Liam opened his mouth, no doubt with another excuse or defense she wasn't in the mood to hear, she held up both her hands. "Forget it. What is it you want my help with?"

"I need you to help with the weddings this weekend." He raked a hand down his face, the stubble on his jawline bristling beneath his palm. "I can't do the cake by myself with my hand."

Macy stilled. "Pardon me?"

"You heard me." Disgust filled his tone. "I hate asking,

I hate being incompetent, but there's no way in hell I can make this cake with one hand."

"How in the world do you think I can help with my two? Remember who you're talking to here."

Liam offered a slight grin. "I know exactly who I'm dealing with and I'm going to be with you for each step and we're going to do this for my brothers, for Cora and Sophie."

Macy had no idea what he was thinking asking her, but Sophie and Cora were expecting their wedding to be amazing and Liam clearly couldn't do this all himself.

"They wouldn't be upset if you ended up asking one of your chef friends to make it."

Liam cocked his head, lifting his brows. "Chef friends? I wouldn't ask anyone else to do this. I'm going to get this cake done with or without your help. It will just be a hell of a lot easier with you."

"I don't see how."

Liam closed the space between them. "Because I have faith in you and I'm your teacher."

That set jaw, those intense eyes, and that husky tone . . . How did any woman ever say no to this man? How did *she* say no?

"Fine. But I'm only doing it for them."

Liam's lips twitched. "Not me?"

"No." She stepped back, needing the distance both physically and emotionally. "Because after the wedding you're gone and I need to get on with my life. You've already mentally checked out."

Liam nodded. "Fair enough. Come up to my apartment after work tomorrow."

"You can come here," she retorted. Childish, but she was done bowing to his every whim. "I need to keep Lucy in familiar surroundings and Dad will be here to help watch her while we work."

Before she knew what his intentions were, he reached out and wrapped an arm around her waist. The force had her bent over backward, with his torso resting on hers. That mouth was mere inches away. The devil himself wasn't this tempting.

"I'm not leaving right after the wedding," he murmured. "I still have a while before I go. So don't think I won't touch you or kiss you every chance I get."

When his lips slammed down onto hers, Macy shoved him back. "You can try, but you'll fail."

Liam let her go and she stumbled before she caught herself on the accent chair.

"We'll see," he told her, throwing her a glance over his shoulder. "My need for you isn't over, Macy."

"Does it matter what I want?" she tossed back.

"Oh, I know what you want. We both know where this is ending."

How could he be so casual about this now? After all she'd told him, after all they'd been through. "It's already ended, Liam."

He stared another second before letting himself out. She knew if she'd just crooked her finger they'd end up in bed.

Bed. Just where he'd taught her to overcome her fears. Where he'd shown her what she thought was love.

She'd been so wrong. Opening her heart had been a risk, one she couldn't take back. Honestly, she wouldn't take back their time together even if she could. No matter the heartache she had now, Liam had shown her that she was even stronger than she'd ever thought. She would get over him, too.

Okay, so the words were easy to say, but the execution of actually moving on was going to be a bit harder. He was still here, and she'd still see him every day until he finally left. So knowing the end was coming, yet being near him, was only adding salt to the wound.

She needed to be ready to face Liam again tomorrow. And the real kicker was now they were going to be working together on a wedding cake.

Yeah, fate sure did have a nice way of smacking you in the face.

Chapter Nineteen

Liam pulled the fresh yeast rolls from the oven. Pairing his specialty rolls with a potpie was exactly what this group of elderly ladies had requested on their form when they'd made reservations. They wanted good ol' Southern cooking, specifically potpies or fried potatoes and smoked sausage. Liam preferred getting a little creative with his potpies by making his own crusts.

There were days he could really branch out and try new recipes, then there were times like this where he had to stick with a boring and unimaginative menu.

But he would do his best because that was his job, that was what he was raised to do. Plus, he refused to let himself slack off even for a second. This was Chelsea's dream; her entire life savings had gone into buying this place.

But it was damn hard doing this with one good hand. Thankfully he'd had dough made up in advance. Any seasoned chef had multiple backups and premade options. You never knew when things would go to shit in a moment's notice.

"Need help?" Sophie swept through the kitchen, her gait a little more normal today.

"Have a seat." He gestured toward the bar stools. "I've got it so far. Are all the drinks and appetizers set up?"

Sophie gripped the back of the stool and nodded. "I even took the salads out and the dressings are already on the tables. The ladies are still cooing over your amazing lunch with fried chicken."

Liam slid the rolls into a decorative bowl. "You can take these out and the potpies will be up next."

Sophie pulled the bowl from the counter. When she took a step, she hissed. Liam crossed to her, grabbing the rolls. "Sit down, you're hurting."

"No, it's fine. I just had a showing earlier and there were so many stairs. It's actually easing up."

He stared at her as she sank to the stool. "How much longer are you going to keep working?" he asked. "The resort is a full-time job in itself."

Letting out a sigh, she sent him a smile. "You sound like Zach. I know I need to sell my business. It's just hard to let go of something you love."

And this was going to dive into a territory he didn't want to get into. He wasn't ready to let his dream go. Sophie's circumstances were different. She had an old injury that held her back, or hindered her ability to keep up. But she was determined to do it all.

"I'll take these out."

He managed to get in and out of the dining room while the ladies chatted about the upcoming book club meeting they were going to attend. But he didn't escape before they started discussing someone named Rafe. When Liam heard the words "on page seventy-eight" he realized this Rafe was fictitious.

When he came back into the kitchen, Sophie was at the oven, door open slightly as she peeked inside.

"Trying to take over?" he asked as he grabbed a pot holder.

"These smell amazing." She closed the door and stepped back. "I can help you carry those in."

"I already told you to sit down. Where's Brock, anyway?"

Sophie ignored him, pulling out a serving tray. "He started working for Macy after school. We all decided this was the perfect time for him to start since she is fostering and could use extra hands."

And she hadn't mentioned this to him last night?

No. Why would she? He'd made it clear he was leaving, made it clear there was no future for them, and then he'd had the balls to ask her to help with a wedding cake.

"What's that look for?" Sophie asked as she leaned against the side of the island.

Liam lifted the individual dishes and sat them on the tray. "I just didn't know, that's all."

Was he already getting shut out? Isn't that what he'd chosen? He'd opted to get the hell out of Haven with as few ties as possible.

Still, this was his family. He had discussed a new job with Brock, but to know the plan had been set into motion was altogether different.

"I can get this," Sophie told him. "Really. I promise the pain has eased and I won't splatter your dishes all over the floor."

Liam laughed. "I'm more concerned about you than the dishes."

She lifted the tray and sent him a wide grin. "No need to be concerned with either."

As she headed into the dining room, Liam cleaned up his work area. He'd made up lemon bars and homemade raspberry sorbet in advance, so the dessert was all set. They might like traditional foods, but it was spring and he wanted something to go with the season. He didn't think there would be any complaints over this meal.

And since dessert was done, he could take his leave. When Sophie came back into the kitchen, she was laughing.

"Book club talk, still?" he guessed, slicing into the bars.

"Whoever this Rafe character is, he has them torn up."

All the more reason for him to get himself home. He wasn't interested in any book club chatter, and he sure as hell didn't want to discuss Rafe.

"I have the desserts all set." He pulled out all the items and sat them on the island. "Can you get them all out? I'd like to head home. I have a certain cake to work on for this weekend."

Sophie beamed. "Go, go," she said, shooing him with her hands. "I've got it all covered. But are you sure you can do the cake with one hand? I know Cora and I would totally understand if you can't."

He reached across the island, placing his hand over hers. "No problem. I'm doing it. Well, Macy is helping me."

Sophie raised a brow. "Really?"

"I had to ask. I won't let you down and I know she can do it."

Sophie's smile widened. "Does this mean you're getting closer with her? Because the other day she swore you were just friends, but then I see how you two have looked at each other and it seems like—"

"Don't read any more into this," he told Sophie. "Seriously. I . . . damn it. I have something I need to tell you."

Her brows drew in. "What's wrong?"

"There's no easy way to say this, but . . ." He blew out a breath. "I'm going to be leaving Haven. I'm buying Magnolias."

Sophie's eyes widened. "You're serious?"

Her shocked, whispered question caught him by the throat, rendering him speechless. Liam nodded.

"When?"

"I promised the guys I'd stay until I found a suitable chef for the resort. I won't leave you all in a bind and I'll make sure the transition is smooth."

Sophie sucked in a breath. "I didn't see this coming. I thought for sure you'd be thrilled with the prospect Dax gave us."

"It's not that I didn't appreciate the opportunity," he corrected, hoping she'd see his reasoning. "I've just always wanted my own restaurant and Magnolias is like my own. I was head chef for so long, and now it can all be mine."

Sophie tucked her hair behind her ears as she pursed her lips. "I'm going to miss you."

Closing the gap, Liam pulled her into his arms. "It's not like I'll never come back. Savannah isn't far at all."

"It won't be the same," she sniffed into his shoulder.

No, it wouldn't be the same. Isn't that what he wanted? Didn't he want to be separated from this town and his past?

"Why are you always hugging on my woman?"

Liam glanced over his shoulder as Zach came in the back door. Without releasing Sophie, he grinned. "Maybe she's the one always hugging on me."

When Sophie eased back and looked at Zach, there was no hiding the fact she was upset.

"Oh, hell." Zach instantly moved forward, taking Liam's place and holding her. "You told her?"

"I had to."

"I was hoping you'd wait until after the wedding," Zach scolded.

"No." Sophie kept her arm around Zach's waist and wiped her damp cheeks with her other hand. "I want to know. I'll be fine. I'm just going to miss him not being here."

Zach merely lifted a brow at Liam. The risk was too great to get swept up in all these emotions right now. Liam could so easily let them talk him into staying, but he might never have a chance like this again. And he'd had to tell Sophie so she didn't immediately jump to conclusions where Macy was concerned.

This was just one colossal mess from every angle.

"I need to get going," he stated as he went to the counter by the back door and grabbed his keys and cell. "I have a wedding cake to work on."

"With that hand?" Zach asked.

"I've got it covered."

Before he had to get into the whole "Macy was helping" speech, he pushed open the screen door and headed toward his SUV. Leaving one emotional disaster and heading straight into another wasn't his idea of a good time, but there was no way around it. As soon as he got to Macy's house, he knew he'd be in for it. He needed her help, a fact that pissed him off. He didn't want to ask for help, didn't want to ask her because he knew they would inevitably discuss the turmoil that had become their norm the past few days. He didn't want the tension, didn't want her to have to deal with the negativity.

But he wanted her. Still. Even though he was leaving, Liam wanted the hell out of her. The thought crossed his mind to keep this going, but how was that fair to her? She lived here with a store, fostering a child, and he wanted out. Continuing with their affair would only prolong the inevitable.

Liam pulled out of the drive from the resort and headed toward his apartment to grab some items to take to Macy's. All he could do at this point was try to emotionally survive until he could leave. Once he was gone, he knew he'd be fine.

Out of sight, out of mind . . . right?

* * *

Macy settled Lucy into her high chair. Of course the stuffed dog was nestled right against her. The social worker had called earlier, checking in. So far, Lucy had adjusted remarkably well, considering. Being so young, she couldn't comprehend exactly what had happened, which was both a blessing and a harsh reality.

This poor baby would never remember her mother. Macy recognized that bedtime was rough, so she made sure to rock her, to sing to her, anything she could think of that was calming, nurturing. All the things Macy's mother had done for her.

"How about some peaches?" Macy asked.

She cut up some fresh peaches she'd picked up at the farmer's market earlier. When spring hit, the vendors set up in the park and offered fresh produce, homemade products, and a variety of handmade items. Since her father had been at the store most of the day, Macy managed to sneak out with Lucy and take her to the park to check out the goods.

Of course people cooed over the sweet baby, making Macy's heart soar. She already loved this little girl. There was no way to detach from all the feelings that accompanied being her caregiver.

Macy set the tiny, bite-sized pieces on the high-chair tray. Lucy immediately grabbed one and shoved it into her mouth. Once she chewed that, her slobbery hand reached for another.

"We have a winner," Macy muttered as she cut off a chunk of fruit for herself.

The green beans earlier had been a big, giant no. The green mess might never be fully cleaned from her office at the store. Macy had brought in some leftovers for her lunch and decided to get some veggies into Lucy. Clearly this girl was all about her fruits and the greens could take a hike.

Macy had just sliced up more tiny bites when her doorbell rang. She threw a glance to the clock on the oven and realized it was a little later than she'd thought. She'd actually left the store early when her father decided he'd help show Brock how to close out the register. Macy had been hesitant, but figured her father wanted that time with Brock. It was good for the teen to be working for someone other than his adoptive family. He was a remarkable kid, and from what she'd seen so far, he was going to be quite an asset to her business.

She felt silly calling Brock a kid. He was practically an adult, with life experiences nobody should have had to endure.

Macy grabbed a towel and wiped her hands. The sticky juice from the peaches clung to her fingers, but she'd wash them in a bit.

Time to greet her guest.

When she pulled the door open, Liam stood there with his arm wrapped around a huge box. Macy quickly went to take it.

"I've got it."

Fine. She wasn't going to argue. She moved back, opening the door wider as she gestured for him to come in.

"I wasn't sure what all you had, so I tried to grab everything I could think of."

He headed straight for the island. Lucy's eyes widened when she saw him. Immediately, Macy went to her and picked up a piece of the peach to show her that everything was just fine and normal.

Liam sat the box on the counter and glanced around. "I can get most of this started. I'll just yell when I need you."

"That's fine. She's had dinner. I just wanted to give

her a snack. She seems a little more content when she's preoccupied with something."

Liam stared at the little girl. "Is she . . . has she been okay?"

There was no hiding the hurt in his tone. The hurt of losing his mother, then the years that followed, had clearly shaped the man who stood before her. Did anyone ever recover from such a tragedy?

"She's done considerably well."

Macy picked up another piece and held it to Lucy's lips. She'd yet to take her eyes off the new guest. Macy understood where she was coming from. Liam was a hard man to ignore.

"And you?" he asked, his eyes meeting hers. "How have you been with her?"

"We survived our first day at the store," Macy told him with a smile. "Having Dad and Brock helped, though."

"You didn't tell me Brock was going to work for you when I was here yesterday."

With his good hand propped on the counter, that scar, and those dark eyes, Liam looked every bit the hard man he wanted to portray. Macy knew better. She knew it bugged him that he hadn't known what was going on in his own family.

"It didn't come up," she said, shrugging.

He started to say something else, but just shook his head and started unloading the box. Macy finished feeding Lucy, and by the time she was done, they were both sticky with the combination of peach juice and drool.

"I need to wash her off." She pulled the tray off and sat it in the farm-style sink. "Will you need me in the next ten minutes?"

Liam had already pulled out a huge mixing bowl and was tossing in ingredients like a champ with his one hand. "I'm okay for now."

The tension between them rattled her. The sexual tension they'd initially started with was at least something she could handle, like a stepping stone, because she knew where they'd been heading. Right now? She had no clue what was going on. Part of her wanted to hold out some sliver of hope that he'd stay, but in her heart she knew he wouldn't.

And even knowing all of that, she couldn't just turn off her feelings for him. She'd never felt this way about another man in her entire life. He was everything; he'd shown her everything. How could he think what they had wasn't special enough to fight for?

After stripping Lucy, Macy sat her in the tub and ran the smallest amount of lukewarm water. She tossed in a few toys and let her splash around for a bit. Macy squatted down, picked up a plastic fish and filled it with water. Squeezing the toy, water shot out the fish's mouth and onto Lucy's belly. The little girl giggled, warming Macy's heart. She wanted her to keep smiling, to play and have as normal a childhood as possible.

"You're good with her."

Macy jerked around to Liam leaning against the door frame.

"She loves the bath," Macy stated.

Suddenly this all seemed too much like a family. Too much like what she'd always wanted. Yet the two people in this room who owned pieces of her heart were only temporary. They'd both go and Macy would be left to heal on her own.

"Did you need me?" Macy asked, turning back to squirt Lucy once again.

"Yeah. I do."

The huskiness of his tone had Macy stilling. She closed her eyes, hating how fast she could melt at just the way he spoke. Her body shivered as if he'd touched her.

"I'll be done in a second."

She couldn't turn back to look at him, didn't want him to look in her eyes and see all of the emotions, because there was no way she could hide them. Quickly rinsing the suds off Lucy, Macy let the water out and reached for the hooded duck towel. After she wrapped her all up and scooped her out of the tub, Macy turned . . . and Liam still remained in the doorway.

Definitely too close to a family moment.

His dark eyes held her in place and Macy wasn't even sure she was fully taking in a breath. The squirming baby in her arms was the only thing that kept her grounded and focused on the fact she and Liam were not alone. No matter if they were, though, she couldn't go down that path again with him. And, honestly, she didn't know if she had the willpower to tell him no.

Macy started forward, thankful when he stepped aside and let her pass. Just as she went by, Lucy reached for Liam. His eyes widened as he stared at the outstretched arms, but he didn't hesitate in submitting to the innocence of the sweet girl.

Liam slid his strong hands around the wrapped towel and pulled the little girl to his chest. Macy couldn't help but smile and just accept the familiar burn that came along with all the crazy emotions lately.

"She likes you."

Lucy laid her head against Liam's shoulder and started sucking her thumb. As much as Macy wanted to continue to watch this big, strong man hold a vulnerable child, she could only handle so much.

She eased between Liam and the door and headed into Lucy's room to pull out some clothes. Liam came in behind her, murmuring something to Lucy. Concentrating on the diaper and pajamas, Macy went to the crib.

"You can just put her in here. I'll be out in a minute."

Liam threw her a glance. "Pushing me out?"

"Just trying to keep some distance."

Why not go for honesty? At this point, why play a game? She wasn't going to hide her feelings.

Shaking his head, Liam laid Lucy down in her crib. "This was a bad idea."

Lucy tugged part of the duck towel into her mouth, sucking on the fake beak. Macy quickly put the diaper on and reached for the bottle of lotion in the basket at the base of the crib.

"What part are you referring to?" she asked as she lathered unscented lotion onto Lucy's little legs and arms. "Us sleeping together or you pretending this means nothing to you?"

"Sleeping with you wasn't a mistake," he retorted immediately. "The mistake was me thinking we could work together on the cake. I'll figure out a way to do it on my own."

When he turned to go, Macy called to him. "I'm going to help you. I love your brothers, I love Cora and Sophie. I'm doing this for them. Don't be pissed when you caused all of this yourself."

He took off down the hallway and Macy was sure she heard him mutter, "Maybe I'm pissed at myself."

Chapter Twenty

Finally the wedding day had arrived. The cake was done and Macy had painstakingly spent way too many hours rolling fondant, cutting fondant, cursing fondant.

If she never saw that hellish icing again, she'd die a happy woman.

The truce she and Liam had called was definitely the only way she'd gotten through the week unscathed. But that didn't mean that each evening he came over didn't leave her wanting more. Even Lucy kept reaching for him, getting used to him.

Thankfully, though, Lucy had fallen in love with Phil, too, so at least there was a man in her life who wouldn't be leaving anytime soon.

Macy had let Phil run the store during the morning, then they posted a sign they'd be closing early due to family. And the Monroes were so much like family to Macy. She loved each of them, felt a connection just the same as if they were blood related.

As she turned from side to side, studying her image in the full-length mirror in one of the guest rooms at Bella Vous, Macy decided she actually loved her dress. Loved it even more because the vintage lace looked adorable with her boots. The outdoorsy wedding would be perfect for her bridesmaid look.

The cream lace she'd chosen made her skin look a bit darker, as if she'd actually gotten a tan. As if she ever had time for such things. She'd opted to leave her hair down, curling the ends. A simple amount of shadow and gloss was all she committed to in the makeup department. She looked feminine, but still comfortable. Granted, her favorite lingerie beneath the dress always managed to make her feel sexy.

And she was going to be standing up with two brides, so it wasn't like anyone would notice her anyway.

Smoothing her hands down her dress, she went across the hall where Sophie and Cora were getting ready. Sophie had just zipped up the side of Cora's dress and stepped back.

"Wow." Macy froze in the doorway. "You two are absolutely gorgeous."

Both brides turned.

Sophie lifted her satin A-line skirt and shifted back from Cora. "I'm so nervous," she said with a laugh. "I don't know why. I've waited for this day for years."

"Well, Zach and Braxton are not going to be able to concentrate on vows with the sight of you two."

Cora slid her hands down the sides of her dress. "I love how this feels. I wanted something vintage and classy."

"Lace is the way to go," Sophie agreed.

While Cora's dress was straight with a short train and completely covered in elegant lace, Sophie's was smooth silk with just a touch of lace across the bust and scalloped edging over her shoulders.

A pang of jealousy hit Macy. She couldn't be happier for her friends, but at the same time, she wondered if she'd ever have this moment for herself.

"And speaking of gorgeous, wait until Liam sees you."

Sophie stepped in front of the vanity and picked up a set of pearl earrings. "He's not going to be able to keep his hands off of you."

Macy laughed. "I wouldn't bet on that."

Cora felt along the edge of the king-sized bed until she reached the end and faced Macy. "Is this because he's leaving? Savannah isn't that far away."

"It might as well be Alaska." Macy stepped into the room, heading to the dresser where their flowers were all laid out. She fingered the delicate petals. "We want different things."

"But you want each other. That's pretty difficult to ignore," Cora countered.

More like impossible.

"Well, I can't make him stay and I won't ask him to." Why did her chest ache when she said those words? Why did every aspect of her life lately circle back to Liam, to the mess they'd gotten themselves in? "Besides, we both knew this wasn't going to last."

"I'm sure you agreed to that before you fell in love," Cora murmured. "Am I correct?"

Macy bit her lip, pushing beyond the hurt. "Yes."

Pulling in a deep breath, Macy realized this was not the time or the place to get into her issues. She would not ruin this day for the people she loved, the people who deserved all the happiness in the world.

"Let's not focus on any of that." Macy picked up her bouquet of fresh hydrangeas. "Today the sun is shining, the guests are arriving, and you two are the most gorgeous brides I've ever seen."

"Where's Lucy?" Sophie asked as she adjusted her pearl necklace, her gaze meeting Macy's in the mirror.

"Dad took her for a walk. I didn't want her to get too restless, and if she's in her stroller, she'll probably fall asleep."

"You seem to be adjusting with her in your life." Cora

grabbed Heidi's collar, which had been wrapped in cream satin ribbons. "Has the social worker said if there's a potential life family for her?"

"Her grandmother in Texas has been notified, but I'm not sure if she wants to take Lucy." Macy gripped the ribboned stems in her hands. "I, um . . . I sort of requested that I could be a contender for adoption."

She'd not told anyone yet, not even her father. She didn't want to get anyone's hopes up, but at the same time she seriously needed a support team. What if this didn't work out? Yes, there would be other children and she'd known going in that there would be ups and downs and inevitable good-byes. She just didn't want to let Lucy go.

"Oh, Macy, that's wonderful." Sophie spun from the vanity, her hands clasped together. "Lucy is one lucky little girl to have someone like you in her life."

That's what Macy was banking on social services thinking, and maybe the grandmother didn't want to take in such a young child.

"Don't say anything," Macy added. "You guys are the only two who know."

"We won't say a word," Cora promised. "I'd better get downstairs. I'm sure my mother wants to see me before the ceremony and I told her to wait in the parlor."

Sophie shrugged. "Since my parents still disapprove of Zach, they aren't coming. I have no worries today."

Macy knew Sophie and her parents had always had a strained relationship, but to not come to your own daughter's wedding? Zach was the best thing that had ever happened to Sophie and she totally completed him.

"Let me help you down the steps," Macy offered Cora. But she knew Cora prided herself on being independent, so Macy quickly added, "I know you are well aware of how to get around, but if you tripped on that lace train and fell, Braxton would not be a happy groom."

Cora held out her hand. "I will gladly let you escort me. The last thing I want is to trip over this dress and tear it."

Sophie gathered the two other bouquets. The bundles of tight lilacs and white roses were simple, yet elegant. "I guess it's showtime?"

"Let's go get married," Cora stated with a wide grin.

Once she made it through this day, Macy could focus on Lucy, on the store, on teaching Brock more of the little details that went into the business.

And Liam. There would have to be a recovery period when he left and she needed to brace herself for that. She knew full well it was coming.

As she started down the steps at Cora's side, Macy pushed all thoughts of Liam to the back of her mind . . . or as far as she was able to.

So much for pushing all thoughts of this man away. She not only had to walk up and down the makeshift aisle leading toward the pond with Liam as her escort, she also had to face him during the vows.

Macy had tried to concentrate on the couples, on the beauty of the day and all that this new beginning symbolized. She focused on her father, who sat with a sleeping Lucy on his lap. Anything so she didn't have to look directly at Liam, because standing there, listening to declarations of love, was making her chest ache, her mind filling with thoughts of what-if scenarios.

Now that the ceremony was over, the guests had left and the married couples had gone on their ways—to destinations they were not disclosing. Macy wanted to help clean up so Cora and Sophie didn't have a worry. Phil offered to take Lucy back to the house and play with her. Brock was a huge help and so was Liam, one hand and all.

Brock stacked the chairs and managed to get them all in

the storage room. Liam worked in the dining room and kitchen and Macy went through the house straightening each room that guests had mingled in.

Once she was satisfied the house was back in order, Macy went out the patio doors off the dining room. Dishes clanked in the kitchen, but she couldn't go in there. Facing Liam right now wasn't smart and she really just wanted some fresh air.

She'd had to watch him all day. See him laugh with guests, hold his drink in his right hand because his left was still bandaged, and he'd throw her an occasional side-eye that had her insides churning and her head spinning.

Thankfully no more headaches, though. She'd been faithful in keeping her meds right on her in case of another onslaught, but nothing since the last meltdown.

Macy crossed the brick patio and into the cool grass. She'd slipped her shoes off as soon as the last guest had gone. The blades tickled her toes, but she loved being outside. The moon had come up, sending a sparkling reflection onto the water.

Once she reached the edge, Macy sank down into the grass, pulled her knees up, and wrapped her arms around her legs. She tugged the short, flared skirt around to cover her as much as possible, but other than the ducks, there was no one out here to flash. And she didn't care about grass stains at this point. Her mind was on other things.

What if she asked Liam to stay? What would he do? Would he feel torn or obligated?

On the flip side, if he asked her to come with him, would she? She'd just built a home and she was hoping to adopt Lucy. But . . . he hadn't asked. Hadn't even hinted that was an option.

Macy dropped her forehead to her knees.

"I assume you want to be alone."

Liam's voice behind her had Macy stilling. She clenched her hands and lifted her head, but didn't turn.

"Then why did you come out?"

He came to sit beside her, still in his navy dress pants and navy dress shirt, but the sleeves were rolled up on his forearms. His bandage was much smaller, but he'd still been only using his right hand from what she'd seen. She couldn't help but wonder how injured he truly was.

"Because you've avoided me all day," he replied.

Too close. He sat entirely too close. The soft breeze sent her hair gliding over her shoulders, tickling her bare skin. The woodsy cologne he always wore enveloped her.

"I've been busy," she informed him, keeping her eyes locked on the dark water. Somewhere the family of ducks were wading around, but unless they came into the path of the moonlight, she couldn't see them. "I'm about to go home—just wanted some fresh air."

When she started to get up, Liam placed his hand on her arm. "Don't go."

Macy closed her eyes. "We've gone all week without this. I don't have the energy to argue anymore. It's just time we let go and move on."

His thumb stroked the inside of her arm, the most sensitive place. "I don't want to argue, but I'm not leaving town with all of this pain between us, all of this tension."

She risked a glance his way. "You know when you're leaving?"

His dark eyes met hers. "I have a couple people I'm talking to about taking over here. They both worked for Magnolias for a time, so I know them."

Silence settled around them and Macy waited for him to answer her question. He blew out a breath, raking a hand over the back of his neck.

"I'm hoping to be gone within the next two weeks."

The air rushed from her lungs. That was rather fast. Didn't the sale of properties take more time?

"I found out my old condo building has another unit that's opening next week. I have a few changes I want to make at Magnolias so I need to be there to oversee those. The final sale will go through in about fifteen days or so."

"You've been busy," she murmured. Straightening her legs, Macy leaned back on her hands and willed the hurt to cease. He'd never fully been hers, so how could this hurt so bad?

"I haven't said anything because I wanted everyone to focus on the weddings. But I'll tell them Monday."

Well, at least he'd never lied to her. That was something. Liam had always been up-front and honest about the fact he didn't want to be here, and whatever he felt for her didn't override the dream he had of owning his own restaurant.

"Well, congratulations." Macy pushed off and came to her feet, smoothing her dress down. "I'm heading out."

She'd managed to take two steps before she stopped and turned back to him. Not surprisingly, he was on his feet.

"I know you want this more than anything, and I'm truly happy for you." She fisted her hands at her sides and pushed the rest of her thoughts out before she had the chance to change her mind. "But just tell me, did I ever weigh in on your decision? I mean, what we had, did it mean half as much to you as what it did to me?"

In her head the questions didn't sound so . . . needy. Now that they were out, she cringed. She wasn't that clingy a woman. Hadn't she prided herself on control after she'd been nearly raped?

Liam infuriated her because she lost all sense of control whenever he was around. All he did was get into her mind, into her heart, and she was completely lost.

With slow, deliberate steps, he completely closed the

space between them. His hands slid up into her hair, the stronger hand gripping a fistful as he pulled her in closer.

"You think this didn't mean anything to me?" he ground out. "You think leaving is easy for me? Nothing about you has been easy since I came back, Macy. But if I stayed, I'd always wonder what would've happened if I hadn't taken this chance."

The way he towered over her, his face so close to hers, his grip on her, had Macy sliding her hands around his waist. She needed to touch him, feel him against her. If this was how they were going to officially part, she needed one last bit of Liam to lock away inside her heart.

"I want to hate you." She blinked away the tears. She would put up a strong front. She knew this hadn't been an easy decision for him, but that didn't make the pain any less. "Part of me wishes we'd never started this."

He rubbed his lips against hers. "And the other part?"

"Is glad to have learned how I should be treated by a man."

He eased back, his thumb stroking along her jawline. "You can say that even though this isn't going to last?"

She smiled through the hurt. "I can say that because you showed me that I'm stronger than I thought. I can say that because you never lied to me. The way I feel about you is all on me."

Maybe she was a masochist, maybe she just couldn't bear the thought of never being with him again, but she fisted the bottom of his shirt and untucked it from his pants. When she glided her hands beneath the hem, meeting his taut back, Macy rested her forehead against his chest.

"If Brock weren't inside—"

"He left when I came out here." Liam's hand went to the zipper on the back of her dress and slowly eased it down. "You sure about this?"

Was she? This probably wasn't the smartest idea, but she

couldn't deny him, herself. This one last time. She knew going in that this would be it. But damn it, she wanted him and for tonight, for now, she was going to take this sliver of happiness.

Macy stepped back, letting the loose dress slide down her body and silently to the ground. Standing before him in only her strapless white lace bra and matching panties, she was so glad she'd opted to have a good lingerie day.

His eyes devoured her. The visual lick he gave her had shivers racing all through her.

"Damn. I thought you looked gorgeous in the dress, but out of it . . ."

When his hand went to his buttons, Macy reached out. "Let me. I don't want you to injure your hand anymore."

"Forget my hand. I want to touch you and I need these damn clothes off."

Considering she was in just as much of a hurry, Macy made quick work of ridding him of his shirt and unfastening his pants. He kicked off his shoes and she jerked everything down.

"You better hope no one comes back," she said with a laugh as he stood before her naked and she still only wore her bra and panties.

"They better hope they don't come back or they're going to get quite an education."

Next thing she knew they were on the bank of the pond. Liam rolled over so his back was in the grass as she straddled him. When she braced her hands on either side of his head and lowered herself onto him, she locked her eyes with his.

She wasn't in a hurry, wasn't ready for this night to end.

Liam's hand gripped her waist, his fingertips digging into her skin. He opened his mouth as if to say something, but Macy leaned down, capturing his mouth. No words were necessary. Nothing would change the outcome of this and all she wanted, all she needed, was one last time.

She made love to him under the stars, giving herself up even though her heart was breaking. And when they trembled in each other's arms, Macy closed her eyes and willed the tears away. She would love Liam forever, but she'd never be enough.

Chapter Twenty-One

"And we have a new eight-burner gas stove in addition to the six burner."

Liam took in the familiar kitchen. He thought he'd feel like he'd come home, but that emotion hadn't hit him yet. Granted, Liam had only come in to Magnolias for the day to talk with Mark and go through the entire restaurant to discuss final details.

"John was promoted to head chef when you left," Mark went on. "I know this will be a smooth transition with you both holding the reins."

Liam and John had gotten along beautifully over the years at Magnolias. This would be a perfect match. Liam continued to walk around the kitchen, thankful he'd driven over early, before they opened.

"I heard from the bank and the final papers will be ready on Tuesday of next week," Mark added.

One step closer to his goal. "Great."

Liam passed by the pristine white plates, instantly reminded of the floral ones Sophie had at the resort. The large flat screen over the prep area took him back to several months ago. The orders would come in one after another, unlike at Bella Vous, where he could do his own thing and cater to a smaller, thankful clientele.

"Do you have any other questions?" Mark asked. The older man crossed his arms over his blue dress shirt and leaned back against the stainless-steel counter. "I think I covered everything. I had all of the contents added into the contract. I'll be taking nothing with me when I go. There are several weddings scheduled next month, so you'll be getting back just in time to pick up where you left off."

Weddings. Liam swallowed the lump of emotions. No point in thinking of the past . . . or the last wedding he'd been part of, which had him stripping Macy in the backyard.

"I don't have any other questions," Liam stated.

The more he glanced around the kitchen, after he'd strolled through the dining room and around the grounds, the more he wondered if this was truly his dream or if he was just fulfilling a goal of his mother's.

His cell vibrated in his pocket, but he'd get to it later. He'd promised to be back at Bella Vous by two so he could get dinner started and interview a potential chef. Most likely, whoever needed him was one of his brothers.

"It's going to be great for this place to have you here again," Mark added. "The staff is excited you're coming back, too."

"You have a great staff," Liam agreed.

Mark chuckled. "Now you're going to have a great staff."

Liam merely nodded as the cell in his pocket went off again. He pulled it out, glancing at Sophie's name. He'd get back to her later. Though it wasn't like Sophie to text two times in a row.

"I better get back to Haven," Liam stated, anxious to return to the car to see what Sophie needed. "I'll see you at the bank Tuesday and if I think of anything before then, I'll call."

Mark nodded and stepped forward. "I'm ready to hit retirement and let someone I trust take over."

Liam rubbed the back of his neck, tension building as nerves settled in. He was actually buying a restaurant. And not just any restaurant, but the most prestigious one in Savannah and the surrounding area.

"Any retirement plans?" Liam asked as they started toward the back door.

Mark shoved the steel door open, holding it for Liam to pass through first. "My wife has always wanted to get an RV and just travel the country, so I guess I'll be RV shopping next week."

The bright morning sunshine hit Liam as he pulled his sunglasses from his back pocket and slid them on. "Sounds like a plan."

Liam said his good-byes and headed to his SUV. Once inside, he immediately opened the texts from Sophie. He read them once, twice, then stared at the glaring words. This wasn't happening. Could fate be this cruel?

Liam had no idea what the hell to do at this point, but he knew he needed to get back to Haven immediately. Nothing else mattered.

As he drove away from Magnolias, his heart ached, thoughts whirled through his mind, and he just wanted to make all of this right. But he knew even this was out of his control.

There had only been one other time where the pain was so intense, Macy literally ached. When her mother died, that had been almost unbearable.

But nobody had died this time. Lucy had been removed and was going to live with her grandmother in Texas.

Apparently the grandmother had a falling out with Lucy's mother, but they were related so the woman wanted her granddaughter.

Macy could hardly blame her, but still . . .

She'd just taken the high chair into the garage to store it when her front door opened and closed. It was midmorning and she was always at the hardware store during this time, but thankfully her father had taken over. He'd been at the store with Lucy when the call came in from Laverne.

"Macy?"

Sophie's voice echoed through the house. The empty house. Who knew a week with an infant could turn your world completely inside out? Macy had always respected foster parents, but she had a whole new appreciation now. The emotional battles they faced, the bond, the loss.

Macy stepped up into the kitchen from the garage just as Sophie closed the front door.

"I hope you don't mind I let myself in." She stood in the doorway, a sad smile on her face. "I just . . . I didn't think you should be alone."

Macy nodded, biting her lip so she didn't burst into tears all over her friend. Not only was Lucy gone, Liam was leaving next week. Macy had tried to brace herself for this, had known she was on borrowed time, but for everything to come crumbling down on her at once . . . It was seriously more than she could bear.

"I'm okay. I mean, I'm not, but this was what I signed up for, right?" Macy braced her hand on the corner of the countertop. "Going into foster care is opening your heart to a hurt you cannot describe, but it's so rewarding. I just . . . I thought I'd have more time and I really thought I'd be considered for adopting her."

Sophie tipped her head and crossed the room. "There will be others. You'll bring children in and love them, and when the time is right, you'll get that family you want."

Tears burned Macy's eyes, clogged her throat, and her only response was to nod.

"What can I do for you?" Sophie asked. "You need a girl day? Cora offered a massage. She said she'd rearrange any of our guests and just tell them she made a mistake in scheduling. Let us help you through this. Wine? Chocolate? A dirty movie?"

Macy laughed. "No. I'm just trying to move all the baby stuff. I can't come home every day and look at it."

Sophie glanced around the kitchen, into the open living area. "Let me help you with that. Then maybe we can go get some lunch. Is your dad watching the store today?"

Nodding, Macy headed to the sink to wash the sippy cup and bowl Lucy had used for breakfast. Was that just this morning? So much had changed. Everything had changed.

Macy rested her palms on the edge of the sink, dropping her head between her shoulders. She willed herself not to cry. She'd already cried so long her head threatened to blow up again on her. But it didn't matter. Maybe that pain would take away the ache inside her heart.

Sophie's arm came around her shoulders. "It's going to be all right."

"I know," Macy whispered. "But losing Lucy, knowing Liam is moving back . . . It's just quite a bit to take in all at once." Macy reached up to rub her head—damn headache.

"Take your medicine," Sophie stated. "Go take a nap, go take a walk, or whatever you want to get through this. I'll pick up and you won't have to worry about anything."

"You don't have to do that." Macy turned, rubbed her forehead. "But I am taking my medicine. The last thing I need is a migraine."

She crossed to the narrow cabinet above the refrigerator. She'd automatically moved all medicines up high before she knew the age of the child coming to live with her. She'd put everything out of reach before the first home inspection.

Once she swallowed her migraine pill, Macy faced Sophie, who was filling the dishwasher. "I know you didn't come here to clean my house."

Without looking up, Sophie said, "I came to help with anything you need."

What she needed, her friend couldn't provide.

"I've been wanting to put some new pots and flowers out front on my porch, but I've been so busy."

Sophie closed the dishwasher and started it up. "Then go do it. I promise, I'll put any baby things in the spare room and close the door."

"You're the best friend."

Sophie blew out a sigh and reached for Macy's hand. "Only my parents and Zach know that I cannot have children."

"What?"

Sophie squeezed her hand. "After the accident, and the surgeries, I was told I'd never be able to have children. I know a little of how you're feeling. I always wanted a family, so seeing pregnant women, people with baby carriers, families in the park, it hurt. I won't lie. But I also know everything happens for a reason and now I have Brock and Zach. I wouldn't change my life for anything."

Macy had no idea why Sophie had opened up, but Macy wrapped her arms around her friend. "I'm so sorry. I know you're happy now, but I'm sorry if this brought up bad memories."

Easing back, she met Sophie's soft smile. "I was going to just hide here all day and will the world away," Macy added.

"I figured you'd want to be left alone, but that's usually when you need someone the most."

Sophie was right. Unfortunately, the person she wanted the most was in Savannah looking over his new restaurant and gearing up for the big move.

"Now, go do what you wanted to do," Sophie demanded. "I'll work around here."

"I'll be in the garage if you need me."

Macy knew full well that planting vibrant flowers in the new colorful pots she'd brought home from her store wouldn't ease the raw ache. But at least she'd have something to do to pass the time.

And later, she was going to get a punching bag, because she had some serious frustrations to take out on something.

"Would you make up your damn mind?"

Liam rubbed his hand over his jaw. "I've made it up. This is it."

Braxton and Zach both stood across from the center island and glared at Liam. He'd come back to Haven earlier than expected, after Sophie's text regarding Lucy. But he hadn't come straight to the resort.

"My plans are all in place," he went on.

Zach narrowed his eyes. "Why the change of heart?"

There were too many reasons to list. The heart in question had gone through a complete transformation. He was no longer the man he'd been even a month ago. Even with the uncertainty of his injured hand and his relationship with Macy, Liam knew he was exactly where he should be.

His brothers had questioned the status of his hand, but he quickly brushed them off. As much as the nerve damage scared him, he refused to dwell on the fear.

"Does it matter? I'm here, I'm staying."

"Have you told anyone else?" Braxton asked.

Liam shook his head, not bothering to go into the fact he wanted to explore the whole prospect of opening his own bakery as an expansion of Bella Vous. He had no clue what the hell was going to happen with his hand. So far, he still couldn't feel a damn thing on his palm and a portion of his fingers. He knew the injury would require more time to heal, but the unknown terrified him. Despite these uncertainties, he refused to give up his dream. The dream he'd once held had shifted somewhere along the way and a new one had taken its place.

The intense stare from his brothers unnerved him, but he wasn't sorry he'd made the decision. His entire life was here in Haven, as was his future.

Zach didn't let up on his skeptical gaze. "Something happened in Savannah."

More like something had happened in the past several months, but Savannah was a smack in the face—one he'd needed to wake him up. The text from Sophie had simply solidified his decision. He wasn't sure when he'd fully decided not to take the offer in Savannah, but now that he had turned it down, he had no regrets.

Liam had been so anxious to get to Magnolias this morning, but once he'd arrived and was really able to comprehend exactly what life would be like, it didn't take long for him to see that perhaps his goal had changed. That was definitely something he hadn't seen coming.

The homey kitchen he'd gotten used to at Bella Vous fit his life better now. Liam wasn't quite ready to get back to the hustle and bustle of long hours and a staff that was good, but not family. Besides, he figured he'd miss the elderly ladies discussing books or the bachelorette parties and their quirky requests.

He needed to call Mark as soon as possible. First, though, he had a few other things that were slotted higher on his priority list.

"You haven't told Sophie or Cora?" Braxton asked.

"Or Macy," Zach added.

"I had to tell you two first." Liam swallowed. "And to make sure you weren't pissed and planning to change the locks and take my key."

Zach snorted, crossing his arms over his chest. "We're pissed, but we wouldn't lock you out. And since you came to your senses, we're not as pissed."

A wave of relief flooded Liam. Not that he'd expected his family to turn him away, but he'd been ready to leave, to turn his back on them. Sending money to keep supporting the financial aspect of the resort was one thing, but actually being here and getting his hands in the family business was another.

"I guess I won't be needing to interview this afternoon for my replacement."

"I'm going to go tell Cora." Braxton headed for the wide hallway leading to the front of the house. He stopped, gripped the door frame as he threw a glance over his shoulder. "I hope you didn't actually believe we wouldn't welcome you back."

Liam watched his brother walk away, then turned back to Zach. "What?"

Zach merely shrugged. "Just glad you finally realize where you belong, that's all."

Liam still had work to do in the resort kitchen, no matter how much he wanted to get to Macy. Pulling out the bowls of ingredients he'd put together last night, he started finishing up what would be dinner in a few hours. The numbness in his left hand was beyond frustrating, but if he kept dwelling on the negative, he'd totally miss what was happening now and all the possibilities awaiting him.

Besides, he could learn how to work without the feeling in his left hand. He'd damn well make sure he did because he wasn't about to let his family—or Macy—down.

"You don't have to look so smug," Liam muttered.

"I just enjoy being right."

Liam couldn't help but laugh, but then sobered quickly. "Have you seen Macy today?"

"No." Zach eased onto one of the bar stools. "Sophie

went over there and then texted me. She said Macy is doing okay, but she's heartbroken."

Liam knew how much she wanted Lucy. The love Macy had for Lucy was undeniable. Macy had gone into fostering with her heart wide open, just as she'd done with him. Twice she'd been crushed and he'd have to live with the guilt of doing his part to hurt her.

"Why don't you leave this," Zach stated, waving a hand at the various bowls. "What the hell is it anyway?"

"I was going to do roulade."

Zach tipped his head. "A who?"

"Never mind."

"Can it keep until tomorrow?" Zach asked. "Sophie and I can whip something up. I do a mean spaghetti."

"Spaghetti? A jar of sauce and box noodles will not be served from my kitchen." Liam shook his head. "I'm going to get this roulade done. Macy doesn't want to see me right now, and as long as she's not alone, that's all that matters. I'll go see her when the time is right."

Later. Much later. He needed to figure out what the hell he wanted to say to her. Assuming she even wanted to see him again was presumptuous on his part. They'd pretty much parted ways after the double wedding.

Right now she was hurting. If he told her he was staying, she might think he was staying out of guilt. He just needed to figure out how to approach her, how to help her heal and move beyond the hurt she faced now. He couldn't botch this up.

"I'll leave after I get dinner ready and you and Sophie can serve the guests." Liam stirred in more spices, gripping the bowl with his good arm. "That work?"

"So long as you go straight to Macy." Zach flattened his palms on the counter. "I have no idea how you left things, but she loves you. Five minutes with you two and it's obvious."

Liam stilled, refusing to look up. "I'll go see her. I just . . . I need to get my head on straight."

If he told her he was in Haven for good, he didn't want to just assume they'd pick up where they left off. She might not want to give him another chance. He'd hurt her—he felt responsible for that. She'd wanted him to stay, but she hadn't come out and asked. From here on, he had to be honest with her and tell her everything that was on his mind, in his heart.

Over the next couple hours, Liam figured the words would come to him while he cooked. At least, he hoped they did.

Since Macy's dad had filled in for her at the store, she didn't mind that he'd asked her to come in and finish up the invoices. It wasn't as if she had to get Lucy in bed early. Macy actually welcomed the distraction.

As she pulled into the store lot, she noticed Liam's SUV sat in the back. The hurt in her heart actually burned. She rubbed her chest as she shut off her engine.

Most likely he was up there packing the rest of his belongings. Considering all of the boxes he'd left unpacked, it shouldn't take him long.

Her thoughts had bounced back and forth today between wondering how Lucy was adjusting to another home and if Liam was already falling in love with his upcoming changes. He'd gone to Savannah, but she didn't know if he was working out restaurant details or if he was checking out the condo. Either way, he was moving on, pushing forward, and whatever they'd had would just have to remain a memory.

Just like Lucy.

Macy rested her head against the steering wheel and pulled in a deep breath. Perhaps she'd just get the paperwork and take it home. At least there she could put on a movie, have some wine, and hide. She could ugly cry on her couch and nobody would have to know.

The tap on her window startled her. Macy jerked around to see Liam standing there. She unbuckled her seat belt and opened her door.

The last thing she wanted today was to come face-to-face with more pain. There was only so much she could handle.

"Can you come upstairs for a minute?" he asked.

Macy smoothed her hair away from her face, jerking it all over one shoulder. "I'm tired and I still have invoices to work on."

"No, you don't."

Confused, Macy propped her hands on her hips. "My dad stopped at my house and told me—"

"I asked him to get you here somehow. He already did the invoices, but that's all he could think of to get you here."

Macy's heart quickened; nerves churned in her stomach. "I'm emotionally drained. Today has been—"

He put a finger to her lips. "I know." He removed his hand, then gripped her shoulders. "I heard. Just give me five minutes, Macy. That's all."

He slid his bandaged hand down to hers, holding on to her fingers.

When he started toward the back steps, she followed, trying not to read too much into this. In her heart she hoped he was going to tell her he was staying, that he wanted her and nothing else mattered. But that was absurd. He wanted that big-time restaurant, not a small-town resort that hadn't ever been a blip on his dream radar.

He released her hand as he climbed the steps. He probably wanted to discuss moving or packing or something else that would take him away. But why go to the trouble of having her come back?

When Liam eased the door open, Macy stepped inside. The wall of boxes were still stacked, but there had been more added. A man staying would have unpacked those final boxes. Her heart sank. Even his free weights were missing from beside the sofa.

"Follow me." He didn't leave her much choice as he headed toward the bedroom.

Okay, not what she was expecting. Slowly, she made her way down the short hall. When she rounded the corner, Liam stood there with a pair of boxing gloves, bright yellow ones, actually.

"What are these?"

He gestured for her to take them. "Yours. I bought them for you as a going away gift and I actually have a heavyweight bag being delivered to your house."

Macy rubbed her head, but didn't take the gloves. "You called me here to give me a going away gift? Are you serious?"

Anger bubbled up. "You're leaving, so you get me a stress reliever. How ironic. Did you think I actually wanted to come here and see you again? I thought we left things the way that was best for both of us, considering."

The burn in her throat, her eyes, was inevitable. Tears were a staple in her life today. She wasn't even sorry for the display of emotion—she was human.

"I had to hand over Lucy today. Just hand her over like she didn't make a huge difference in my life. I had to think about where she was going, if they knew she liked to be rocked and sang to before bed. Then I'd start thinking of you and what you were doing. And the people who'd come into my life were going in different directions and I'm here. And . . ."

Macy's voice broke as the sob spilled out of her. "I can't do this."

She spun around, heard Liam curse behind her a second before he wrapped his arms around her from behind. Pulling her against his chest, he kissed the side of her head.

"I know you're hurting," he whispered. "I didn't mean to be insensitive. I just thought you might want to get some of that tension out. Or you can punch me, I don't care."

"I'm tempted." Macy closed her eyes, dropping her head back against his shoulder. "But punching you or the bag won't fix my problems."

"It won't bring Lucy back," he agreed. "But I was hoping if we took one of your spare bedrooms and turned it into our boxing room—"

Our boxing room?

Macy spun around. "What?"

Liam swiped her damp cheeks with his good hand, then tipped her chin up. "I'm staying in Haven."

She had to have heard him wrong. The migraine she'd battled earlier had clearly messed up something in her mind.

"You just went to Savannah today." Way to state the obvious. But she was too stunned to come up with anything else. "What made you change your mind?"

"Everything." He released her, stepped back, and shrugged. "The resort, my family, you. I wasn't feeling at home in that kitchen like I thought I would. As my boss and I were talking, something was just off. Then there's my hand."

"You never talked about what the doctor said, but you still have a bandage on it."

Liam nodded, the muscle in his jaw clenching. "He's not sure if there's permanent nerve damage, but . . ."

Oh, no. Her heart hurt for so many reasons, but now she literally ached for what Liam was possibly facing.

"Liam, I had no idea it was that bad."

His brief nod spoke volumes as to how much he didn't want to discuss just how "bad" the injury truly was.

"I'll make this work. For Chelsea, for my brothers, for you. I'll make everything work out. I was already thinking of everyone back here when I was in Savannah, then Sophie texted me about Lucy."

Realization dawned on her. Macy held up her hands. "If you tell me you're staying out of guilt—"

"No." His firm tone stopped her. "I'm staying because I love you."

Macy dropped her hands. "You just figured that out today?"

He smiled, as if she needed another reason to melt into a puddle at his feet. "No. I've known for a while, but I couldn't trust myself. I was in love once. She didn't feel the same, though I was clueless. She used me and I swore I'd never fall in love again."

"Yet here you are."

He closed the gap between them, reaching for her once again. "Here *we* are. Everything we have is brand new to me. I botched it up because I was afraid. My ex, Angela . . . she hurt me, more than I wanted to admit. I thought she loved me, and I was ready to spend my life with her, but she was just using me as a stepping stone until someone with more money, better looks came along."

Macy hated this faceless woman, but was thankful she'd moved out of the way. "She won't find a better man," she told him, fully believing every word. "Her loss."

"I see that now," he explained. "I see it because of you. I didn't want to get close again, but I had no choice. I couldn't stop myself from falling for you, Macy."

In ways she'd never thought possible, they'd healed each other. Her heart had never been this full.

"I only paid my rent through the end of the month," he

murmured, holding his gaze steady with hers. "I'm looking for a place to stay."

And there went that flood of tears again. The emotional roller coaster that summed up this day was more than she could bear.

"Macy." Liam framed her face, catching each tear as it fell. "I'll foster every kid you want, we'll adopt them, have our own—I don't care. But I want you to know I'll get you through this and when you're ready, we'll bring in more. You did what Lucy needed at the time and she is now somewhere where she is equally loved."

Macy nodded, unable to speak for fear that he'd never make out a word she said as she continued to sob.

"But I won't leave you again," he continued. "You're it for me. I should tell you that I've been offered a chance to open my own bakery at Bella Vous that serves to the public. I need to wait and see about my hand, but that's an avenue I'm definitely exploring."

"That sounds perfect." Macy threw her arms around his neck and held on tight. "And I think I know a place you can stay."

Liam gripped her waist and nuzzled her neck. "Is that right?"

"The rent is free, but I hear the landlord is prone to emotional meltdowns."

Sliding his hands to her backside, he jerked her hips against his. "I've only heard she loves cowgirl boots and sexy panties."

Arousal shot through her as she backed him up toward the unmade bed. "I believe we're talking about the same landlord."

Liam stopped, nipped at her lips, and murmured, "I plan on changing her title from landlord to wife as soon as possible."

Macy jerked back. "Wife?"

Those captivating eyes held hers. "Are you rejecting my proposal?"

"Are you proposing?"

Liam drew his brows in. "I got you yellow boxing gloves. What more do you want?"

Laughing, Macy pushed him down onto the bed. "I'll show you."

Epilogue

"Too late to turn back now."

Liam tightened his hold around his bride as he pulled her flush against his body. The setting sun cast the perfect orange glow all around his beautiful wife. When Macy smiled wide everyone around them ceased to exist.

"I'm not going anywhere. I've waited a long time to become Mrs. Liam Monroe."

His heart swelled. In the past month of planning this whirlwind wedding, he'd only grown to love her even more. She'd healed him in so many ways. His hand and career might still be in question, but each day he was getting more feeling back and hoped to make a full recovery. His family was quick to pitch in when he asked, and he'd had to swallow his pride and let others come to his aid.

Macy had taught him that. She'd shown him so much.

Thankfully they had had one day in the schedule that nobody was booked for the resort. She'd wanted to get married in the backyard by the pond just like his brothers.

So here they were on a Wednesday evening and he'd never seen her more beautiful. He couldn't wait to peel her out of that simple, straight gown with lace over her slender shoulders. He knew for a fact she'd bought a pair of brand new cowgirl boots for the wedding. Of course his Macy wouldn't want something as traditional as heels.

She'd wanted simple, by the pond, at sunset. Those were her only requirements. Liam didn't care if they got married at a drive-thru window. He just wanted Macy to be his— forever.

The preacher had already left and Liam and his family, Macy and her father were all still enjoying this perfect spring day in the backyard of Bella Vous. No decorations were needed when the setting was naturally enhanced with mossy oak trees and flower beds bursting with color, thanks to Sophie's eye for plants.

Liam grew to love this place more and more each day and he totally understood where Chelsea's vision had come from.

"Can I give my condolences to the bride?"

Liam looked up to meet Zach's lopsided grin. "Don't touch my bride."

Sliding his arm around Sophie's waist, Zach shrugged. "You've hugged on my wife enough."

"We're all damn lucky," Braxton chimed in as he moved to the group. Cora had one hand on Heidi's collar and her other hand loosely wrapped around Braxton's elbow. "I'd say Chelsea would be pretty pleased at how things have worked out for all of us."

"She's smiling down on us, I'm sure." Sophie's eyes misted. "I'm so happy for you guys."

Phil moved in on the other side of Macy, and Brock came to stand by Sophie. She reached down to take Brock's hand.

"I hope it's okay if I share some news," Sophie announced. "It's just . . . we're all here and this is such a beautiful, perfect day."

"Of course," Macy stated, leaning into Liam's side. "You're beaming. What's the good news?"

Sophie's gaze darted to Zach, and he gave a nod. "We're adopting a little boy. He's two and his name is Isaac."

Liam laughed, then shot a glance to Macy, who winked back at him. "We put in for adoption as well," Macy exclaimed. "We obviously just got the ball rolling, but this is something we're passionate and excited about."

"I guess we can't keep the secret any longer." Braxton's smile widened as he placed a hand on Cora's abdomen. "We're looking at our own miracle around Thanksgiving."

Macy and Sophie both squealed and rushed to hug Cora. Braxton, Zach, and Brock shifted out of the way and came to stand next to Liam. As Liam watched the women rejoicing, he couldn't believe what was taking place all because his late sister had a vision.

"Hope we didn't spoil your day by . . ." Braxton muttered.

Liam cocked his head toward his brother. "By announcing we're all going to start another generation of Monroes? Not possible."

Brock groaned. "I hope you all don't expect me to babysit. I'm already working at the store and the resort."

Phil laughed, slapping Brock on the back. "You want to save for that new car, don't you?"

"We won't make you watch all three at the same time," Liam assured Brock. "We can set up a schedule for a rotation."

Brock's eyes narrowed. "You wouldn't."

Liam met Macy's eyes across the group.

"With Liam hoping to open the new bakery part of Bella Vous in late summer, we may need extra help with the little one," Braxton stated.

Macy shook her head. "Don't listen to them, Brock. I need you more at the store than I do changing diapers."

Diapers. Liam had never imagined his life with a beautiful wife, a bakery of his own on the horizon, and a head chef position at a resort. Soon he'd be a father. His life was beyond full and as Liam watched his wife of only thirty minutes laughing with his family, he knew he'd finally come home. For good.

Macy caught his attention and mouthed "I love you." Liam couldn't wait to leave his own wedding so he could show her just how much he loved her, too.

Connect with Us

Visit us online at
KensingtonBooks.com
to read more from your favorite authors, see books
by series, view reading group guides, and more.

for sneak peeks, chances to win books and prize packs,
and to share your thoughts with other readers.

facebook.com/kensingtonpublishing
twitter.com/kensingtonbooks

Tell us what you think!

To share your thoughts, submit a review,
or sign up for our eNewsletters, please visit:
KensingtonBooks.com/TellUs.